D.A. Dwinell

Path of the Guardian

Guardian of the Stone
BOOK FOUR

D.A. Dwinell
Path of the Guardian
This book is a work of fiction, and the events, incidents,
locations, and characters are products of the author's imagination or
are used fictitiously. Any resemblance to actual persons, living or
dead, businesses, companies, organizations, events, or locales is
entirely coincidental.
Copyright © 2022, DA Dwinell
Self-published

Scripture quotations taken from The Holy Bible, New
International Version® NIV®
Copyright © 1973 1978 1984 2011 by Biblica, Inc. TM
Used by permission. All rights reserved worldwide.

First Printing, 2023

This book is dedicated to my parents and my brother. God truly blessed me when He put us together.

Special thanks go to Audrey, Mark, Deborah, and my father.

One

My respect for my grandmother, Lillie, has grown since finding her underground operations room. I will never forget the thrill of finding this well-hidden room under the bench on the stairs. The room contained her journals. The journals revealed a lot about my grandmother's secret life. I have continued her tradition of journaling by writing my own. A lot has happened over the last year.

Since I became the protector of the Bloom of Dreams, my life has changed immensely. It was difficult to remember them all, but I did help put Anthony Granaldi III and his son, Joseph, in prison for stealing paintings. I could not have done it without Tony's help. Then there was my cousin Phillip. He stole diamonds from a lovely lady. Oh, I can't forget Eleni Kostopoulos. She is someone I don't wish to mess with again. I was able to scare her off by threatening to expose her money-laundering scheme, which would have crippled her financially.

It took me several days to get all the events documented. I included details about the things they did to people to let the next guardian of the stone know what they were capable of. The worst was my cousin Kevin being locked in a small box for days. Kevin and his parents, William and Lainie have been helping protect the Bloom of Dreams. They were worried about him when he went missing.

My cousin Allison was able to help locate Eleni and Kevin. Kevin was traumatized by his torture. Thank God he is doing better. I did the best I could to remember the dates of things. My last journal entry was about finding this room. The journal is next to my grandmother's journals on the shelf. As much as I wanted to learn more about my grandmother's life and her experiences with the

Bloom of Dreams, I needed to find out who murdered my grandmother. It was summer, which meant I had a few months to collect as much information as possible. Once school starts back up, I will have a harder time following up on leads.

I had the feeling the Bloom Keepers would not be much help. Greg was working with Austin and Bill at the farm for the rest of the summer. Jacob had an internship with IBM and Juliet was babysitting twin boys.

One day I will read all the journals in order, but my priority was finding the person who murdered my grandmother. I pulled out the last journal she wrote in and flipped to the last few pages to see what she wrote.

April 15

Imelda Lombardo, Anthony Granaldi III's cousin, contacted me. She knows he is evil and suspects her son was dead because of him. It amazed me when she provided me with blueprints of his home. She overheard him talking to his wife about a secret room in the house. I started searching for the room.

April 28

I think Marshall Blaise may have figured out where I live. I have warned Phyllis to keep an eye out for any strangers lurking around. I will head to France to see what I can find out about him.

I'm looking forward to passing the Bloom on to Brooke. She will be 18 soon. I plan to take her to Italy to meet Isabella and Leonardo. She must rely on them. They will assist her with anything she needs. Brooke will be shocked to find out she will inherit millions. We will need to travel to Japan to connect with Asahi Abe. Her training will begin with him immediately after she graduates. She will only have the summer to train with him before college.

May 2

Imelda Lombardo told me her son, Federico, had died. She wants me to help her figure out who did it. She stated they found him stabbed in Villa Fiorelli. It's a park in Rome, Italy. He had gone to Rome with Anthony and his boys. Anthony claimed he and his sons were not with him. Anthony told Imelda; Federico left them to go out with friends. She has been a great asset. I need to help her find the truth.

Per Isabella's request, I dropped by the villa. Marshall Blaise stopped by there to see if he could find out when I would return to Italy. Isabella explained I had not made a reservation yet. All she could tell me was he spoke English with a French accent.

May 3

Overheard Anthony and Tony talking. They seemed to talk in code. Anthony said, "You're sure there's nothing that could lead to us?"

"I took care of him. I did what needed to be done before he flips," Tony assured him.

Unfortunately, I need more evidence. I can't be sure he was talking about Federico.

May 4

A man with a French accent stopped by the house, wanting to see me. Phyllis told him I was out of town and asked for his business card. He did not provide one. He told her he was only in town for the day and explained he would try to contact me another time. It sounds like Marshall may know where I live. Phyllis believed this was Marshall Blaise.

The stone started heating in the church. Phyllis and I looked around discretely to see if we could figure out why it was warning me. Phyllis discovered the Frenchman sitting behind us to the right. As the service ended, I handed my purse to Phyllis and hurried to catch up with the Frenchman. I placed my arm through his arm as if I knew him and said, "Mr. Blaise, it's a shame you and I haven't met before. I understand you're looking for me. What can I help you with?" He played along and walked me to the side of the building without saying a word. The stone became warmer with each step.

He smiled and politely said, "I want that stone. Name your price."

I smiled and said, "It's not for sale, Mr. Blaise."

He placed his hand on my arm, and with a smile and a tight grip he said, "I will have it one way or another."

I concentrated on moving through his arm and moved toward the front of the church. "We're done here. Thank you for your offer, but I'm not interested." I do not think that is the last of him.

I should find Imelda Lombardo. She might know something about Marshall Blaise. Grandma also wanted me to meet Asahi Abe. I will need to do some research to find him. It says I will train with him. I think he might teach martial arts.

Jacob was at work, so I called Juliet to see if I could stop in for a visit. She was at the park babysitting. On a piece of paper, I wrote Imelda Lombardo and Marshall Blaise. I took off toward the park to meet her.

She was standing on the edge of the playground watching several children run around. I walked up to her and joked, "How does it feel to be a mom?"

Startled, she turned toward me. "I thought someone seriously thought these boys were mine. They are sweet one-on-one, but together they are like a hurricane coming at you." At that moment, a boy ran between us and pushed us both aside. "Ryan, that was not funny!"

At that moment, another boy did the same thing. "Let me guess, that's Davy," I said with a chuckle as Juliet rolled her eyes. "I need you and Jacob to find two people for me." I handed her the note with the two names.

Juliet looked at the note. "Who are they?"

I explained who they were, and I gave her the little information I had about both of them.

Juliet seemed to scan the playground. "Where's Davy?"

"He's right there," I said, pointing to a boy on the swing.

"That's Ryan," she said.

"I don't know how you tell them apart."

"Their shoes are different colors."

At that moment, we both noticed Davy on top of the close circular slide. Juliet leaped on top of the slide and made her way to him. Just as she reached him, he fell. She grabbed him in the nick of time. Juliet told him to climb on her back. Slowly, she climbed down and brought him to safety. She snatched his hand. "Ryan, it's time to go."

Ryan did not move. Using my power of persuasion, I told Ryan to follow Juliet. He jumped from the swing and caught up with them.

"I'm sorry, Brooke. I need to get them home."

"I understand. They've got a lot of energy," I said as I helped her into her car.

"Jacob is coming over for dinner tonight. I'll let him know what needs to be done," Juliet said just before shutting the car door. She walked to the driver's door. "I hope I survive the summer. I don't know how moms manage." Juliet took a deep breath and climbed in her car.

When I returned home, Phyllis was unloading groceries. I helped her with the bags. We put away the groceries. I asked her if she knew anything about Imelda or Marshall. She told me about Lillie warning her about Marshall, but she knew nothing about Imelda. Once she found out about her being Anthony's cousin, she suggested I speak with Leonardo and Isabella. I continued putting groceries away.

"Go."

I looked over at her, puzzled.

"Go, see them. If you hurry, you might get to speak with them before they serve dinner," Phyllis said, taking the bag of sugar from me.

I smiled and gave her a kiss on the cheek before heading to my room to change. I arrived in my room at the villa in Italy. The bed reminded me of the night we brought Kevin here after we rescued him from Eleni Kostopoulos. Kevin is doing better every day. I strolled out of my room and began searching the villa for Isabella and Leonardo.

I found Isabella at the front desk. She was cleaning the counter. "Surprise!"

Isabella looked up, "Hello Brooke. What brings you here today?"

"Could we talk privately?"

"Of course," she said as she came out from behind the counter and walked toward her private quarters.

As soon as she closed the door, I heard Leonardo ask, "Izzy?"

"Excuse me, Leonardo is not feeling well," she said before heading to her bedroom.

Not wanting to be rude, I remained in place and waited for her return.

She returned a moment later and picked up the phone and called to have a bowl of soup delivered.

I asked, "May I see him?"

"Of course," she said, motioning me to the bedroom.

Leonardo was lying on his side. He looked horrible.

I asked, "How are you feeling?"

He said, "Not well.".

I reached out to touch him. "May I?"

He nodded.

I placed my right hand on his head. I held the Bloom of Dreams against my chest with my left hand. The stone immediately heated up. After about a minute, Leonardo rolled over on his back. Life appeared to be coming back into his eyes.

After another minute, he sat up. "Thank you. I feel so much better."

"I'm glad. I don't want to take up much of your time, but I need to know if you know anything about Imelda Lombardo or Marshall Blaise"

"We know Imelda well. She is a lovely lady. Nothing like her cousin," Isabella said with a smile.

That was good news. I asked, "Do you have a way to contact her?"

"We do. Imelda doesn't know you. She's a private person because of Anthony. Perhaps I should call her. I will set up a way for you to meet her. I will let you know when I have the details," Isabella informed me.

"Thank you. What about Marshall? Do either of you know anything about him?"

Leonardo cleared his throat and said, "He came by here once looking for Lillie. We have not seen him since then." He sat up some more. "I feel a lot better. Thank you, Brooke" He pulled the covers off himself revealing his blue and green plaid pajama pants. "Will you excuse me, ladies? I'm going to get dressed."

I walked out, followed by Isabella, who shut the bedroom door behind her. 'Yes, thank you. I was really worried about him." She looked like she was on the verge of tears.

"You know you can always call me if you need help," I said as I hugged her.

"We don't want to impose on you."

"It's no imposition. I love you both. You are family now. If you need something, ask," I insisted.

There was a knock at the door. As Isabella opened the door, Leonardo came out of the bedroom looking healthy. A server stood at the door, holding a tray with a bowl of soup. The server looked confused when he saw Leonardo.

"I'm not sure we are going to need that now," Isabella told the waiter and then looked over at Leonardo.

"Speak for yourself, I'm starving," Leonardo said as he took the tray from the man.

Isabella thanked him and shut the door.

"I am going to get going. Let me know about Imelda and call me if you need anything.," I said as I pulled out my mirror.

"I will contact her in the morning. I need to get everything set up for dinner," Isabella said as she waved goodbye.

Two

I woke up with birds chirping outside my window. This was one of my favorite things about living here. It was a peaceful way to wake up. I glanced at the clock and realized my alarm would go off soon. It was getting too warm to work out in the afternoon. I quickly dressed and went down to grab a small bite to eat before my run.

Phyllis and Mom sat in the kitchen chatting when I entered the room. "Good morning," I said cheerfully.

"Good morning, sweetheart," Mom said before she took another sip of her coffee.

Phyllis smiled and prepared me a cup of coffee. I sat down next to my mother. Phyllis placed my coffee and a small bowl of fruit with Greek yogurt in front of me. "Thank you, Phyllis. What are your plans today?"

Mom answered, "We are meeting some ladies from church for lunch. Would you like to join us?"

Mom needed to make more friends, and I already had plans. "Greg and I are going to work out this morning. We might try to see if Juliet and Jacob want to do something later. I hope you have a great time."

We continued chatting for a few minutes until Greg knocked on the back door. Mom let him in while I scarfed down the rest of my breakfast. He greeted everyone before coming up behind me and greeting me. Phyllis offered to make him something to eat.

"You know I love your food, but Mom made a big breakfast for everyone this morning," Greg stated.

"I am so glad she is doing better. She made an amazing recovery. Praise God," Mom said.

I cleaned my dishes and kissed Phyllis and Mom on their cheeks. We better get to it. Greg and I exited the house through the back door. As soon as we were out of their eyesight, Greg pulled me to him and kissed me.

"Did you miss me?"

"Hum, you, or the livestock. It's tough to say," he said with a smirk on his face. He pulled me in closer and whispered, "I miss ya every minute we're apart." He kissed me again, and he took off running. "Come on."

I started following him. "We didn't even stretch." Greg was going slow enough, that I could catch up with him. Occasionally, one of us would say sprint and we would take off. We had to count out twenty seconds before we could return to a jog. At the first block, I yelled, "Sprint!" Greg must have been expecting it because he sprinted past me. We finished our run and went up to my gym on the third floor. It was nice not working out in a garage with the mats on the cement floors. I grabbed us some water to quench our throats before we started sparing.

The sparing drills began after we put our gear on. We were practicing our foot patterns to get used to the way we move our feet to expect what our opponent might do. We added punches in after we warmed up. Greg swung his leg around, causing me to lose my balance. I was able to counter and knocked him on top of me. He went to get up, and I grabbed his shirt and pulled him to me for a kiss. He gently pressed his lips against mine.

It was Intense. The heat kept building between us. Greg's body was covering mine. I wanted more but knew it was wrong. I was lost in the moment. *This needs to end before we regret it.* I turned my head away from him. He pulled himself up some. I grabbed his right shoulder and wrapped my leg around his right leg. Pushing my body to the left, I rolled over and positioned myself on top of him.

"I'm sorry," Greg said, not attempting to counter my move.

"You have nothing to be sorry for. We were both lost in the moment. Greg, I love you. We both want to wait and need to."

"I love you, too. The last thing I want to do is upset you or not to wait till we are married," he said, moving my hair behind my ear.

Did he just say married?

"I now understand why people in Jesus's time married so young. The temptation is hard to resist," Greg said. He closed his eyes and appeared to be praying.

I prayed and asked for forgiveness. My phone rang. I ran over to the table and answered it.

After a quick greeting, Isabella said, "Imelda will meet with you. She said Lillie told her you might help her. Lillie made sure Imelda knew she could trust you. She wants to meet at the villa today. Will you be available in a couple of hours?"

"Yes, of course,"

"When you get to your room here at the villa, call the front office. I will send her to your room."

We said our goodbyes. I told Greg what was going on and told him I needed to shower and think about what I needed to talk to her about.

Greg said he understood and went home.

As I showered, I had a thousand things on my mind to ask her. I dried my hair. *What would one wear in Italy during the summer while on vacation?* I wore a white sundress. I still had another forty-five minutes until I needed to be there. I returned to Grandma's secret room. I randomly grabbed a journal and read.

December 13, 1991

As hard as I try, I have been unsuccessful in getting Sandra to want to learn the skills she would need to take the stone. She is a great deal like her father. Phyllis even tried to persuade her. Brooke seems to be more like me. Perhaps she will be my successor. If not, Allison is my only other choice, and she does not want the responsibility unless she is my only choice.

I visited Asahi Abe today. It was nice catching up with him. He had aged a lot. I need to visit more often. I would not be who I am today without him.

I put that journal back and randomly grabbed another.

December 23, 2010

Sandra, Jeremy, and Brooke arrived here after dinner. We did not get to spend much time together because they were tired of driving all day. I wish they would move to Kentucky. Brooke has gotten so big. I can't believe she is seven already.

December 24, 2010

Phyllis fixed a fantastic meal. Brooke and I spent some time alone today. She shows real promise. I gave her some puzzles, and she easily figured them out. She also has an adventurous side like me. I need to convince Sandra and Jeremy to move back to Kentucky. Brooke needs to develop the skills she is going to need when she becomes the Guardian.

Jeremy seems to drink a lot these days. I am concerned. Sandra asked him to slow down when she thought I was not in the room. I am concerned about their marriage. They seem to snap at one another or just not talk.

December 25, 2010

The morning went great. Everyone seemed to like their gifts, but this evening I was heading to my room and heard Jeremy and Sandra fighting. As much as I wanted to not get involved, I heard him putting her down and she said nothing. It broke my heart. When Sandra answered the door, it appeared she had been crying. I walked past her and confronted Jeremy. He needed to sober up because he had too much to drink. I told him that Sandra was staying in the guest room on the third floor for the night. He got belligerent and said she wasn't going anywhere. I asked Brooke to give us a minute. Brooke closed the door when she left. I let him know how badly he was treating my daughter and he had the nerve to put his finger in my face. He is regretting that now.

I glanced at my phone. It was nearly time to head over. I put the journal back and returned to my room at the villa. My room was as beautiful as always. I called the front desk to let Isabella know I had arrived. Imelda was on her way.

It did not take her long to make it to my room. I offered her a seat at the small table. "I'm sorry for your loss. Lillie was a wonderful lady," Imelda said to me.

"Thank you. I miss her. It is my understanding you believe Anthony Granaldi III had your son killed."

Imelda squirmed in her chair a bit and looked around the room. "Yes, but there's no way to prove it. Besides, he's in jail."

Secretly, I chuckled because he was in prison because of Greg and me. "Do you have any leads that could prove he had him killed?"

"Unfortunately, I don't," Imelda said, looking disappointed.

"I can't make any promises, but I will see if I can find anything out. Do you know a man named Marshall Blaise?"

Imelda seemed to think. She said, "I don't think so. Who is he?"

I wanted to say he killed my grandmother, but at this point, I did not know that for sure. "That's what I'm trying to figure out."

"Here is my contact information if you find anything out about Federico."

We said our goodbyes. I was about to find Isabella to thank her for setting up the meeting when I received a text.

GREG:　　　　　　How did it go? RU still there? Jacob & Juliet want to hang out tonight.

Rather than text back, I popped back home and called him. No one could decide what to do. Greg was going to tell them to meet at my house and to dress nicely, but casually. I had an idea, but I wanted to surprise them. My outfit was fine from being at the villa.

While I waited for their arrival, I searched the internet for Asahi Abe. My search was unsuccessful. I trotted down downstairs to see what Mom and Phyllis were doing. They sat on the sofa in the sitting room, giggling. "What's going on here?"

They both looked at one another and laughed. "You tell her," Phyllis said and appeared to be blushing.

"It appears Phyllis is being pursued by the butcher," Mom informed me.

I must admit that caught me off guard. Phyllis is quite the catch. "Tell me more," I said.

"Apparently, my selections at his market impressed him. He has frequently asked me for recipes over the years. His wife passed away two years ago. He wasn't his cheerful self for a long time, but lately, he seems happy again. Well, he asked for my number and has been texting me all day," Phyllis informed me.

The doorbell interrupted our conversation. Jacob and Juliet came in and greeted everyone. Mom told me she had a date with Lance and would not be joining us for dinner. Phyllis jumped up and said, "I need to get dinner ready. How many will there be tonight?"

"We may go out. I will let you know soon, but we can just order a pizza if we stay in," I informed her. "Please send Greg to the library when he gets here," I said as I walked toward the stairs with Jacob and Juliet right behind me.

The three of us settled in on the sofa and began discussing dinner. I did not want to say anything to them about the plans I had for us until Greg arrived. I asked Jacob if he had located Marshall Blaise.

Jacob pulled out a piece of paper and handed it to me. It contained an address in France.

"I couldn't find a picture of him. He's kind of mysterious. Marshall has investments all over Europe. Some businesses and a little real estate."

The door flung open. Greg jumped through the doorway, and asked, "Miss me yet?"

I jumped. Fearing my mother was coming through the door. "What took you so long?"

"I ran into Lance outside. He's a cool guy," Greg said as he assumed his usual position leaning against the front of the desk.

"Did my mom leave yet?"

"Yeah. I think I may have made them late for the show they are going to," Greg said as he crossed his ankles.

I ran to the top of the stairs and hollered, "Phyllis!"

Looking annoyed, she popped her head into view, and asked, "What is it, child?"

"I have a surprise. Please come to the library," I said with my begging face.

As soon as she was in the room, I began, "Tonight I am taking us to the Hard Rock in Hollywood, Florida, for dinner. We are going to the Bae Korean Grill. Mechelle's parents took me there once. It was delicious." Everyone seemed excited about my surprise.

Juliet asked, "Have we dressed appropriately?"

I assured them we were. Mechelle and I spent a lot of time exploring the hotel grounds and I knew the perfect place in the stairwell to arrive. I brought Greg and Phyllis and returned for Jacob and Juliet. We exited the stairwell. My excitement for the evening building up as I looked around the hotel. As we walked toward the restaurant, the girls chatted about the many shops. Every store had glass along the front of them, allowing shoppers to peak in for a

14

glimpse of what they offered. The walkway was light marble. Stunning was the best way to describe the Hard Rock.

At the entrance to the Korean Grill, a large statue of a warrior on a horse greeted you. The aroma of the food made me hungrier. We only had to wait a few minutes before we were seated. The decorator had done an excellent job of making the décor cozy.

Everyone began asking about the round grill in the middle of the table. "I want you to experience the unique dining experience. The food is amazing. All you need to do is select a protein or you can have something vegetarian," I said, remembering how my stomach was in knots when I thought about trying Korean food when I ate here with Mechelle's family. Thankfully, it opened me up to trying new foods because everything tasted fantastic.

This time I was excited as I listened to the waiter explain about the Shinpo Grill table. My stomach growled in anticipation. After some conversation, we ordered our food. The waiter came by and lit the grill. When the food came out, it surprised everyone it was raw, except for the items served on the side. In small bowls, there were a variety of items to enjoy. Several items in the bowls tasted pickled, while others had hints of toasted sesame seed oil or fish sauce. Phyllis and I laid a few pieces of our meat on the grill. The sizzle released a wonderful aroma. Everyone else followed our lead. Such unique flavors in Korean dishes. After the first bite, my mouth began to salivate in anticipation of more.

We had a wonderful time discussing which of the side dishes we preferred. The evening was filled with laughter and love.

We returned home before my mother. We gathered around the dining room table and played dominos. I asked Jacob to help me in the kitchen with everyone's drinks. When we were out of earshot of everyone, I whispered, "I need to ask you a favor, but you can't tell anyone. Not even the other Bloom Keepers."

Jacob squinted his eyes and leaned his head back. "A top secret mission. I'm interested. Count me in."

Jacob filled a few glasses with ice. I grabbed a piece of paper from Phyllis's notepad and wrote "Asahi Abe," on it. I took a glass from him and handed him the note. "Can you find this person? It's very important. He was a friend of my grandmother's. The only thing I know about him is he lives in Japan. I need this as soon as possible."

I started filling the drinks, and he continued adding ice to the remaining glasses and told me, "I'll work on this tonight after I drop Juliet off." He picked up a few of the filled glasses. "You can always count on me, Brooke. You've changed my life." He turned and walked back to the dining room.

We continued playing until Mom arrived. We chatted with her and Lance a bit before everyone started heading home.

Greg hung around to say goodbye to me after everyone left. "Thank you for tonight. It was a great surprise," he said as he grabbed my hands and began rubbing the top of them.

"It was as much fun for me as it was for you," I said, looking down at our hands and lifting my eyes to his. We said goodnight, and I went straight to bed.

Jacob awakened me at nearly 3:30 in the morning by calling me. In a drowsy voice, I asked, "Are you okay?"

"I'm fine. I finally found the mysterious Asahi Abe," Jacob said, abounding pleased with himself.

I immediately sat up and was wide awake. "Really? Can I come over now?"

"I am anxiously awaiting your arrival."

I jumped out of bed and quickly dressed before grabbing my compact mirror and stepping through the full-length mirror in my room, "Show me everything."

"He was hard to find. I could only find this old picture of him. He looks to be in his forties. This is his son, Akio. Look at the article. He saved a young girl from a dog attack. They lived in Higashi Chaya District," Jacob said. He turned to look up at me.

I was peering over his shoulder, looking at his computer screen. "Thank you." I had Jacob scroll through some photos to get an image of the place. The village was within the volcano walls. The landscape was stunning. There were not a lot of pictures of the area. It was the smallest town in Japan. It was an island made from a double volcano.

"Look at this, there are no restaurants and only one store there," he said, sounding surprised.

I tapped him on the shoulder and said, "Good job, Jacob. I need to get back to bed. Thanks again."

Three

The next morning after church, Phyllis, Mom, Lance, and I went to lunch. This was Lance's first time joining us. We went to First Watch. I loved their Chicken Avocado Chop Salad, but Mom wanted to come here for their Pesto Chicken Quinoa Bowl. After lunch, Mom and Lance wanted to head to the mall, so Phyllis and I took her car home. I told Phyllis, Greg, and I would spend the rest of the day together. I told her not to plan on me being home for dinner.

As soon as I parked the car, I received a text.

GREG: I'm ready to go when you are.

BROOKE: Give me 15 min to change.

What does one wear to Japan? I started looking through my clothes. *What time is it there?* I grabbed my phone and looked up the time difference. It was nearly midnight in Japan. *Perhaps I should rethink this.* I picked up some jeans and a top and changed. I threw on some sneakers and my outfit was complete. A quick glance in the mirror told me I needed to brush my hair. As I was fixing it, I heard Greg say, "Are ya decent? Phyllis sent me upstairs."

"Come on in. I'll be out in a minute," I hollered back as I finished grooming myself. I took one last look at myself before going to greet Greg. "Hello, handsome."

Greg kissed me and asked, "Did ya come up with any ideas on what we should do today?"

"I did, but after some research, I'm not so sure it is a good idea." I felt like I was a balloon, and someone just stuck a pin in me.

He sat on the bed and asked, "Let me decide if it's a bad idea."

"I found out my grandmother wanted me to meet a man named Asahi Abe. He trained her in martial arts. I'm not sure where he even lives, but the last known place he and his son Akio lived was Aogashima in Japan. It is the most isolated inhabited island. There are only 170 people living there. I want to meet him and see if he will train me like he did my grandmother," I began explaining.

"What's the problem?"

"Japan is like ten hours ahead of us. It's 3:30 am there," I said, frustrated.

"I don't understand the problem. We'll just head over after we have dinner and check the place out. See if anyone knows him or his son. With only 170 people living there, everyone should know them, and the locals should assume we are just more tourists," Greg reassured me.

He always knows the right thing to say. "What do you want to do until then?"

"I've wanted to go to Frankfort Avenue," I said, hoping he wanted to go.

Greg seemed to ponder the idea before replying, "For you, anything."

We strolled down the historical neighborhood, admiring the many shops and restaurants along the avenue. We did a lot of walking because the shops were spread out. Some restaurants were offering small samples of their food. Greg and I ate at The Hub. We grabbed the Buffalo Cauliflower as an appetizer. It came with Korean BBQ sauce. It was amazing. Greg ordered his usual burger, and I had the Bucatini Primavera. After dinner, we rushed back to my house to head to Japan.

As soon as we entered the house, I transported us invisibly to the next building I had seen in one of the pictures. Greg followed me behind the building.

Once we were out of everyone's sight, I made us visible again. We walked down the road and were about to pass a man. I asked, "Excuse me, do you know Asahi Abe or his son Akio?

The rather short man looked at me and said, "Yes."

This was good news. "Do you know how I can find him?"

"Akio works at the salt mine."

I noticed Greg staring at me. I turned back to the man and asked, "How do I get there?"

He pointed down the road and said, "Just follow the road."

I thanked him. We moved fast toward the mine.

"It's so strange listening to you speak in Japanese," Greg said as he took my hand. It was not that far of a walk. The island is only three-square miles. When we arrived at the mine. There was a man outside. I asked him about Akio. He said he would go get him.

About fifteen minutes later, a man came out. He looked at me and seemed to stare at the Bloom of Dreams.

"Thank you for speaking with us, Mr. Abe," I said.

"You must be Brooke Garrison," he said as he looked at the Bloom of Dreams.

"You know me?"

Akio began speaking in English, "I have known your grandmother my entire life. How is she doing?"

I filled him in on her passing and introduced him to Greg.

He seemed genuinely upset about the news. "My father will be heartbroken," he said. He seemed to be in deep thought, "I'll be right back." Akio turned and rushed back into the salt mine. About ten minutes later, he returned. "Sorry, I needed to let my boss know I was leaving for the day. Follow me." He started walking at a blistering pace away from town. Greg asked, "Where are we going?"

"Sorry, I should've told you. I'm taking you to see my father. He lives outside of town," he explained. "I think he will know when he sees you with the Bloom of Dreams that something is wrong. I don't want him to find out from a stranger. He and Lillie were very close," he said and stopped. Turning to me he inquired, "May I ask why the stone is in a different setting?"

"My grandmother had been looking for this setting for many years. Greg and I finally found it." I did not want to disclose to him the additional powers it possessed.

We continued walking until we came across a narrow pathway hidden in the brush. After dodging the fifth branch that nearly slapped me across the face, I asked, "Do you see your father often?"

"No, I live in town and as you can see, he likes his privacy. Occasionally, I will bring him supplies or he will meet me in town. He is the only reason I still live here. There are only a few options for employment. Most work at the salt mine," he said as he unintentionally flicked another branch toward me.

Without warning, it rained. Akio did not seem to notice. By the time we arrived at the small hut, there was not a dry place on my body.

Akio called out to his father. A man who I believed to be in his seventies appeared on the porch. He called out to Akio, but I did not understand what he was saying because the sound of the rain pounding the dense vegetation nearly drowned out his voice.

As Greg and I caught up with Akio, I noticed the man staring at me. Akai introduced us to his father, Asahi Abe. Immediately, Asahi's eyes filled with tears. He walked over to me and placed his hands on my shoulders. "There's only one reason you are here without Lillie," Asahi said as a tear fell down his cheek.

I was not sure if it was seeing how heartbroken he was or if something in me was stirring up my emotions, but my eyes filled with tears. Regrettably, I told him all the details about her death, including the fact that I suspected someone murdered her. I neglected to introduce Greg, so Akio introduced himself to him. He invited us into his home. We took off our shoes and socks and left them on the front porch. Asahi handed us some towels to dry off. His home was beautiful. The tables and chairs seemed to be handmade. I asked, "Did you make this furniture?"

He nodded and said, "It is too expensive to ship things here or to even visit the other islands. I like many of my ancestors, survive with what God has given us."

Greg asked, "You don't study Buddhism?"

Asahi chuckled, "I did. Lillie told me and my family about Christ. I'll always be grateful for her telling me about what He did for us." He arose and walked to the table and brought back a Bible. "Lillie even brought me this Bible."

"How did you meet my grandmother?"

"Fate. She went to Japan to find someone to train her in Jujitsu. She met Michi. He was born and raised here, but like many, he left to make a living for himself and his family. Lillie asked him to train her, and he did for a little while. Michi figured it was a simple job. He would instruct the rich kid in a few moves until she got bored. However, Lillie didn't get bored. He discovered she was not a typical tourist. Lillie's dedication to learning the skills allowed her to pick them up quickly. Increasingly, she wanted more of his time. She never explained to him why she needed to learn to defend herself. Michi was neglecting his other customers and told her about me. He told her I was much better, and that she could learn more from me. She paid to bring him here so she could meet me." Asahi stopped and turned to Akio. "Please make us some tea."

Akio did as he instructed. Asahi continued, "At first, I was not interested. I figured Michi brought her here to help me earn some money and get her out of his hair. Lillie showed up at the strangest times and saw me working. She would step in and help. Lillie never said a word. If I was making a fire, she would collect the wood. Lillie even got on the roof and helped me repair it. I finally started talking to her, and she convinced me to help her in exchange for free labor. During our training, she taught me about God, and I taught her Jujitsu. We developed an amazing friendship. She even became like an aunt to Akio. We lost his mother when he was born. There is only a small clinic here. When she gave birth, they could not stop her bleeding in time."

Akio handed out wood-carved cups of tea.

"Lillie came to check up on us after my wife passed. She was a quick study. After she completed her training, she returned about once a month to say hello and occasionally brought Akio and I small gifts," he said as he wiped a tear from his eye. "She became my best friend and, like a second mom, to Akio."

"My grandmother wanted to bring me to see you on my eighteenth birthday," I informed him.

"I knew as soon as I saw you without her, something had happened. I don't have the means to call her. I knew one day you would come here," Asahi smiled.

The tea was delicious. Not like our hot tea at home. It was warm. I waited for it to cool.

"Brooke, perhaps you and I can have a private conversation," Asahi asked as he looked over at Greg. He let me in first. "Please don't disturb us. We have a lot to discuss."

I smiled. "Greg and I do not have secrets."

"Akio, entertain Greg while I speak privately with Brooke." He rose and motioned for me to follow him. I placed my tea on the table and followed him to his backroom.

The room was beautiful. There was a bed, a dresser, and a chair. He leads a simple life with minimal distractions. The hut did not appear to have electricity or running water. He shut the bedroom door and motioned for me to be quiet. He pulled the corner of the bed frame up. The bed moved to the side, revealing a narrow stairwell under the home into what appeared to be a cave. He motioned for me to enter. At first, I hesitated.

I looked at Asahi. *Brooke, you need to trust him. Grandma did.* I proceeded down the secret stairwell into the dark cave. Once Asahi was clear of the bed, it returned to its original position, leaving us in the dark. He lit a match, followed by a torch I had not noticed mounted on the wall. He moved ahead of me. We walked for about

21

four minutes, moving downward deeper into the cave. Ahead of us were two passages. One to the right and one to the left. We took the passage to the left. We walked for about another minute and entered an enormous cavern. Asahi asked me to stay where I was. He walked around and lit several other torches. The light flickered across the room, revealing what appeared to be a training room. It was cool down there and I could hear a trickle of water.

He hung the torch on the wall and motioned toward some pillows along the far wall. "Please have a seat."

I sat down and looked around. It was as if Asahi had a secret lair. He sat across from me.

"Akio does not know about the power of the stone. However, he has mastered the art of Jujitsu. I find it hard to keep up with him." He leaned in and said, "Don't tell him I told you." He leaned back and chuckled. "It is up to you if you would like him to know about the stone. He is trustworthy and loyal. He, like me, will honor any commitment he will make with you or your family. Lillie wanted me to teach you the art of Jujitsu. I do not wish to waste our time if you are not interested. Is this something you would like to learn?"

"Yes. I need to learn as much as I can to protect the Bloom of Dreams."

"Very well. We will need to discuss when the training will begin. What kind of shape are you in?"

I smiled and commented, "I'm in great shape. Greg has been working with me. He has been training me in Karate."

"Good. Perhaps he can join us from time to time. My son is unaware of this room. I found this cave when I was young and have slowly worked in it and my home over the years. When my son moved out, I moved in here. Lillie helped me over the years with the hut. She wanted to pay someone, but it would not mean as much if I had not used my own hands to create this sanctuary for myself. If you wish to let Akio know about the stone, I'll reveal this place to him. There's no need for it otherwise. Whenever we train, I'll meet you down here at our designated time. There are matches on that small table if you arrive before I do. Matches are scarce around here. I may need you to bring them occasionally."

"Regarding Akio, do you think he should know?"

Asahi took a deep breath and bowed his head for a few moments. He said, "I do. You may need him because I am getting old. I vowed to your grandmother I would keep this place a secret until she was ready for me to bring him into assisting your family. I think Lillie thought we would never get old. We rarely trained together over the past few years. We spent our time talking about our lives and a great deal about you."

"I suspect there's no time like the present," I said as I stood up.

"I suppose you are right," he rose and placed his hand on my shoulder.

"I take it you have done this before?"

"Yes. I've been on a few missions with Lillie over the years," he said with a smile and gently squeezed my shoulder. "Bring us to my bedroom."

We arrived and joined Greg and Akio, who had moved to the porch. I told them, "Please join us inside. We have much to discuss."

As we moved back to our seats, telepathically I told Greg what was going on. He looked over at me and smiled.

"Akio, you know honor and commitment are important. You also know Lillie was our family. She had a secret that she has passed on to Brooke. Brooke would like to share that secret with you."

Akio looked shocked. His eyes moved from his father to me. He appeared to be waiting for more information.

Asahi continued, "Before we move on, you must vow to protect this secret with your life. If they need you to assist Brooke or her family to protect this secret, you must do it without hesitation."

I interrupted, "Sorry, but you must also agree to assist the Bloom Keepers as well." Asahi looked confused. "I'll explain later."

He nodded and turned to Akio. Everyone's gaze moved toward him.

There was a long pause. Akio looked at me, "I'm honored you would trust me with such a secret. Forgive me, I'm very confused. Could I have a little more information before I make my decision?"

"Few people are aware of my secret and a few aware of it have tried to kill me and one was successful at killing my grandmother. This secret could put your life at risk," I informed him.

Akio turned to his father and asked, "You have been protecting such a secret?"

Asahi bowed his head. "It's been a great honor. I'll protect it until I die, as you should."

Greg looked over at Akio. He informed him, "I'm so glad you speak English. I found out about it by accident. I can assure you this secret will change your life. It certainly has changed mine for the better. I truly feel this secret was a gift from God."

"My curiosity about this secret is eating away at me. Father, could we talk privately for a minute?" Asahi and Akio excused themselves and went into the bedroom. When they returned, Akio stood before me and bowed his head. "It would be a great honor to serve you in whatever capacity you would need me. You have my word; I'll keep your secret and protect you and it until the day I die. Oh, and the Bloom Keepers. I'll protect them as well."

I jumped up and hugged him. "Thank you. We'll protect you as well."

Akio chuckled.

Using telepathy, I asked Asahi if I could take everyone to the cavern. He nodded. "I guess the best way to show you my secret is to show it to you in action."

Akio looked puzzled. I wrapped my hand around his arm and pulled out my mirror. Greg stood behind me and placed his hands on my waist. Asahi placed his hand on my shoulder opposite Akio. I looked up at Akio. He seemed confused and possibly a little scared. I focused on the cavern and teleported us to it.

Akio, "What just happened?" He looked around. "Where are we?"

"Your father will tell you about the location. I am the guardian of the Bloom of Dreams and its cradle." I lifted the necklace from my chest to show him. This stone and its cradle have powers that allow me to transport myself and others to locations I have been to or seen. There are a few that know of its existence. I must protect it with my life. It is never to be used for evil things."

"I feel like I am in a dream," he said as he looked up at us nervously.

"The teleporting gets easier the more you do it," Greg assured him.

"Dad, how long have you known about this?"

Asahi placed his hand on his son's shoulder and looked him in the eye. "Many years, my son. You were just a young boy when I found out."

"This is crazy," Akio said, shaking his head. His fear seemed to turn to excitement. "What else can that thing do?"

I grabbed his arm and concentrated on the mirror. "We'll be back." I took him to my room.

Akio looked around. "Where are we?"

I explained to him we were in my room. I grabbed Akio's arm again and concentrated on the Eiffel Tower, but made sure we would be invisible.

The Eiffel Tower appeared in the full-length mirror in front of me. "Just observe. Don't say a word or touch anyone. They won't be able to see you." I stepped through the mirror and pulled Akio behind me. He was like a young child after they learned how to ride a bike for the first time. He looked over at me. Using telepathy, I told him he could talk to me with his mind.

"We're here. I can feel the breeze." Akio looked around. "Brooke, there are no words."

After a minute, I brought us back to the cavern.

"Dad, I went to America and France," Akio said and shook his head again. "Are you sure there was nothing in that tea?"

"You made it," I laughed.

We talked a while longer before I told them we needed to head home. Asahi and I worked out our training session schedule. Greg and Akio would join us when they can. We said our goodbyes.

Akio hollered, "Wait! Aren't you going to take us back to my dad's house?"

I smiled and looked over at Asahi.

"Son, we are still at my house." Akio puzzled. "Help me put these torches out, and we will head back."

I concentrated and brought us back to my room.

"That was fantastic. Thanks for bringing me along," Greg said with a smile. He and I spent the rest of the night watching movies and discussing how different life was in Aogashima, Japan.

Four

I walked into the kitchen after my morning workout and found Phyllis leaning up against the counter, giggling at her phone. This was like watching the rare sighting of an extinct bird. Phyllis occasionally used her phone and when she did, it was short and to the point. She never searched the internet or played games. "What's going on?"

Phyllis looked up quickly and returned to her phone. She glanced up and asked, "What?"

"What has got your attention? You're never on your phone for more than a minute," I said as I tried to peek at her phone screen.

"It's Hal. He is sending me the cutest things. Look at this," Phyllis said, turning her phone toward me and revealing a picture of a horse wearing glasses.

"Is Hal the butcher?"

"Yes. He's still trying to take me on a date with him," Phyllis said, almost blushing.

"Why don't you go?"

"I haven't dated in many years. I wouldn't know what to say or do," she said, putting her phone down on the counter.

"Is that the only reason you haven't said yes?"

Phyllis grabbed a glass from the cabinet and filled it with ice water. "Yes. I like him, but what if I say something wrong?" She handed me the glass.

I drank my water and contemplated grabbing her phone and texting Hal back. "Would it make you feel better if I went with you?"

"It would, but I would be even more embarrassed if you went with me. What would he think?"

I chuckled, "You know I could go, and he would never see me. I would be happy to help you with your words."

Phyllis smiled and said, "That's a great idea. Would you do that for me?"

I did not think she would take me up on it. I was joking, but she needed me to help her. "Yes, if I'm available. I'm about to do some training." I filled her on Asahi and Akio.

"Japan, how exciting," Phyllis said as she took my now empty glass.

I kissed her on the cheek and went to my room to freshen up a little before teleporting to the cavern.

The cave was lit with torches, but I did not see Asahi. I placed my towel on a small table by the pillows. I stretched out while I waited. As I was coming up from the ground, I heard a noise behind me. Immediately, I put myself in a position to defend myself. Asahi came at me with full force. I was able to dodge many of his strikes. He grabbed my shirt and flipped me over his shoulder. He pinned me down. As hard as I tried, I could not get up.

"You've impressed me. Greg taught you well. Lillie had virtually zero skills when we met. Karate is a striking martial art, whereas jiujitsu is a grappling art. My father taught me both. He lived in Brazil for twenty-three years. We moved here when I was a teenager."

We trained on a variety of things, including stance, chokes, and throws. While we spared one another, Akio showed up.

Akio stood in the distance and watched for a few minutes. He hollered, "Would you like to spar with me?"

Asahi whispered in my ear, "Don't hold back. Use what you've learned today and your Karate."

I nodded. Turning to Akio, I answered, "Sure." He stood before me, and I bowed to him.

Akio immediately started trying to grab me, but I got a punch in and swiped the back of his leg, bringing him to the ground. That was when things turned on me. Being on the mat was his zone. He pinned me down and had me in a throat choke within seconds. *I can't breathe. I can't talk.* My mind was not thinking about telling him to stop. I struggled with him. Everything went black.

"Brooke. Brooke, wake up. I'm so sorry." I heard Akio saying over and over.

I opened my eyes. Akio and Asahi were both beside me.

"She's coming to," Asahi said, sounding relieved.

"I'm sorry, Brooke. I didn't mean to make you pass out. It's been a long time since I've done that move," Akio said as he ran his hand across my forehead. "Please forgive me."

I sat up. Feeling a little lightheaded. "I'm fine." I could feel the stone healing me. My head cleared.

Akio's face showed genuine concern. He asked, "Are you sure you're, okay?"

"Yes, I'm fine. Shall we try this again? Only this time no throat chokes," I said, laughing.

They laughed with me.

"I think that is enough for one day. Brooke, you're an amazing young lady. Lillie would be proud," Asahi said as he gave me a side hug. "How about some tea?"

I started heading toward the secret entrance to his home when Akio stopped me. He asked, "Can't we do your special way?"

At first, I was confused. I quickly realized he wanted me to teleport us, which I did. Asahi and I talked about my grandmother and Akio made us blackened eggs. Asahi told us the eggs were cooked in volcanic steam. This process turns the outer shell black. I enjoyed the eggs' smokey flavor.

During our conversation, I discovered Asahi knew Leonardo and Isabella. "Lillie had me stay there to ensure they were safe. I pretended to be a cleaning man. This prevented anyone from suspecting why I was there. Anthony Granaldi III showed up there one night and took them to the wine cellar. Fortunately, Leonardo gave me a master key. I unlocked the door and caught them questioning Leonardo in a not-so-friendly way. Let's just say they were not in any hurry to come back after I escorted them out. Isabella contacted Lillie. She came and healed Leonardo of his injuries."

I promised to bring them both to the villa to see them.

Akio seemed excited. "Where's their villa?"

"Italy," I said, knowing he would be thrilled.

I enjoyed visiting with them, but I needed to head home and not wear out my welcome. I told them I would be back the next day.

As soon as I arrived home, I jumped in the shower. As I dressed, I ran the various moves I had learned in my head and occasionally performed them. Jujitsu differed from Karate. I grabbed my phone and saw I had missed a few texts while I was gone.

JULIET:　　　　　I need a spa day. These boys have too much energy.

I texted her back an image of a bubble bath with candles surrounding it. *I hope she survives the summer with the twins.* Greg sent me a picture of his bloody hand in front of a blackberry bush.

GREG: Ouch.

An idea popped into my head. I finished getting dressed and stood in front of my full-length mirror. I concentrated on the image Greg sent me. The image barely disclosed the field. *Please let this work.* I arrive invisibly next to a blackberry bush. I hope this is the right field. There was a rustling in the distance. I followed the path toward the sound. They had picked the blackberries in that area. There was an opening in the path and in the next row, I could see a few men wearing hats. Moving to stealth mode, I made my way toward them. Austin and his father, Bill, and another man were blocking the direct route to Greg. I focused on using telepathy to speak with Greg. "Surprise."

In a surprised and loud voice, Greg said, "Brooke?"

I was so shocked my eyes widened.

"Dude, I know ya love the gal, but ya don't need to be screaming out her name," Austin hollered down toward him. All the other men laughed.

Greg looked so embarrassed.

"Tell them you forgot something you need to tell me, and I'll follow you," I said to him in his head.

Greg told them and walked away from them. Making sure not to stir up the dirt as I walked, I followed Greg. When he was well out of their view and not in earshot, Greg turned around and whispered, "Brooke?"

I grabbed his face and kissed him. His arms wrapped around me and pulled me closer. When we finished greeting one another he leaned back. His hands moved from my back to my waist. "This isn't weird at all," he said with a quirky smile.

"I thought it would be nice to surprise you," I said before giving him another peck on the lips.

He appeared to be looking me up and down and said, "I love ya came here. How am I supposed to kiss you? I can't see you."

"I was so lost in the moment I forgot I was invisible."

He felt around for my face and positioned it between his hands. "This is kinda cool." He attempted to kiss me on the lips again but missed and kissed my nose.

We both laughed. I took his hand and looked at the cut he had. "Let me heal that for you."

Greg quickly pulled his hand away. "Ya can't. The guys already saw it. Bill told me to wear my gloves, and I forgot to put them back on after lunch."

We kissed for a few more moments before he returned to the group and me to the comfort of my room. I took my shoes off and banged them out on my balcony to assure I did not make a mess in the house.

My heart was still fluttering from my secret escapade with Greg. I skipped down the stairs toward the kitchen. The blackened eggs did not satisfy my stomach. I could hear humming coming from the kitchen. I tipped toed over to see what was going on. Phyllis was dancing around, putting groceries away.

I ran up and caught her and began acting like I was her male partner. She stopped and blushed.

"Look at us, we both seem to be having fantastic days," I said before spinning around.

"Why are you having such a great day?"

I filled her in on my surprise visit with Greg. "I'm guessing you're in a great mood because you saw Hal at the store."

Phyllis showed her embarrassment again. "His schedule's different every week. We are going to have lunch on Friday." Phyllis grabbed my hands and said, "Please tell me you're available."

"I will be there. Give me the details," I said as I sat down at the counter. Phyllis filled me in on how he asked her out again. It surprised Hal when she said yes. Phyllis and I chatted a bit before going out to get her a new outfit for her date. We found the cutest pink dress. Luckily, she had a pair of cute sandals to wear with it.

We had lost track of time, so we planned on ordering Chinese food for dinner. Mom was home when we arrived. She was at the desk by the front door. It appeared she was working on her bills. "Hey ladies. I found out I need to leave first thing in the morning and head to California for business. I should be back on Friday night, but that is still up in the air." She licked an envelope and stuck it in a pile with some other mail.

Mom looked overwhelmed. I asked her, "Do you need me to get you from the airport?"

"No, the company driver will bring me home. Phyllis, would you make sure this pile of envelopes gets in the mail tomorrow? I need to head up and pack. When is dinner?"

31

Phyllis said, "We're going to order Chinese. Do you want your usual?"

"Yes, please. Thank you. Please call me when it arrives," Mom said as she grabbed her things and proceeded up the stairs.

I grabbed my phone and noticed a text.

JACOB: I've got the info.

It was nearly 5:30 pm.

BROOKE: Can you come over at 7:00 pm?

JACOB: Can Juliet come?

I assured him they were both always welcome. My stomach growled. I ordered a smorgasbord of food for us.

It took forever for our food to arrive. It was nearly 6:30 when it showed up. Mom joined us. She scarfed down her food like she had not eaten all day. We had Egg Rolls, Wonton Soup, Vegetable Lo Mein, Hunan Beef, Pork Fried Rice, and Sweet & Sour Chicken. Everything was amazing. We usually eat with chopsticks, but Mom did not seem to want to fuss with them tonight. As soon as she finished devouring her food, she rushed back upstairs. Phyllis and I were taking our time enjoying everything and chatting about her date on Friday.

The doorbell chimed. Phyllis answered it. She returned with not just Jacob and Juliet, but Greg as well. Everyone sat down and Phyllis offered everyone to join us, which they did. It surprised me I had ordered enough for them to each get a decent amount of food.

Jacob looked around and asked, "Where's your mom?"

"She is upstairs packing. With her room on the third floor, it is unlikely she can hear us. I can't hear anything from my room," I assured him.

Jacob grabbed his computer. Everyone watched as he set it up. "Marshall Blaise is a tough man to find. I found his daughter, Misty Blaise. She lives in Miami. Her mother is American. She and Marshall never married. I can't find all the details. She has never lived in France. I couldn't even find a passport for her."

Juliet held her hand up and asked, "Are you telling me you can hack into our government databases and find a person's passports?"

"Those words never came from my mouth," Jacob chuckled. "Who am I dating?"

32

At that moment, we all began laughing. We had not noticed my mother coming around the corner holding a shirt on a hanger.

She smiled and asked, "What's so funny?"

"Juliet is consistently being surprised by Jacob's computer skills," Greg said with a smirk on his face.

Mom seemed confused. "Phyllis, would you mind ironing this for me? I need to take it on my trip."

Phyllis got up and took the blouse. She walked quickly toward the laundry room.

Mom turned back to us. "It was nice seeing all of you. Have fun," she pivoted and immediately left us. We heard her running up the stairs.

"That was close," Jacob said, looking almost afraid to continue.

I asked, "Do you have a picture of Misty?"

"Tons of them. She likes social media. Misty is attending Miami International College. She is a sophomore and with the number of pictures she has of her partying, I'm amazed her grades are so good."

I looked at the pictures. I said, "The campus is huge. Do you know where she lives?"

He handed me a sticky note with her address and apartment number.

"I know she is going to a party on Friday night," Jacob said with a grin.

"A party on a Friday night. I think we should all crash it," Greg said as he leaned back in his chair. He appeared to be proud of his suggestion.

Juliet chimed in, "It's been a long time since we all have worked together on a mission."

I pivoted my head toward Jacob and asked, "What, you've nothing to add, Jacob?"

"Actually … I do. I think you are going to need me to help you locate this shindig. Oh, and you know I'm here to keep you safe," Jacob said, making a Karate move with his hands.

We all had a good laugh. I looked at each of them and realized they were anxiously waiting for my response. "I don't know. There is a lot to consider." I intentionally wanted to make them wait for my answer. "I think it's best… if we all went to Miami for a fun evening."

Everyone was beaming with excitement. Phyllis strolled by the dining room with Mom's ironed shirt in hand. I wanted something sweet. "How about some dessert?" After two nods and a yes. I grabbed a few of the Chinese food containers and went to see what I could serve everyone.

I was looking through the pantry when Phyllis showed up with more containers and our plates.

Phyllis asked, "Can I help you find anything?"

"I was looking for a dessert for us," I replied.

"Sorry, I did not have time to make one today, but I have an idea," Phyllis said, as she went into the pantry and pulled out some chocolate and sprinkles. She melted the chocolate in the microwave and asked me to get the box of ice cream sandwiches from the freezer. She grabbed five small plates and placed them on the counter.

Phyllis cut the ice cream sandwiches in half. She dipped each half in the chocolate. She had me add sprinkles to it. Phyllis placed them on the plate with one laying down and the other leaning against it.

Phyllis helped me bring them out. She returned with ice water for each of us. Her quick thinking impressed everyone.

"Phyllis, I want you to adopt me," Jacob said as he grabbed the sandwich and began eating.

"I'll consider it," she said with a grin.

We continued hanging out until Jacob informed us, he and Juliet needed to leave. They had to work the next day.

"I didn't realize it was so late. Yah, I need to go too. I need to be at the farm early," Greg spouted.

Phyllis grabbed the dishes and said her goodbyes. I walked everyone to the door. Greg stayed for a moment on the porch with me for a goodnight kiss.

"Bill told me he would pay you to help pick the blueberries if you are interested," he said as he drew me closer to him. "I told him your hands are too beautiful for such work." He lifted my hand and kissed it.

We did not linger with our goodbyes, because Greg was exhausted.

I got ready for bed and began thinking about Misty. *Does she even know her dad? Will she be able to tell us anything that will help us locate him? How will I get her to talk about him?* I prayed about it. *It's in the Lord's hands now.*

Five

I spent the week training with Asahi and occasionally Akio. Fortunately, Akio did not knock me unconscious again. We even did some training in the jungle. I climbed trees and did flips off them or leaped over limbs. Asahi had us leaping from one tree to another. Akio followed me along the course he had me on. He missed one jump to another tree. I know I shouldn't be, but it made me proud that I could do something he couldn't. He was amazing to watch. It was much like parkour. They were both impressed and asked if I had been a gymnast. Neither of them had ever heard of parkour. I promised to take them someday.

This morning at breakfast, Phyllis did not seem to act like herself. She was nervous about her lunch date today. Because of the date, I did not train with Asahi. Instead, I went early to the parkour training center and got a good workout.

As I stood in my closet trying to figure out what to wear on Phyllis's date, it hit me. *No one is going to see me.* At my realization, I rolled my eyes. I threw on some shorts and a t-shirt. I wore my Vans because they were the quietest of my sneakers.

I pulled my hair back in a ponytail and went downstairs to wait for his arrival. Phyllis had not come downstairs yet. I plopped myself down on the sofa in the sitting room and began scrolling through social media. About fifteen minutes later, the doorbell chimed.

I opened the door and discovered a man wearing jeans and a green plaid short-sleeve shirt. He nervously said, "Is Phyllis here?"

"You must be Hal. Please come in," I said as I opened the door to let him in. He stood and gazed up at the grand entrance of our home.

"I'm Brooke. Follow me." I led him to the sitting room. "Have a seat. I'll tell her you're here."

"Wait. This is her home?"

"Yes. Phyllis has been living here for as long as I can remember. Why?"

Hal seemed puzzled. He asked, "I didn't know she came from money. Maybe I should leave."

I explained the situation to him but assured him she was like family to us. The explanation appeared to be good news. I excused myself and went to retrieve her.

Phyllis's door was open. She stood in front of her dresser smelling perfumes. I knocked on her door frame. She spun around. "He's here, isn't he?" The look of fear come over her.

"Yes, but you don't need to worry. I'm going to be there with you. You and he talk fine on the phone, right?"

"Yes," Phyllis said, as she seemed to choke on her words.

I looked down at the perfume and asked, "Which one did you choose?"

Phyllis pointed to a small bottle. I smelled it and handed it to her to put on. "I'll ride over in the back seat of his car. If you want to talk to me, talk using your mind. I'll hear you," I said. I kissed her on the cheek. "I'm going down to tell him you will be down in a minute." I walked to the door and turned to look at her one last time. She smiled at me.

When my foot hit the last step, Hal stood. "Please sit down. She'll be down in a minute." He returned to his seat. "Where are you going for lunch?"

"I thought I would take her to Chili's. Unless you think there is somewhere else, we should go," he said, fidgeting with the keys in his hand.

"I'm sure she will be happy wherever you take her." Chili's is not a good place for someone of her age for a first date. *Should I suggest somewhere else?*

Before I had time to consider another place, Phyllis entered the sitting room. Hal leaped up and greeted her.

Hal looked at her. "You look beautiful, Phyllis."

She thanked him.

Using my power of persuasion on Hal, I tried to convince him to take her to a nicer place. I, however, could not think of a place to suggest.

Hal asked, "Where would you like to go for lunch?"

After a small conversation, Phyllis suggested hibachi. He agreed. I held the door for them. Hal's truck was a single cab truck without a back seat. I told them to enjoy themselves and shut the door.

Moving out of view of windows, I teleported to the bed of his truck. Hal opened Phyllis's door and waited as she buckled up before closing the door.

While he walked around the truck. I poked my head through the cab. I said quietly, "I'm here, but I'm going to use telepathy…" Hal interrupted me opening the door.

We pulled out of the driveway. I waited patiently for one of them to say something, but neither of them did. "Phyllis, tell him how you like the cute photos he sends you, or tell him he looks nice."

"You look nice," she muttered.

"Thanks."

This is going to be a long lunch. "Phyllis, you need to get him to talk to you. Ask him an open-ended question."

"A what?"

"A question that requires more than a one-word answer. Like, what made you become a butcher?"

She asked. Hal began telling her about his stepfather being a cattle farmer. "He butchered his own cattle and, well, he taught me when I was younger. He was a great mentor," he smiled at her.

I was just relaxing and did not notice he turned. My body slid toward him. I tried to brace myself, but it was hard since the stone was allowing me to go through things.

"I've never had hibachi. You mentioned it was on this road. How much farther?"

Phyllis looked around. "It's on the next block in the shopping center."

The silence had returned. With my head still through the cab of the truck to hear, I found myself lunging forward every time Hal hit the brakes. He nearly missed the turn. He braked causing me to slide toward him. I hit his arm with my head. Hal looked down to see what hit him, but thankfully, he could not see me.

Without warning, my body flung upward. I came back down and let out an "Oh" and Hal heard me.

Hal turned to Phyllis, who looked like a deer caught in headlights. "You, okay?"

"Yes. That was a big speed bump," Phyllis said, trying to cover for me.

"Sorry about that," Hal said as he pulled into a parking spot.

Phyllis sat in the car waiting for him to open the door. He seemed to wait at the back of the truck for her. Using my powers of persuasion, I told him to open her door. It was cute how nervous they both were.

Once they were away from the truck, I teleported to the door of the restaurant and followed them in when they entered. They were sitting at a hibachi grill with only one other couple. They both seemed to study the menu.

I suggested, "Phyllis, ask him what he is considering getting?" She did.

"I'm not sure how this works, but I think the steak and shrimp. How about you?"

In a panic, Phyllis asked, "Brooke, what should I order?"

"Look at the price of the steak and shrimp. Remember, never order a meal that costs more than his meal. It's the polite thing to do," I advised.

"I think I'll have the same," she said to Hal with a smile.

The chef came over and asked everyone for their orders. A server brought their drink order. They began chatting and getting to know one another.

My phone vibrated. I missed a call from Juliet. "Phyllis, I'll be right back."

Her eyes widened. "Don't leave me," she screamed with her eyes.

"It may be important. I need to call Juliet back," I said. I teleported to my bedroom and called Juliet.

In a nervous voice, Juliet said, "Thank you for calling me back. I think Ryan slammed Davy's finger in the door. It looks broken. Can you please come here and fix it?"

"I don't know where you are?"

"My car is in their driveway. Ring the bell when you get here," she said. I heard a cry from a young boy. I assumed it was Davy.

I teleported to her car. I looked around to make sure nobody would see me. The coast was clear. As instructed, I rang the front doorbell and waited for Juliet. The door flung open, and she grabbed my arm and pulled me in. We were moving so fast I was not sure she even closed the front door.

She pulled me from room to room until we reached the kitchen table. Davy was crying at the table while Ryan sat trying to console him.

In a calm voice, Juliet said, "Davy, you remember my friend Brooke? She is very good with booboos. Can she look at your finger?"

He lowered his hand under the table.

"Davy, I promise I won't hurt you. If you show me your hand, I'll show you a magic trick," I said, trying to get him to show me. He wasn't budging.

Juliet looked over at me and pleaded, "Please do something."

I looked at Davy. Think Brooke. Using persuasion, I asked Davy to trust me and to let me hold his hand. He finally permitted me to touch it. It was apparent the finger had broken. I gently placed his finger in my cupped hand. The stone warmed. I watched as his twisted finger moved back into its original position. It surprised me it did not hurt him as it healed. Once the stone was no longer warm, I asked, "How does it feel?"

He began moving it. "You fixed it! Look Ryan, it's fixed!" He jumped from the chair and gave me a super tight hug, nearly knocking me to the ground.

Juliet mouthed, "Thank you."

"I need to get going, but I'll see you later," I said.

I attempted to walk to the front door, but Davy wrapped himself around my legs. Ryan's eyes widened. He grabbed my other leg. Davy said, "Don't leave. You said you would do magic."

"You said that Brooke," Juliet agreed.

"Fine. I will magically disappear," I told them.

"No one can do that," Ryan informed me.

"I can, but remember, magic is not real. It is an illusion. A good magician never discloses the secret to their trick," I informed them.

"Brooke, come into the living room and do your trick," Juliet encouraged me. When we entered, she knocked me with her elbow and looked at the mirror above the mantle.

I smiled to let her know I understood what she was showing me.

"Have a seat," I instructed. They leaped onto the sofa.

I stood between the sofa and the mirror. "Juliet, would you mind standing here?" I pointed to the area between me and the mirror. She stopped but blocked my view of the mirror. I motioned for her to move a little. Put your hands on your eyes when I say and count to three super-fast. I concentrated on the mirror. "Count to three." It then sucked me into the mirror and onto the walkway outside of the restaurant. I confirmed in the window I was invisible before walking through the door. Phyllis and Hal were laughing with the other couple and seemed to enjoy themselves. She did not seem to miss me. I watched them. It brought a smile to my face, knowing she was out there dating again. I have known Phyllis my entire life. She had been alone, or at least I had not known her to date. *Wow. So, sad.*

I felt like a voyeur. Using telepathy, I told Phyllis, "I'm back. Things seem to go well. Do you need me to stay?"

She looked at Hal and smiled and shook her head.

"I'm out of here then. You behave," I said jokingly. I returned to the pantry because I was starving. *Hum, a peanut butter, and jelly sandwich sounds good.* I fixed the sandwich and grabbed an apple and a bottle of water. I strolled out to the patio. It was such a nice day. I sat enjoying my lunch scrolling through my phone when Karen suddenly appeared before me.

"Where have you been? I hardly see you?"

I swallowed the bite of my apple and replied, "I've been around." I motioned for her to have a seat. "What are you doing all summer?"

"Hanging out with my friends. They're all busy today," Karen said, looking down at a small stone next to her. She began moving it around with her foot.

I thought about how I could entertain her and myself until I had to get ready for tonight's mission. "How about a makeover? If you don't think your mother would mind," I asked.

"Really? She won't mind. I can wear makeup. Mom rarely wears it and never showed me how to put it on right. I would rather not wear it than feel embarrassed by the way I apply it."

I finished my lunch and brought her to my room.

"This house is amazing," Karen said as she entered my room.

Despite being Greg's sister and my next-door neighbor, she had never had a tour of the house. She sat down. I went to my bathroom to get my makeup. I sat on the coffee table, leaning over toward her, and began applying the makeup. We laughed and she confided some things to me. I stared at her and thought, this could be my future sister-in-law. The thought brought joy to my heart. She was an amazing person.

We were having an outstanding time and nearly lost track of the time. I told her I needed to get ready for my date. She wanted to stay and watch me do my makeup and hair. I gave her a few outfits to choose from. She picked a skort and a blouse I recently purchased. I curled my hair and put it up in a high ponytail. "How do I look?"

Karen looked me over and went into my closet. She returned with a pair of my sandals. "With these, you'll look gorgeous."

I agreed. She had to leave when her mother called her and told her she needed help with dinner.

The Bloom Keepers agree to have dinner on Miami Beach before heading to the party. I researched places to eat and where we could appear. I had only been to Miami a few times, and I had never been to Miami Beach. After ten minutes of researching, I discovered the restaurants were very expensive. It was difficult to find one everyone could afford. *Finally!* I located a Latin restaurant. The prices were perfect for a bunch of college students. I looked for pictures of places in the area to teleport to. I found a picture of the restaurant. *We will teleport to the door invisible and find a place to become visible after we arrive.*

I relaxed until it was time to leave.

Six

We would grab dinner at 8:30 pm because college parties typically started late. It would be easier to blend in with the group of students than be the first to arrive. The Bloom Keepers arrived about 8:15 pm. Juliet looked amazing in her Hawaiian Jumper. The blues and greens in the material complimented her skin tone. She even had her hair up. Jacob wore black pants and a blue button-up short-sleeve shirt. Greg wore his usual jeans, a nice western shirt, and cowboy boots.

"I hate to say this, but you might want to change," I said to Greg. Greg looked at his clothes and back at us. "There are not a lot of cowboys in Miami. We need to blend in with the locals."

Greg agreed to change. He returned with a black shirt and sneakers. Everyone gathered around me. We teleported to the door of the Latin restaurant, invisible. Fortunately, only a few people were on the sidewalk, but there were a few people in the restaurant. We held on to one another as we walked through the door and made our way to the men's restroom. I had them go through the door first and only had my arm enter the room. There was no way I wanted to enter the room and take a chance on seeing anything I shouldn't. Juliet and I went into the ladies' restroom. Two women nearly ran into us as they exited the room. Using telepathy, I told Jacob and Greg to let me know when they were in a stall.

"Brooke, there is only one stall," Greg muttered to me.

"Don't worry. I got this," Jacob assured me. A moment later, "We are ready."

I made each of us visible. "Look in the mirror before you leave the room to make sure you can see yourself," I told everyone, using telepathy.

Juliet and I exited our stalls and moved to the mirror. It was nice to see our reflection and know no one saw us. We exited the bathroom, and a man exited the bathroom quickly. Something seemed to bother him. The man sat down with a few other people and pointed to the bathroom.

Jacob and Greg exited the bathroom. They also seemed bothered by something. I smiled and suggested, "Let's get in line for our food."

Greg pulled me aside and whispered, "We need to go somewhere else to eat."

"Why do you not like Latin food?"

Greg seemed distracted by the man in the bathroom. "Latin is fine. Jacob and I should leave."

Using telepathy, I asked Greg to tell me what happened. Apparently, the man that exited the bathroom before them watched them come out of the same stall. He thought they were doing some hanky-panky in there. I looked over at the table the man was sitting at and, using persuasion, I attempted to have everyone forget about Greg and Jacob.

It appeared the glances toward them stopped. "I think we are good now. Let's get our food."

"Are ya sure? I would feel better if we sat somewhere else," Greg informed me.

I explained to him this was the cheapest restaurant in the area. We could not afford to go anywhere else. He finally gave in and ordered our food.

While we waited, Greg became rather affectionate. He kept hugging me and kissing the top of my head. I looked over at Jacob, who seemed to act similarly. Greg grabbed our tray of food and lead us to a table crammed in a corner away from the man and his friends.

My food looked amazing. Black beans, rice, pulled pork, and plantains were just what I needed. Everything tasted amazing. Greg and Jacob had never had plantains. They like them.

Everyone seemed to enjoy the dinner. It was a little hard to talk about our mission, with our table being close to everyone. Our conversations were more about Jacob's internship, the twins, and Greg wishing he had a more challenging job. He did state Bill paid him well.

We sauntered outside and found an alley to teleport to the party. There were two men in the alleyway chatting. I led everyone in their direction. They did not seem to want the company and scurried away. When the coast was clear, I took everyone to some bushes beside the home. We moved closer to the middle of the house, away from windows to appear. Greg and I walked toward the entrance first. The stucco home had a large, circular brick driveway. Juliet and Jacob would follow us shortly. The driveway was already full of vehicles. People were still arriving. We fell behind a couple of guys as they walked in. Once in the home, we moved out of the walkway and waited for Jacob and Juliet.

It was not long before they came in. The music was so loud they did not hear us call out to them. Using telepathy, I told Juliet to turn around and head back to the front door. She spotted us as she entered the foyer.

Jacob suggested, "We should split up and try to see if we can find Misty. In a large group, it is easier for everyone to tell we are not here with anyone that was invited."

Everyone agreed and split up. It was a large house on the intercoastal. As I looked around the living room, I could tell Greg would have stood out in his boots and plaid shirt. Some people were in nice shorts and shirts, while others looked dressed to go to a nightclub. Several people were sitting in the living room on beige sofas. One man leaning against the wall smiled at me. I smiled back and walked over to him.

"Hello beautiful," he said, looking at me from head to toe.

I played stupid and ignored his flirting. I politely said, "I'm looking for Misty Blaise. Have you seen her?"

"I don't know who she is, but beautiful, you can hang out with me till she gets here."

I smirked at him with a half-smile and removed myself from the living room. His flirting was nauseating.

The dining room was just off the living room. The table sat eight and had high-back chairs. There were a few people there chatting. I listened to their conversation for a few minutes and did not hear anyone mention Misty. This group had a lot of young ladies, and I did not want to approach them out of fear she might be the one I was asking.

Toward the back of the house, Juliet spoke with a short guy who looked to be about eighteen. Juliet waved me over.

"Brooke, this is Bernard. This is his house," Juliet informed me.

He looked up at me and awkwardly said, "Actually, this is my parent's house. They are out of town," Bernard said.

"Bernard told me Misty is not here yet. Her best friend is here, and she told us she should be here soon," Juliet added.

I looked at Bernard. He lacked confidence. The party and it seemed most of the people here were superficial and were probably using him. I don't like people taking advantage of others. "I know you don't know us, but do you mind us just dropping in on your party?"

He looked around the room and said, "I don't know most of the people here. It's still early and people just keep coming. I am going to get in a lot of trouble. My parents told me I could have a couple of friends over. I invited five people from the University. I guess they invited these other people."

Juliet asked, "Did you invite Misty?"

"Yes, she has always been nice to me. Her boyfriend bullies me a lot. He will probably show up with her," Bernard told us, looking around the room again. "Excuse me, I need to make sure everything is okay."

"That poor boy is going to be in so much trouble with his parents. It would not surprise me if a neighbor contacted them to tell them what is going on here," Juliet said as she looked around.

"We need to help him, but not until Misty arrives. We can't take a chance on her not showing up."

Juliet nodded her head in agreement. She suggested, "Let's find the guys and let them know what is going on."

We found Jacob and Greg in the kitchen eating some chips. Juliet filled them in on what was going on, and I went to the foyer to wait for Misty to arrive.

Misty arrived with a large man who was the size of a pro football player. He was huge and appeared to be solid muscle. Everyone seemed to know him when he arrived. While distracted by his friends, I approached her.

With a smile, I asked, "Excuse me, Misty? Misty Blaise?"

She looked confused and asked, "Do I know you?"

"No, but I have an urgent matter I need to discuss with you regarding your father, Marshall Blaise."

Misty raised her hands in the air and snapped, "I don't want to discuss him. The man did nothing more than get my mother pregnant and disappear. He is slime. No, he is worse than slime. He is the sludge at the bottom of a dumpster!"

"I agree with you, which is why I need to talk to you," I said as I noticed she seemed bothered by me.

Her wall of a boyfriend walked over and began bullying her, "I told you, you're not to talk to anyone." He grabbed her arm and pulled her away from me.

Misty looked back at me. Her eyes screamed; I'm scared. I followed them into Bernard's backyard. He shoved her down in a chair and sat down next to her. Misty had her head down, staring at the ground. She looked defeated.

She needs our help. Using telepathy I said, "Greg, Juliet, Jacob? Are you there? Come to the patio."

Anxiously, I looked for them to come through the doorway. Greg came out first, followed by Jacob and Juliet.

As soon as Greg was near me, he asked, "What's going on?"

I didn't want to repeat myself. I waited for Jacob and Juliet to arrive and explained the situation to them. "Misty needs our help, and we need to get her to trust us. She seems fearful of her boyfriend."

"I've been watching him interact with the others. Everyone seems to move away from him as he moves about the house. It's like their afraid of him," Juliet informed me.

"I know I am," Jacob said with a worried face.

"Brooke, you get Misty. Jacob and I'll deal with him," Greg suggested.

Jacob's face looked shocked by Greg's comment. "Greg, I know I just mentioned I'm afraid of him, too."

Juliet hugged Jacob's arm. She told him, "You have been training and are doing great. Trust your instincts."

"My instincts are telling me I should head home," Jacob said with his eyes wide.

"I need you to back me up. Juliet you too. Help in whatever way you can," Greg said. He tapped Jacob on the shoulder and started heading over to the area Misty was sitting in. I followed Greg. Juliet pushed Jacob on the back, and he lunged forward in our direction.

"Misty, we're not finished with our conversation," I said as I stood in front of her.

She looked up at me and mouthed, "Don't. Please."

There was fear in her eyes.

The man got up and said, "Misty, tell your friend to leave."

As I stood next to him, I became very aware of our size difference.

"Please leave," Misty pleaded.

I turned my attention to him. "Misty and I have something serious to discuss. Family business, this doesn't involve you," I informed him.

He stepped closer to me. As he looked down at me, I could feel his hot breath.

"Excuse me, sir, why not just let the two ladies talk for a moment," Greg said as he moved me out of the way of the man.

"Come with me," I said, trying to get Misty up and out of the area. She would not move; I used the power of persuasion to get her to move. She stood up, and the man lunged for her. I pushed her aside and kicked him in the stomach.

The man seemed shocked. I looked over at Misty, whose face appeared to be in shock. "You're in trouble now," she said, trying to pull me away from the area.

He started moving toward me. Jacob tripped, causing him to lunge forward. He swung around and started moving toward Jacob. Jacob moved out of the way for Greg to come at him with another punch that did not seem to faze him.

Out of nowhere, Juliet took a nine-foot pool skimmer net and placed it on his head. She gave it a pull with all her force. This caused him to move away from Greg. He grabbed the pole and yanked it away from her. She released it, causing him to lose his balance. The crowd around us grew.

Bernard came up to me and asked, "What's going on?"

I barely heard him; my attention was on the fight. The man had his back to me. Using a move, Asahi and Akio taught me. I jumped up on him and squeezed his neck as hard as I could until he passed out.

Juliet ran over to me. She asked, "Girl, where did you learn that?"

I instructed them, "We need to get everyone out of here. Juliet, take Misty to the house. Greg, I need you and Jacob to get everyone to leave."

We told everyone to head home. As soon as everyone was out of sight, I grabbed the man and took him to the only place I knew in the area. The ladies room at that Latin restaurant. He was coming to and seemed shocked and confused. Thankfully, he was still groggy.

Using the power of persuasion, I said to him, "If I even hear about you being near Misty again, I will be back. I can assure you we won't be so nice next time. Forget you know her." He leaped toward me, and I went through the stall door."

"Are you a ghost, or a witch, or something?"

"I'll be your worst nightmare if you bother Misty or Bernard again. Perhaps next time, I'll bring you to an area out of this country. A large volcano or even the moon would be too good for you. I'll drop you off and leave you somewhere foreign." He did not know that I could not take him to the moon. I moved closer to him. "Do we have an agreement?"

I focused on moving through things as he swung at me. His fist went right through me.

"Let me make this a little clearer to you. You can't hurt me, but I can put you in the wall and leave you there."

This seemed to worry him.

"How would you like to be put in the middle of a mountain? No air, no way to escape."

"Fine. I'll leave her alone." He looked around. "Where are we?"

"Well, you're in the ladies' room somewhere in Miami." I pointed to myself, "Me, well, I'm out of here," I said as I waved goodbye and, like that, I returned to Bernard's home.

As I walked into the home. It was oddly quiet. I realize everyone had left. Bernard, Greg, and Jacob were cleaning the home. Misty was chatting with Juliet.

Misty jumped up and looked behind me. She nervously asked, "Where's Junior?"

"He's gone. I don't think he will bother you anymore," I said with confidence.

"Thank you for your help with Junior," she said as her eyes watered.

"I know you don't know me, but we have something in common and I need your help," I said as I sat down next to her on the sofa.

"Help with what?"

"I need to be honest with you. Your father murdered my grandmother. I need to find him."

Jacob interjected, "Your dad doesn't have much of a digital footprint."

She looked down for a moment. When she raised her head, everyone gathered around to hear what she was going to say.

"My father has had little to do with me. I haven't seen him in a couple of years. He shows up for important things like my high school graduation. My mother gets money periodically and in exchange, she writes to him to tell him about important things going on."

Jacob asked, "How does he send the money?"

"I'm not sure. Sometimes she gets mail from him or packages. He sent me a doll when I was a junior in high school."

Jacob continued his questioning, "We need to find out where she mails letters to him and if he is wiring the funds to her, I need one of their account numbers."

"I'll see what I can do. How do I get in touch with you?"

Jacob informed her, "We'll get in touch with you. How much time do you need to look?"

"Mom moved out of Miami two years ago. She lives in Anderson, South Carolina now."

I smiled and asked, "Would you mind giving us her address?"

"Sure, but my mom says nothing bad about him. I think she still loves him," she informed us.

"Look, I can't say much, but we'll take care of getting the information about the account. If you need our help with Junior, put something on social media saying you miss your friend Brooke and we will come and help you," Jacob said. "Come on, let's go home."

"Bernard, it was an interesting party. Don't let others talk you into things you don't want to do. You're a cool guy. Find better friends," Greg said, shaking his hand. Jacob shook his hand as well. Juliet and I hugged him before heading back to the side of his home to leave.

Seven

I crashed into the sand from the overwhelming heat from the sun as I walked through a desert. There was no one around except the scorching hot sand. Sweat ran down my face and disappeared as soon as it reached the burning sand.

"Beep. Beep. Beep."

As my alarm awoke me, I realized my sheets were wet from perspiration. Even after removing my covers, I discovered the house was unusually warm. I went to the bathroom and washed my face. It was uncomfortably warm. I changed into some shorts and a t-shirt.

As I moved downstairs, I discovered it was a little cooler. Phyllis was in the kitchen making breakfast looking as well as one could while they were sweating. "Why is it so hot in here?"

"The air conditioner is not working. I made coffee," she said as she chopped fruit.

The thought of drinking hot coffee did not appeal to me. I grabbed a glass and filled it with ice and began making myself an iced coffee.

"Good morning," Mom said as she entered the room. She glanced at my iced coffee. "That is a good idea. She began making herself one. Mom asked, "Phyllis, when will your friend be here?"

"He should be here soon.

I looked at her with my eyes widened and eyebrows lifted. "Friend? You have a friend coming over."

Phyllis threw a kitchen towel at me. "Git your mind out of the gutter. Hal is coming over with his son, who is an air conditioning repairman."

No wonder why she looked so good on a Saturday morning. "Will he be joining us for breakfast?"

Phyllis turned around and gave me a look that said not a word. "He will be."

I gulped down some more coffee. "What's for breakfast?"

"Coffeecake, fruit salad, and bacon wrapped puff pastry twist."

"Sounds great! Do you mind if Greg joins us?"

"Of course not. That boy's always welcome," she said, smiling. "Brooke, please take this to the table." Phyllis pointed to the bowl of fruit. I grabbed a paper towel and blotted the sweat from her forehead. As I washed my hands, the doorbell rang. Immediately Phyllis looked panicked. Mom told us she would answer the door.

"What do you need me to do?"

She pulled the bacon from the oven and asked me to place it upright in the few mugs she had set out. Once it was in the mugs, it looked so cute. It was amazing how she took something so simple and made it adorable. I could not resist the bacon and ate a piece. It was amazing. There was even cheese in it. I took the bacon to the table. Phyllis followed me with the coffee cake.

Mom, Hal, and Hal's son were standing in the foyer discussing the air conditioning. Hal introduced us to his son, Eli.

Phyllis asked, "Eli, would you like to join us for breakfast before you get started?"

"No, thank you, mam. I can't eat a lot when I work. The heat turns my stomach," Eli explained.

I took him to the air conditioning units and texted Greg on the way about breakfast.

GREG: I'll be right over.

Mom was opening the windows in the dining room when I returned. Phyllis entered from the kitchen with Greg behind her carrying a pitcher of orange juice.

Greg put the pitcher on the table and gave me a kiss. "Did you already work out?"

I explained to him why I was so sweaty as we sat down to eat.

Mom was fanning herself with her napkin and asked, "Greg, would you mind blessing the food?"

Greg did as she instructed.

The heat really seemed to bother my mother. She was unusually quiet but asked about their date. As they each told a little about it. I remember to keep my mouth shut.

The breakfast was mainly us talking about how amazing the food was. Greg and I both agreed we ate too much to work out. Besides, my motivation was gone. Greg and I moved to the back patio because it seemed cooler under the roof with the light breeze. My phone alerted me I had received a text.

JACOB: I have photos.

Greg and I had nothing planned for the day. I texted Jacob, Greg, and Juliet.

BROOKE: Anyone up for a trip to South Carolina?

Everyone agreed to meet at my house at 1:00 pm. Juliet had some chores to complete. Greg and I sat on the patio catching up on the week's events. His parents were planning a trip to celebrate his mother being cancer-free. He would be responsible for Karen during that week. I offered to help. He said he would let me know when they had confirmed a date. He would be taking the week off from work.

Phyllis came out and informed us the air conditioning was back on and asked if we would help close the windows. We had a couple of hours to kill and tried to think of things we could do until everyone arrived. I knew I needed a shower before then. We thought about working out in my training room, but the house had not cooled down enough. We sat in the library trying to come up with ideas when Mom walked in.

Mom leaned against the door frame, "I thought you were still home. I'm free today. Would you both like to go do something?"

"We are free for a little while, but we have plans with Jacob & Juliet at 1:00 o'clock," I informed her. She looked disappointed. "Is Lance busy today?"

"Lance is a great man but I'm not sure it's going to work out. He has a problem with my job. He thinks I work too much, and he hates that it requires me to be out of town so much. By the way. I'll be gone all next week. I forgot to tell you. I will be spending my days working in Hawaii," she said proudly.

"I'm a little jealous," I told her.

"You know you could come with me. I'll be working a lot, but you could go site seeing while I work. I should warn you. I may be back to the hotel late," Mom said as she moved closer into the room.

"Tempting. Perhaps another time. Touring Hawaii alone does not sound like much fun. Besides, you and I both know you will be working even when you are at the hotel," I told her.

"Well, if you don't mind sharing a bed with a friend. Perhaps you could bring Juliet or someone."

"She has a job for the summer. Thank you though. I will be fine here," I told her. Secretly I wished Juliet, and I could take that trip.

"I guess I'll head up and start packing."

I knew she wanted to spend time with me, "We could play a game for an hour or so. If you're interested.

We played scrabble until it was time for me to shower. Greg went home to get cleaned up also.

I had been blowing my hair dry when I heard my name, "Hello."

"It's Juliet. Can I come in?"

I walked into my room to greet her, "Sorry, I didn't hear the doorbell."

"Jacob and I have been out front ringing it. We finally walked out back and found Phyllis with a man on the porch. She told me to come up. Jacob is waiting downstairs for us. Who is the man?"

I filled her in before I finished blowing my hair dry.

I went up to my mother's room and told her we were leaving. She hugged me, "Thank you for spending some time with me today. How about we have a mother-daughter day soon?"

"That sounds great. Will you let Phyllis know I left? I don't want to bother her and Hal."

"Sure. Have fun sweetheart," she said before returning to her suitcase.

I returned to my room. Everyone was there waiting for me. Jacob showed me the picture of Misty's mother's house. Everyone placed their phones in my drawer before we stepped through my full-length mirror. We arrived in a wooded area behind her home.

From the backyard, there was not an entrance or even a window low enough for me to investigate. There was a small balcony, "Wait here. I'm going to go around the front and see if anyone is home." There was a small pathway between her home and the home next door. There was not a car in the driveway, but she had a two-car garage.

I walked past the front door of the brick home to a window opposite the garage. I looked in and could see it appeared to be a spare bedroom with some gym equipment in it. I leaned in and tried to cup my hands to see in better, but my hands did nothing because they were invisible. *That was stupid of me.*

I approached the front door to see if I could peer through the glass windows on either side of the door. The blinds were closed on both. I took a deep breath and entered the home. I leaned only my head through the front door hoping to hear something. Silence. I pulled myself the rest of the way through the door. There was a table to the left. Stairs to the left, just past what must be the garage entrance.

I stepped further into the room. To the right of me was a fireplace and just past it was a small hallway that led to the front bedroom, an office, and a bathroom. Past the stairs were two doors. The first one was closed. I gently opened it. It was a closet. The second door led to the master bedroom. It had massive furniture. The room had a large closet and a beautiful bathroom.

I returned to the living room and walked toward the opposite side of the home. The dining room had a stunning view of the wooded area my friends were in. Just past the woods was a boat dock and a lake. Opposite the dining room was the kitchen.

Using telepathy, I told them to come to the front door. I met them at the door to pull them through it. Greg stayed out front and be our lookout. A large sailfish mounted above the television caught my eye.

"We need to find an address or banking information that will lead us to Marshall Blaise," Jacob reminded us. Each of us had our gloves on to ensure we did not leave prints anywhere.

"I'm going to go see what is upstairs," I informed them. This contained another bedroom, along with some storage boxes. I went through some boxes and found photo albums and childhood mementos, but nothing that would lead me to Marshall.

I returned to the office. "How's it going in here?"

"Nothing yet," Juliet said as she continued to focus on what she was doing.

"I'm going to the master bedroom and look," I said.

I stood in the doorway. *Where would I put something important here?* I started with the nightstands. A bottle of sleeping pills, some lip balm, a box of tissues, and a variety of perfumes were all the secrets it held.

Suddenly, I heard the front door fling open. I quickly shut the closet door.

"If he thinks he can pull one over on me, he's mistaken."

I tiptoed over to the doorway to the living room. A woman was on the phone. "Look, I moved up here to be with you. The least you could do is to be a little more understanding."

Brooke, think! What should I do? I thought about getting everyone and heading home, but I was sure they had not found anything. They needed more time. I wanted to know what she was mad about and who did she move here for.

Using telepathy, I told them to keep looking I was going to distract her. I also reminded them to be exceptionally quiet.

"Look, I can't explain that to you. Where I get money from is none of your business," she said, sounding annoyed. "No, I'm not doing anything illegal."

A sound came from the office. She turned and said, "Hold on."

"Greg, ring the doorbell," I said in a panic. I pulled my mirror. The doorbell rang. I teleported to the front door, visible. I motioned to Greg and told him to hide. "Everyone, you're visible now," I said as she answered the door.

"Can I help you?"

"Yes, I'm a friend of Misty's. I'm in town and wanted to know if she was home," I said.

"Misty stayed in Miami. She has an apartment there. She won't be here for months." She looked passed me. "When was the last time you talked to her?"

She must be on to me. "It's been a while. She knew my family lived here and said to stop by if I was ever in town. I knew her a year ago. We had a few classes together."

My stomach began growling. I forgot to eat lunch. "Do you have a way for me to contact her?"

Misty's mother asked, "Where's your car?"

How did you get into the neighborhood? Think Brooke. "I left my car outside the gate. I didn't have the code or a number to call Misty for her to let me in," I told her.

She still seemed suspicious, but I began providing me with her contact information. "Sorry, unlike most people my age, I've never been fast at texting." I slowly put the information from my phone.

She returned to her phone. "Sorry, some kid was at the door." The door slammed shut. Without hiding, I teleported to the bedroom and took Juliet and Jacob back to the woods, invisible. I returned to Greg, who was hiding behind a tree in the vacant lot next door.

"Why didn't you warn us?"

"Brooke? Where are you?"

I grabbed his arm.

"I tried, but the telepathy thing was not working," Greg informed me.

"Interesting. So, I just need to focus on it the entire time to hear you."

I took him back to the others.

Greg asked, "Did you find anything?"

"We found some banking information. We are going to need to return it when we are done. I had nothing to write it down on," Jacob said. He showed us a handful of papers.

"Thanks for tapping on the window, Greg," Jacob told him.

Greg and I explained the error of our plan and returned to my room. Everyone grabbed their phones and Jacob went to his car to get the laptop. Everyone settled into our usual spots in the library. My stomach growled, so I ran to the kitchen to grab something to eat. I gulped down a peanut butter and jelly sandwich as I made snacks and grabbed a few water bottles to bring to the library. I placed everything in one of Phyllis's shopping bags. No one was around, so I teleported back to the library.

"Brooke, you really need a warning system when you do that. You startled me," Juliet said, trying to catch her breath.

I apologized and placed everything on the desk for anyone who wanted something. While Jacob looked for Marshall Blaise's information, we discussed what had transpired at Misty's mother's home.

"Rebecca Riley," Jacob spurted out.

We all looked confused, but Juliet asked, "Who?"

"Rebecca Riley is Misty's mother's name," Jacob said, putting his computer down and getting up to grab a bottle of water. "The money is not being wired to her. Well, at least not to the account we have. It's possible she has another account, but it's not at that bank."

Greg moved the chips aside to make room for him to sit on the desk. "So, we need to go back?"

"Yes. It doesn't appear she works. Money's going into her account, but they're cash deposits. Occasionally they put in a money order, but not a steady paycheck. I don't know how she's making money," Jacob said as he returned to his seat.

Everyone seemed to take a deep breath.

Juliet sat up and said, "We really don't have a choice. She's our only chance of locating Marshall."

"Juliet's right. I don't think it's safe for all of us to go back. She can come and go," I advised. I lowered my head.

Jacob asked, "Do you think Misty would help?"

Juliet sat up quickly. "I think she would. She seemed sincere when she thanked us for helping her with Junior."

"I think ya gals should speak with her. She seemed to like ya both," Greg suggested.

"I agree. The last thing that girl needs is a guy demanding her to help him," Jacob concurred.

I asked Jacob to contact her on her social media account. We would hold a meeting tomorrow after church. Juliet and I both agreed to go.

I took Jacob back to return the papers before she noticed them missing. We spent the rest of the day hanging out and training. It impressed me with how much Jacob had learned in such a short span of time.

Eight

During church, I ran conversations through my head about how to approach Misty. I needed her help, but the last thing I wanted to do was to make her feel like I was using her. My mother accidentally dropped her pen. As I reached down to help her retrieve it, it occurred to me I was not paying attention to the service. I tried to focus on what our pastor was saying.

Pastor Ellis said, "We are called to love one another. Our gifts are used to serve others in a way that gives the glory to God. 1 Peter 4:10 says, 'Each of you should use whatever gifts you have received to serve others, as faithful stewards of God's grace in its various forms.'"

I thought about those words. With all my heart, I knew God had given my family the Bloom of Dreams to protect and to help others. I also knew it was to help defeat evil. This passage made me more curious about the sermon. I began listening intently.

When church let out, my mother's friend, Deborah, stopped her. Phyllis and I waited by the door for them to finish their conversation. "Phyllis, I have an assignment," I said, making quotations with my hands. "I need to be in Miami in twenty minutes. Would you mind covering for me?"

"Of course not," she said with a smile. "You're so much like Lillie."

"Any suggestions where I could exit the area from?"

Phyllis leaned over and whispered, "The family restroom. Just don't lock the door when you go in."

I hugged her, and as I was about to make my way to the restroom, Deborah and my mother approached us. "Happy Sunday ladies," Deborah said as she hugged us both. We returned the greeting.

"I invited Deborah to join us for lunch today," Mom informed us.

"That's wonderful. Brooke can't join us. She and Juliet are helping a friend with a problem. I believe Juliet will be here soon to pick her up," Phyllis said, as she grabbed Deborah's arm and started leading her out of the church. "I wanted to talk to you about your Lemon Cookie recipe. Rumor has it yours are the best."

"I guess I'll see you later. I need to catch up with them," I said.

Mom kissed me on the cheek. She began speed walking to catch up with them.

I did as Phyllis suggested. I teleported from the family restroom into Jacob's closet. Juliet was on his bed playing on her phone when I arrived. "Where's Jacob?"

"He went down to get something to eat. It amazes me how much that boy can consume. He doesn't even gain a pound," Juliet said as she sat up.

"Where are we going to meet her?

"She suggested her apartment."

The door flung open. "Hey Brooke," Jacob said as he stood there with a bag of BBQ chips.

I moved closer to his computer. "Do you have a photo for us?"

Jacob put his bag of chips down and pulled up a picture of an apartment building.

"Any suggestions on how we can become visible? There's nowhere to hide here."

Jacob quickly chewed and swallowed a chip. "The building has an elevator. I suggest there. Oh, she's in apartment 315."

Juliet stood up and grabbed my hand. "See you soon, cutie." She blew Jacob a kiss.

We arrived in front of the apartment building invisible. I walked through the door when Juliet pulled me back. Confused, I asked, "What's wrong?"

Juliet asked, "What if they've cameras in the elevator?"

"Good point. We'll figure something out." I grabbed her arm and pulled her through the secured door to the building. Immediately, I began looking for cameras. As I looked around, I noticed this was not a slum, nor was it a high-end building. It did not appear they had the funds for security cameras. Juliet pushed the elevator call button with her elbow. We stepped inside the elevator and moved against the back wall. Just as the elevator door opened, a man came in. He went to the third floor as well. He exited the elevator.

I changed us back to visible. "We should allow him time to get to his apartment before exiting," I said. The door suddenly opened, and the man was standing before us. *Did he forget something?*

"Wow, you got to this floor quickly," he said as he waited for us to exit.

We strolled out of the elevator. I watched as the door closed.

"Perhaps he got off on the wrong floor," Juliet said.

I shrugged. Thankfully, he did not see us reappear. "We need room 315."

"It's this way," Juliet informed me as she motioned me toward the left of the elevator.

Juliet knocked on Misty's door. A moment later, a smiling Misty seemed happy to see us. She invited us in and asked us to have a seat. Her apartment was what I would imagine a typical college student's apartment to be. It was decorated with used furnishings.

"Misty, we couldn't get the information about your father," Juliet said in a peaceful voice. "We need some help, or at the very least, advice."

She seemed unfazed by the question, "Sure, what do you need?"

Misty seemed very comfortable talking with Juliet. I let her lead this mission.

"We either need you to let us know when your mother will be away for an extended period or we need you to bring us there with you for a day or two," Juliet informed her.

Misty seemed to think about the options in her head. She said, "Well, my mother rarely goes anywhere. She moved there to save money. It's expensive living here." Misty took a deep breath and exhaled slowly. "I think we should…"

The front door flung open. A beautiful, tall, slender young lady came in smiling. With a bubbly personality, she said, "Hey there. I'm Bailey, Misty's roommate." She laid her keys and backpack down on the table.

We both said hello to her and looked at Misty for a clue what to do, but she didn't seem bothered by Bailey's intrusion.

She looked at each of us. Bailey said, "I'm parched. Does anyone want some Kool Aid?"

Everyone seemed to think that was a good idea.

Misty turned and said, "A trip to South Carolina sounds fun. I don't have classes till the fall."

Bailey poked her head around the corner, "Did someone say road trip? Do you mind if I tag along?"

"Bailey, you are the perfect person for this trip," Misty assured her.

I turned to Misty. "Your mother believes I'm in town visiting right now. Juliet and I'll meet both of you there. We'll find someplace to stay. Just let us know when you'll be there."

"It's probably best we surprise my mother. Otherwise, she'll try to talk me out of it. She thinks it's dangerous to drive that far," Misty informed us.

Juliet asked, "Financially, can you afford to do this?"

"It'll be tight, but we'll manage," Misty assured us.

Bailey returned with our drinks. Misty explained to Bailey what we needed, and she was all in on helping us. She seemed to understand Misty's anger toward her father.

We got to know the girls better. I even ordered us pizza as we created our cover story. Fortunately, I had gotten into the habit of carrying cash. I did not want anyone to track the charges on my account if I used a debit or credit card. Once we had everything worked out, Juliet and I rushed back home. The girls planned to leave early in the morning. They would spend most of the day driving. We decided we would go to her mother's house in the evening the day after they arrive. Juliet still had her job watching the twins.

The next day, I teleported to Japan to see Asahi and Akio. When I arrived, they were not at the hut. I made my way to the cave and found them sparing with one another. I watch them for a bit before revealing myself.

Asahi asked for us to follow him through the forest. He took off running and began climbing tree. He glided from one limb to another. Occasionally, he would do a flip and land on his feet. Akio could follow him without hesitation. I stopped. I debated on doing the flip.

Akio hollered, "You can do this, Brooke."

Lord, please help me land on my feet. I trusted God and went for it. It was not a pretty landing, but I did it. "Thank you, Lord," I said before catching up with them.

When the opportunity arrived, I did not hesitate to flip off the branch. We continue with what I was now referring to as Jungle Parkour. We made our way up and over the edge of the volcano and down toward the sea. Branches would occasionally break my skin and the stone would heat and heal them. Asahi suddenly stopped and motioned for us to hide. We each hid in the foliage. I looked to see what had his attention. A boat was unloading its cargo.

"Father, they're putting it in the cave," Akio said.

"Yes, and they're not locals. Many of the older locals don't discuss the caves. Some are superstitious about them," Asahi said. He moved to get a better view. "Brooke, can you get me closer?"

"Yes, but I don't think I should chance taking all three of us. I don't know the terrain and I don't want them to discover us," I said as I grabbed my mirror and flipped it open. "Are you not afraid of the caves?"

Asahi answered, "No. Neither are the young people."

'Akio, wait here. I'll come back and get you if we need you," I instructed.

I looked at the area of the boat and discovered a rock to the right of the boat we could arrive on, "Be prepared for uneven footing when we arrive."

We both barely fit on the rock. Asahi hopped to another rock and made his way to the edge of the water. Two men were exiting the cave, and a third was on the boat looking through binoculars.

The man with the binoculars hollered to the other two men, "It looks like we have an unwelcome guest."

The larger of the two men took the binoculars and began staring up at Akio. *Oh, no! they spotted him.* The man with the binoculars said, "We need to take care of him. We'll go after him." He returned the binoculars. "Bring the boat around to the port. We'll meet you there." He jumped off the boat and the two men began making their way up the volcano.

Using telepathy, "Asahi, I'm going to get Akio." He nodded and moved toward the cave.

When I arrived, Akio was watching the two men heading toward him. "They're coming for you. I need to get you out of here," I said, concerned for his safety.

"No. I'll be fine. You and my father need to find out what they put in the cave. I'll lead them away from here. I'll meet up with you at the hut when I have lost them."

"They're meeting the other man at the port after they've dealt with you. Be safe," I said. He nodded and continued watching the men. I returned to the cave entrance to find Asahi.

They had broken the plants that once concealed the cave to allow them passage. I entered the cave and found Asahi standing in front of a locked cage with two young girls inside. They looked frightened. I grabbed Asahi's hand and teleported us to the outside of the cave.

"Why are they caged like animals? Those poor girls. We must do something," I said in a panic.

"You must calm down. They'll hear you. We need to get them out of here and to safety," Asahi instructed.

"I can't just pull them through the gate. I must be discreet with the powers."

Asahi nodded and commented, "They must have the key on the boat. I'll stay with them. You go find the key."

I did as he instructed. The man was still heading toward the port. I went below and began searching through the cabinets and drawers. The necklace moved across my chest. I looked at the stone. *I could use some help finding the key.* Nothing happened. I continued searching. I found a necklace that appeared might belong to one of the young girls. For a moment, I was caught up thinking about them and what my grandmother might do in this situation. She would always tell me to pray when I lost something.

I prayed. *Lord, thank you for all you have done to bless me and my family. Please help us return these girls unharmed to their families and could you please direct me to the key to the cage?*

A moment later, it was as if God whispered in my ear. *The large man had the key.* I need to find him. I returned to Asahi and, using telepathy, told him. "Those men chasing Akio must have the key."

He told me the girls had seen him. He told them we were getting them help.

I asked, "Where do you think Akio will lead them?"

Asahi said, "My guess would be toward the northern end of the island. He wouldn't want them in the town."

I nodded and rushed back to the path we were on before we discovered the men. We had headed north and then turned toward the east. I looked at the ground and found some of our footprints. I continued following them until I saw them shift directions to the east.

There were no other footprints in the area. I continued moving north. Trusting Asahi, I made my way north. The foliage was thicker and harder to move through. It appeared few people explored this area. I climbed a tree to get a better view of the area.

In the distance, I noticed some movement in the brush. I teleported to another tree in that area. The men were looking for Akio. I did not see him. I moved in for a closer look at a mound of rocks. The large man approached from the east. Just as he was about to climb on the rock. I jumped on him and wrapped my legs around his neck and leaned back to bring him down on his back. Unfortunately, I broke his fall. *Not a good plan, Brooke.* I fought the pain and squeezed my legs together tightly and waited for him to pass out. The stone healed me quickly.

"Brooke?"

Akio was hovering over me. I asked, "Where's the other guy?" I released my hold on the man and made myself visible. Akio helped me get out from under him.

"He's tied up right now," Akio chuckled.

I began going through the heavy man's pockets.

Akio laughed and commented, "Getting a little friendly with him, aren't you?"

I shot him a look. "We're trying to find a key."

He rolled the man over and checked his back pockets. "Nothing."

"Take me to the other guy," I instructed.

He was not too far away. Akio had tied the man to a tree with vines. *Oh my.* I tried not to laugh, but it was funny.

As soon as the man looked at me, Akio punched him. He was out cold. Akio went through his pockets and found a key attached to a small piece of twine.

I grabbed Akio's arm and teleported us just outside of the cave. "Two girls are in a small cage just around the corner. They look to be about thirteen," I said.

Akio handed the key to me and said, "You should be the one to talk to them."

We walked into the cave. Asahi said to the girls, "See, my friends are here to help me get you out of here and back to your families."

I walked up to the cage with the key in my hand. The girls seemed to recognize it. I introduced myself, "I'm Brooke. What're your names?" There was no response. "I'm going to let you out, but you need to stay close to us. Those men are still on the island. We'll bring you to safety and get you some food."

I unlocked the cage, and the girls pushed me over and ran past us to the edge of the water. I walked out slowly to them. They just stared at us. Suddenly, one of them pointed up and said, "They're coming back." The taller girl grabbed the other one's arm and ran back into the cave. They got behind me.

"We need to get them out of here," Asahi informed me.

I knew what he meant. Grabbing my mirror from my pocket, I said, "I'll be back for both of you in a minute. Girls, grab my arms and don't let go." I ordered. They both looked at me, confused. "Now!" They seemed surprised by my demand, but they did as I instructed. I brought them to the hut. "You'll be safe here. I'll be right back."

As I returned for Akio and Asahi, I could hear the men just outside the cave. I grabbed Akio and Asahi grabbed my shoulder. We left before they entered the cave.

The girls looked frozen in their place. When we returned, they stared at me.

"I believe these two could use some food and perhaps a drink," I said, as I nodded my head to see if they would acknowledge me. They nodded back.

Asahi went and got them a sliced-up pear and some water. They devoured everything. Everyone sat down and tried to get the girls to tell us where they were from, but they said nothing. Using telepathy, I tried talking to them. Their eyes just widened as they looked around and then stared at me.

Finally, I tried my power of persuasion. This worked. The girls were friends and taken from a park near their home. They were from Osaka, Japan.

I turned to Asahi. "How do you suggest we get them back home?"

"I think Akio should stay here with them. I'll go into town and get the police. Akio should stay out of sight until we know they have left the island. They'll easily recognize him," Asahi suggested.

"One of them will recognize you," Akio said to me.

"That's true. I can't stay here. Asahi, we need to make sure they get home safely. Do you think you could stay with them until can find their parents?"

"I'll try," he said.

"Girls, please insist on him staying with you. You can trust him," I said before turning to Akio and Asahi. "I need to head back. It's late."

The girls ran over and gave me a hug. They clinched me. One said, "Don't leave us."

I knelt in front of them and said, "I wish I could stay. It is not possible for me. Akio and Asahi will take excellent care of you. You can trust them." I gave them both hugs. "I promise to check up on you. Asahi will make sure I can." I looked up at him. He nodded.

Nine

I had some time to kill before Juliet was off work. After my workout and shower, I teleported to Italy to see Isabella and Leonardo. They were busy when I arrived. I motioned toward the patio and went out for a stroll through the property. Everything was so beautiful. The villa appeared filled with visitors. It seemed strange so many were not out touring the country. I found a seat under the canopy of a tree and took in the vineyard's view.

A short while later, a server approached me with a glass of water. He said, "Ms. Brooke?"

"Yes."

He handed me the glass of water. "Ms. Isabella will be with you shortly."

I took a few sips of the water. The two ice cubes in it were already melting. I watched a few others enjoying the warmth of the sun. One couple appeared to be having a disagreement. Four women were sitting at the table near the entrance to the villa. They seemed to be interested in something going on inside the building.

Isabella popped her head through the doorway and appeared to be looking for me. I waved my arm to attract her attention. She swiftly walked over and sat in the chair next to me. Isabella said, "I'm sorry. It has been a little hectic this week."

"What's going on?"

"We have a couple of famous opera singers. When word got out about them being here, many decided not to travel into town, hoping to meet them." She took a small cloth from her pocket and blotted the sweat from her forehead. "What can I help you with?"

"Have you ever heard of Marshall Blaise? He's from France," I said, sitting up.

"Marshall Blaise… his name does not sound familiar. I can search our database."

"That would be great. I suspect you don't have time now. Let me know if you or Leonardo know anything about him. I'm going to get out of your hair," I said as I got up and gave her a hug.

She darted back inside. On my way back to my room, I handed a waiter my glass.

I returned home and trotted down the stairs to see if Phyllis needed help with anything. As I hit the bottom of the stairs, I could hear voices coming from the kitchen.

Juliet? I entered the kitchen. I found her and Phyllis decorating cookies. They both looked up at me.

Juliet smiled, "Hey there. Look at this." She lifted a cookie decorated with a couple of flowers. "Phyllis showed me how to do this."

"Wow! That looks fantastic," I said as I looked over all the decorated cookies. I went to grab one.

Phyllis gently slapped my hand. "Those are for the BBQ."

Confused, I asked, "BBQ?"

"Greg's parents invited us over to join them on Saturday. They are having a BBQ for their friends. I figured Greg said something to you," Phyllis said as she finished up decorating the last cookie.

"No, but he has been working late. He said he was helping Bill add a room on to their house. Apparently, his mother-in-law needs to move in with them," I advised her. I turned to Juliet. "Why aren't you at work?"

"The twin's mother came home early today because they will be leaving town tomorrow. A family member passed away. I'm off the rest of the week," she said, smiling.

"That's fantastic."

Before heading to the library, we helped pack up the cookies. We caught up on a few things before discussing when we should head over to Misty's mother's home. I grabbed the five hundred dollars I had stowed away to give to Misty. We went over early.

Fortunately, Rebecca lived in a gated community. This gave us a logical explanation to why we walked up to her home. We appeared in the wooded area across the street from her home and walked toward the front entrance. When we were sure no one was watching, we appeared and began walking down the road to her home.

It appeared everyone in the neighborhood was still at work. Juliet rang the doorbell. A moment later, Misty and Bailey showed up at the door. She said nothing and motioned for us to come in. "Moms in the shower. I told her I had friends coming over for dinner. She fussed about it, but I told her I would get pizza." She leaned over and whispered, "I told Mom we were going to take her out to dinner tomorrow. We will keep her out as long as possible."

I sat down. "That would be great. Perhaps we could get her to talk about him some while we were here. Do you think you could help get the conversation started?"

"Sure," she said as she plopped down on the other sofa next to Bailey. Juliet sat next to me.

I reached into my pocket and pulled out the cash I had brought for Misty. "Here, this is for you. It should help with expenses."

Misty fanned the hundred-dollar bills out and her eyes widened. She asked, "Are you sure you can afford this? This is way too much."

"It's fine. Please put it away before your mother sees it," I instructed.

Misty shoved it in her pocket. Just in time, too. She barely had her hand out of her pocket when Rebecca's bedroom door flung open. Misty introduced everyone. Her mother seemed surprised to see me.

While we waited on the pizza, Misty asked her mother, "Hey Mom, why doesn't Marshall have anything to do with me?"

Rebecca nearly choked on her pizza. Her eyes widened as she glanced around at each of us. She swallowed her bite and looked at us again. "He lives in France." She took another bite. It was apparent she was uncomfortable with the questioning.

Misty rolled her eyes, "Mom, there are tons of ways he can contact me. Yet he doesn't," she said as she stared at her mother, waiting for a response.

Rebecca put her pizza down and took a deep breath. "He is a very private person. Over the years, I have questioned what kind of businessman he is. He told me it was best not to ask questions. Until your 18th birthday, he sent me money to help with our expenses. Those funds have stopped."

Misty looked confused and asked, "How are you affording to put the funds in my account?"

Now Rebecca looked confused. "What funds?"

"Mom, I get five hundred dollars deposited on the 15th of every month."

Rebecca leaned toward Misty. "Seriously? It's not coming from me. Are you sure it's not from your scholarship?"

"It's not scholarship money. I thought it was you," Misty said.

Juliet and I looked at each other, knowing this might lead us to Marshall.

Misty pulled out her phone and showed her mother and us the funds that were being deposited.

"It has to be Marshall," Rebecca said as her eyes teared up. "I thought he had abandoned you."

Bailey looked over at Misty and suggested she send him a thank-you letter. "Maybe he'll want to get to know you."

Misty seemed to understand what Bailey was trying to do. "That's a great idea," Misty said, turning to her mother. "Can I have his address?"

"I have a Post Office box," Rebecca said. She got up and grabbed a notepad and pen and wrote the address down for Misty. "Don't expect a response." She grabbed her water and took a sip. "You girls enjoy the pizza. I'm going for a golf cart ride."

Once we heard the garage door shut, Misty handed me the paper with the address. I looked at the clock she had on the wall. Jacob should be home from work by now. "Excuse me, I need to use your restroom. I walked into the bathroom and locked the door. It had not even occurred to me I should not know where the room was located.

I teleported to Jacob's closet and knocked before opening the door. Jacob seemed surprised to see me. I handed him the paper and asked him to copy the address down. He did. I quickly explained what was going on with Misty's mysterious deposits and the mailing address and teleported back to the bathroom. When I came out, I told Juliet, using telepathy, what I had done.

There was no reason to stay because her mother could return at any moment. We also had a lead to find Marshall, but we were having a great time hanging out with Misty and Bailey. Misty seemed so much happier now that Junior was no longer bothering her. Bailey was the type of person with a contagious personality. She was a positive person. Never negative. She made everyone feel welcome and loved. Had she lived closer to me, we would have become great friends.

Bailey wanted to make a video for social media of us dancing together. As much as that sounded like it would have been a lot of fun, we could not risk being seen there. Sadly, we had to decline.

Rebecca had returned an hour later. Without a word, she went to her room.

Juliet turned to Misty and asked, "Do you think your mother is okay?"

"I worry about her. She has said nothing bad about my father other than his questionable business practices. She rarely dates. When she does, she usually only goes out with a person one or two times," she said as she cleaned up the table. "I think she still loves Marshall. For a long time, she had a picture of him displayed."

That could help us. I tried not to show too much excitement when I asked, "Do you have the picture?"

"I'm sure she has it here somewhere. I'll look for it tomorrow," she said, sitting back down.

"It's getting late. We should get out of here," Juliet informed me.

I slipped the paper with Marshall's mailing address to Bailey. I told her to give it back to Misty when she was at home. I couldn't help but wonder if one day she would like to talk to him. She deserved answers.

I told them; I would contact them if we needed anything additional. Misty said they would be visiting for the week.

We said our goodbyes and walked toward the front of the neighborhood. There was a group of guys about our age hanging out on the bed of a truck playing fetch with a black Labrador named Ranger. Ranger did not seem to like to return the stick to them. I could not resist but use telepathy to talk to the dog. "Ranger, bring me the stick."

Ranger followed the instructions and brought me the stick. He sat down and waited for me to take it from his mouth. I grabbed the stick and threw it near the truck. Immediately, he returned it to me. "Good Boy," I said as I petted him.

One guy asked, "We have been trying to get him to do that all night. How did you do that?"

I just smiled and told Ranger using telepathy to take the stick to the man. He did.

Juliet and I walked past the gate and snuck into a wooded area just past the entrance to the development and teleported to Jacob's closet.

Immediately, Juliet and I lost our footing and we're doing all we could to stand on a bunch of clothes that stank like a gym locker room after a big game.

Without warning, Jacob opened the door, and we tumbled out. He held his finger to his mouth and shushed us.

"Jacob, what was that? Are you okay?"

"I'm fine Mom. A box fell in my closet," Jacob hollered back. He helped us up and locked his bedroom door. "Moms in her room. We need to be quiet," he whispered. Jacob sat down at his desk, "I've located the Post Office Box. It's in Annecy, France. Here are some pictures of the area." Jacob scrolled through a few pictures. The city was beautiful. It appeared many of the roads were waterways.

"It's gorgeous. Brooke, who cares about finding Marshall, let's go tour the town," Juliet giggled.

"I would love to take you on a date there," Jacob said, looking up at Juliet. She leaned over and kissed him.

Juliet told him about the photograph we were hoping to get. I said goodnight and waited for them to finish their goodbye before returning home.

I received a few text messages while I was away.

GREG: I love you, baby. Care to go for a walk? I'm exhausted but want to see you.

Awe, such a sweetie.

MOM: Are you home? I want to talk to you.

MOM: Please call me.

PHYLLIS: Your mother is looking for you. She can't believe you left your phone at home.

Yikes. I showed Juliet the text, "We need to leave and walk into the house." I read the remaining text.

GREG: I'm guessing you're not back yet. My bed is calling. Hope to see you tomorrow.

I put my phone back and grabbed Juliet's arm and we went through the full-length mirror and teleported to the garage. When we came out of the garage, we could see Mom and Phyllis in the kitchen. Fortunately, it was dark, and she could not see us.

"I'm going to head home. It's getting late," Juliet said as she turned toward her car.

I waved and strolled into the house through the backdoor.

The moment I opened the door, my mother spun around and said, "Brooke, I have been worried about you. It's not like you to leave your phone at home. Fortunately, Phyllis told me you were with Juliet and Jacob."

I walked over and gave her a kiss on the cheek. "I'm fine."

"Greg even came to see you," she added.

"I'll call him tomorrow. He's probably sleeping. Beside it's late and I'm tired. I love you both," I said as I kissed each of them on the cheek and went to my room.

I grabbed my phone to put it on the charger and noticed another missed message.

MECHELLE: I have a surprise for you. Call me.

I changed into my pajamas and went out on my patio to enjoy the evening breeze. I did not have time to say hello because as soon as Mechelle answered, she began telling me the news.

"I'm so glad you called me back. Our parents have been talking and if it's okay with you, Mom and I are coming up there this weekend," she said without taking a breath.

"That's fantastic!"

"That's not all. We are going on a tour on Monday at the University of Louisville. Brooke, my parents might let me transfer there."

"That would be outstanding," I said. Mechelle started giving me the details about their arrival. I expect them on Friday afternoon. We caught up on a few things before hanging up.

As I lay in bed thinking about what we could do, it occurred to me we had plans to go to Greg's house for a BBQ on Saturday. Looks like two more will be attending. I was so excited about her visit that I had a hard time falling asleep.

Ten

I slept through my alarm. I looked at the clock it was 10:06 am. It had been a long time since I got up so late. I ambled down to grab breakfast. I had expected to see Phyllis, but she left me a note.

Brooke,
There's yogurt and a granola fruit cup in the refrigerator for you. Today is Hal's day off. We are spending the day together. A cleaning crew will be here in the morning.
Love,
Phyllis

Cleaning crew? Strange. I grabbed my yogurt and a coffee and sauntered to the patio to enjoy my breakfast. It was then I realized I left my phone upstairs. As I ate, I could smell freshly cut grass mixed with the aroma of my coffee. Oddly, it was comforting. The smell of the grass brought back the memory of my grandmother's funeral. I couldn't believe it was over a year ago.

I wondered what she would say to the new improved me. There was no doubt she would be proud of me. I had not thought about her journals lately, but I still wondered what secrets they held.

After cleaning up my dishes, I rushed back to my room to get dressed. Before getting in the shower, I glanced at my phone.

JULIET: Let me know when I should come over.

BROOKE: I'm jumping in the shower now. Text me when you get here.

I completed my morning routine in record timing. I grabbed my phone and teleported down to read some more of my grandmother's journals. She had an entire lifetime in these journals. I grabbed one from the middle of the bookshelf and randomly opened it.

January 18

We received two feet of snow last night. Phyllis and I have several of the fireplaces burning to take the chill out of the air. I wish this room had some heating, but it's not possible without making others aware of its existence. This reminds me of the many people my family has protected by hiding them in this room. For now, I feel the stone is safe. I thank God daily for him feeling I'm worthy of protecting such a gift. I don't believe I mentioned it in a previous entry, but I had an angel come to me in a dream and warn me of danger headed my way. The angel told me, "Protect the stone and it would protect you." That was soon after I received it. Whoever takes over after me, always remember you're doing God's work. Keep yourself in His word and talk to Him often.

Reading this stirred the Holy Spirit in me. God just convicted me that I needed to read my Bible more. It occurred to me I had not read it in a while. I flipped to the front of the journal. *Wow, this is from 1969.* That was before my mother was born.

JULIET: I'm here.

I teleported to the pantry to prevent anyone from seeing me through the windows and made my way to the front door.

"Hey there," I said as I opened the door.

Juliet smiled and handed me a small piece of paper with the address and box number. "I figured we would be out late. I told my mother I was sleeping over. Do you think we could get some sightseeing in while we're there?"

"That was a good idea. You can have the spare room on the second floor. I hope so. I need to leave Phyllis and Mom a note," I said, turning to head to the kitchen. Juliet went to the spare room to drop off her bag. I wrote a quick note making sure I included the information about Juliet sleeping over. I waited for her in the kitchen. Once she arrived, we went into the pantry to teleport to the post office in Annecy.

We arrived invisible just outside of the post office. We followed someone inside and made our way to the bathroom. To become visible. We walked out. There was a man behind the counter. He looked to be in his thirties. I asked, "Excuse me. What do I need to do to get a box?"

"You need to fill out a card and provide an ID," he explained as he kept glancing at Juliet.

Using telepathy, I asked Juliet to flirt with him. She looked over at him and tipped her head down a bit and looked up at him with a smile. This put a smile on his face.

"Sir, is our information kept in a safe location?"

He looked at me, "Yes, everyone's files are behind these gates and are entered into our secure system."

"Thanks," I said, grabbing Juliet's hand and turning to the door.

"Hey, don't you want a box?"

"Not today. Thanks"

As we exited the door, Juliet stopped me. "It is so strange listening to you speak in French. I didn't understand a word of what he was saying," she explained.

"Oh sorry, I don't hear it in French. He said everything was on the computer and they locked the original files up back there with him. Which direction should we head?"

"It doesn't matter. So, I gather we are coming back after hours"

I linked my arm with hers and started heading down the street. "Yes, unless Jacob can get into their system."

We made our way to the area we had seen in the photos. It wasn't far. The old buildings and foliage reflected in the water, giving the illusion we were in a fairytale. The water was remarkably clean. It appeared the buildings looked as though they had been there for decades and gave that old-world charm.

"I was reading up on this area. It's known as the Venice of the Alps," Juliet informed me.

Juliet and I spent the day going in and out of the shops. Hunger was becoming a problem. Without a phone, I did not know where to go to convert the money I had with me. Juliet asked if she could wear the stone to ask where to convert the money. I agreed. She walked up to a storekeeper and asked how much we needed to be converted. Juliet talked him into exchanging our cash for the euro.

"That is amazing. He was talking French, right?"

I confirmed for her he was but told her she was also.

"I could've really used this during my Spanish exams," she joked.

Juliet and I stopped at the Auberge de Savoie to grab a late lunch. We both had the salmon, and it looked like a piece of art and tasted phenomenal.

We went into shops and tried on outfits and created amazing memories. Sadly, we could only share this experience with the Bloom Keepers. I did not take the necklace back from Juliet until the evening. She was like a kid with a new toy. Juliet wanted to talk to everyone. She said she was in the bathroom and successfully walked through a stall wall to the next stall.

Once it was dark, we hid in an alley and teleported, making sure we were invisible, to the side of the counter with the customer information. I pulled rubber gloves from my pocket and handed Juliet a pair.

Each of us looked for the files that would contain the personal information for Marshall's box. Without Jacob, there was no way we were getting into the computer. He knew the plan and would help us if we needed him.

Surprisingly, the only lock appeared to be on the door to the room. There were several filing cabinets. Juliet began looking at the one closest to the door and I had the other one. My cabinet appeared to contain shipping records, lists of supply shipping inventory, and forms.

"Brooke, I can't read these. It looks like it might be what we are looking for," Juliet asked quietly.

I closed my drawer and looked over her shoulder at the item she was showing me. The top of the card read Box Rental Form. "Yes, this is it. See if you can find his box." I handed her the paper with the box number.

Juliet flipped through the cards until she came to the box number. "Here it is," she said as she pulled the card out and handed it to me. The card was for a Louis Dupont. It had a driver's license number on it, along with an address and phone number. "I need to write it down."

Juliet grabbed a pen and a piece of paper from a nearby desk. "Here."

I wrote the information down. Juliet grabbed the card and tucked it back into its place in the drawer. She grabbed my arm, and we immediately went to see Jacob.

He was sound asleep. Juliet gently woke him, saying, "Jacob, sweetie, wake up." She repeated this process several times before he opened his eyes. He grabbed his glasses from the nightstand and sat up.

I handed him the paper with the information and explained it did not need to be done tonight. Juliet and I returned to my room. We were both exhausted and went straight to bed.

A text awakened me at 6:55 am.

JACOB: Got it! I need to leave in 20 minutes for work.

I wanted to go back to sleep but knew I needed to see Jacob.

BROOKE: Be Right there.

I grabbed a robe and popped into Jacob's room.

"So, Louis Dupont's Driver's license is fake. The address on it is for a vacant lot, which is owned by the city," Jacob informed me.

"So, we are at a dead-end again," I said, disappointed.

"No. You mentioned the post office had a computer system. I took advantage of that and found out they are keeping track of when mail is placed in the boxes. Like we can do here. You know how you can get emails to notify you when mail is coming. Only they do not set this account up for it. That didn't stop them from tracking it. I can see every delivery in the past few months."

I was excited. "What did you find?"

Jacob swiveled his chair around and pulled up the scans of the mail. I looked over at them and noticed Rebecca had sent him several letters. A letter without a return address was delivered yesterday. I looked at the time on his computer. The post office was already open.

"Thanks, Jacob," I returned to Juliet's room. "Juliet, get up. We need to get dressed," I urged.

Half-awake she answered, "What? Why?"

"I'll explain later. I need to get dressed, too. Meet me in my room when you are ready," I said as I ran from her room.

We both got dressed in record time. In order not to be detected, we arrived in the restroom of the post office. We quietly made our way out to the area where the boxes were located and found the box. Juliet and I knew it was a slim chance anyone would show up, but we took a chance and waited it out. The good news is we had a restroom available for us. Either of us could slip away without being detected. The bad news is we never ate breakfast, and we were both exhausted.

We had been waiting around for several hours before my stomach decided it needed to notify me it was hungry. Juliet heard it and shot me a look. We were both on the floor. We had dodged a few people that came in for their mail, but we were not in the way of most of the boxes.

Another hour and a half passed. I looked over at Juliet who had fallen asleep. I moved over to her and was about to wake her up when a woman came in and tripped over her foot. Fortunately, the woman was able to recover without falling. She looked around and continued to her box. This, however, did wake Juliet up. Her face showed her embarrassment.

At this point, I had passed the hunger stage. My eyes, like Juliet's, were getting heavy. "Juliet, we should stand up. That might keep us from falling asleep," I told her, using telepathy. She must have agreed because she stood up as well.

About twenty minutes later, a man went in wearing a brown fedora, a button-up collared shirt, and jeans. It was difficult to see his face because he kept it down. It seemed he may have been avoiding cameras. I looked around and noticed several cameras. He went up and opened the box. At that moment, the adrenaline raced inside me. Juliet and I both looked at one another with excitement.

He took the contents from the box and shuffled through his mail Before turning and exiting the building. I noticed he knew exactly where the cameras were and looked in the opposite direction or held his mail up to protect his face. He had done such a good job. I only saw a small portion of his face. We pursued him. He moved swiftly down the sidewalk and looked around before darting into an alley.

He walked in and out of the streets until he came upon a parking lot and got into a car with an unusual emblem. I was not familiar with this brand. He sat in the car and looked around before opening his mail. I got closer and noticed the emblem said Peugeot. I opened my mirror and teleported to the back seat of his vehicle.

He was reading a letter from Rochelle. I inched up slowly to peer over his shoulder. I was able to see a small portion of the note. Rochelle was asking why he cut her off. She explained the financial change required her to move to South Carolina. She told him about how well Misty was doing. He sniffled twice while reading the letter. This told me he was Marshall. *Well, hello, Marshall.*

He grabbed the second letter from Rochelle. In this letter, she was frustrated and begged him to help Misty out with her school expenses. This letter was shorter. She signed both letters with all my love. *She still loves him.*

The man opened the last letter. It seemed to be a report of some sort. I leaned in closer because the font was small.

You were incorrect. Neither Sandra nor the maid has the necklace. Sandra's daughter does, or at least she has the stone. It's not in its original setting. Sandra and her daughter are living in Lillie's house. The maid's with them. See enclosed pictures.

The letter was unsigned and did not have a return mailing address. Marshall put the letter on the passenger seat with the other two letters and grabbed the envelope. He peeked inside and tipped the envelope over. A couple of photos of me slid out. The first two were of me jogging. One of them was a profile picture. As I looked closer, I noticed the pictures were taken in my neighborhood. The third picture was taken at night. It was a picture of Greg and me on an evening stroll. It appeared the picture was taken just before sunset. They must have had a zoom lens because they had our faces cropped in the photograph and you could clearly see the Bloom of Dreams and its cradle.

He started the car. As he looked in the rear-view mirror to back up, I could see his eyes. They were brown. The skin around his eyes showed a few wrinkles. I would guess he was about my mother's age. We started moving forward toward the exit of the lot.

Using telepathy, "Juliet, hide. You are going to reappear soon. I will be back for you." I looked back at her and lost sight of her as we pulled out onto the road.

Marshall turned on the radio. About 20 minutes into the ride, my stomach let out a large growl. Fortunately, he was singing and did not notice it. I noticed he was constantly checking his mirrors. I was not sure if it was just his driving style or if he was confirming he was not being followed. Thirty minutes into the ride, we pulled down a dirt road and went quite a way from the main road and came upon a cottage.

From the outside, the home appeared to be run down and tucked well away from prying eyes in the middle of nowhere. However, when he opened the door, I could tell he liked the finer things in life. It was as if the exterior was an illusion to distract people from the true Marshall.

My stomach growled again. This time, there was no way to hide it. Marshall spun around and peered in my direction. Just then, a cat jumped on top of the sofa.

"Oliver, you startled me," Marshall said as though he were talking to a child. He picked up Oliver and began stroking him. "I got some good news today. Misty is doing well in her classes," he said to the cat. We walked into the kitchen. It looked like it had been made for a chef. Marshall placed Oliver on the counter.

"It breaks my heart to know she still loves me. Little does she know I still love her," Marshall told the cat as he made himself a sandwich. He tossed Oliver a piece of ham. "But the necklace will bring me far more than love. Right, Oliver."

The sandwich looked amazing. I needed to get Juliet some food. I pulled out my mirror and returned to the parking lot I left her in. At first glance, I did not see her. I walked in the direction we entered the area from and found her just outside the alley. "Juliet, why did you leave the parking lot?"

"Brooke, where are you?"

I grabbed her arm and pulled her into the alley. "I know where he lives. Let's head back." I teleported us to my kitchen pantry because I knew my mother would not be home.

Without a word, we exited and found Phyllis in the kitchen. She was listening to some music as she made coleslaw. "That looks yummy," I said.

Phyllis jumped and ended up throwing a little of the slaw from the spoon in the air. "Child, you startled me. This is for the BBQ tomorrow."

Disappointed, I opened the refrigerator. "Did you say tomorrow?"

"Yes."

With all that had been going on, I had not realized Michelle and her mother were arriving that day. I glanced at the clock. It was nearly 10:00 am. I needed to be at the airport at 3:00 to pick them up. I filled Phyllis in on finding Marshall while she made us each an omelet. After we had breakfast, Juliet went home to take a nap, and I wandered to my room to take one as well.

Eleven

Despite me not hearing my alarm, I made it to the airport by 3:15. On the ride back Mechelle could not hold back her excitement about possibly moving to Louisville. Her mother barely said anything during the ride. Truthfully, Mechelle did not give her much of an opportunity.

As we pulled down my street, Peggy commented on how much she liked the historical homes in our neighborhood. As we turned down our driveway, I noticed her admiring our home.

As we stepped out of my car, Peggy looked up at the house with her mouth open. She asked, "What year was this built?"

It was apparent by the age of the bricks it was old. "I don't know the exact age, but it was built in the 1800s," I explained.

I popped the trunk. Mechelle and I pulled their suitcase out as Phyllis came out to greet us. Mechelle introduced her to Peggy. Phyllis instructed us to put Peggy into the third-floor guest room and for Mechelle to be in the second-floor guest room.

We walked into the kitchen. Phyllis immediately offered everyone a drink. Peggy stayed with Phyllis while Mechelle and I took the suitcase to their rooms. When we returned to the kitchen, Peggy was sitting at the bar and Phyllis was busy washing lettuce.

I asked, "What kind of salad are we having tonight?"

"It will have walnuts, feta cheese, apples, and pears with a pomegranate dressing," Phyllis replied.

Mechelle's eyes widened. Enthusiastically, she said, "That sounds fantastic!"

"We'll also have Lobster Newberg with asparagus and risotto. For dessert, we will have Bananas Foster," Phyllis added.

Peggy said, "That sounds amazing, but you don't need to go to all that trouble."

"This is normal around here. Phyllis is an amazing cook," I complimented Phyllis.

"Why don't you show Peggy to her room? She can get settled in before your mother gets home," Phyllis suggested.

As we exited the kitchen, Mechelle took her mother on a quick tour as we made our way to the third-floor guest room.

I impressed Peggy with my workout room and the library. We all hung out upstairs until Phyllis texted me to alert me my mother was home. We walked Peggy downstairs to the sitting room and found my mother drinking sweet tea. As soon as she saw Peggy, she jumped up and greeted her. The four of us spent that time catching up until Phyllis called us to dinner.

When we walked into the dining room, I noticed Phyllis did not set herself a place setting. As usual, I brought it up. She seemed embarrassed.

"I've plans this evening and will be having a late supper," she explained.

She had intrigued me. "What kind of plans?"

"Hal and I are going out for a late dinner. I will be meeting him at a restaurant near his work."

I smiled at her and said, "I suppose that is a good reason."

During the first course, we discussed their trip here. Apparently, they had a small child next to them whose mother seemed a bit overwhelmed. They spent their time playing with the child during the flight. When they switched flights in Atlanta, they had some time to kill and had lunch. While in line, they met a lovely lady that was 75 years old and was about to fly to see her first great-grandchild. She told Mechelle what life was like for her when she was younger. During dessert, the University of Louisville was our topic. I told Mechelle about the campus and some of the professors. They explained they had a tour to go to in the morning. I offered to take them to it.

The doorbell rang, and Phyllis went to answer it. She returned with Greg and Austin. As soon as I saw Austin, I turned to looked at Mechelle's reaction. Her face lit up. I introduced everyone to Peggy. We asked to be excused and went outside with them onto the back patio. We settled into the sofas on the back porch. We sat and listened as Austin and Mechelle caught up with one another. As I listened, I noticed Greg seemed distracted. He kept looking into his backyard.

I knocked him gently with my elbow and quietly asked, "What's going on?"

"Karen has a guy over," he said as he pointed to them in his backyard. "He just moved here from Georgia. The only other thing I know is he just graduated high school and is taking summer classes at UofL."

I looked at him and smiled. I walked over to the edge of my patio and hollered, "Hey Karen!" Once she answered, I invited them over.

A few minutes later, Karen and her friend walked up the stairs and greeted us on the patio. She introduced us to Ty. He was a thin guy with his hair cut short on the sides and it went straight up with a wave in the front. He had a thin, short beard that was well maintained. He wore dark-rimmed glasses and had several necklaces along with a Star Wars t-shirt. One necklace appeared to be a white coral, much like you would see people in Florida wearing. The others were on longer chains. One of which was a cross. They sat down and joined us.

I decided for Greg's sake we needed to learn more about Ty. He seemed to be watching him like a hawk. I loved that he was looking out for his sister. "Ty, Greg said you're from Georgia."

"Yes. I was born in Maine but have been living in Georgia for a while," he told me.

Mechelle must have noticed his necklace, too. She told him, "I like your cross."

He thanked her. Karen felt it important to let us know they had met at a church event the week prior. Through our conversation, we discovered Ty was attending the University of Louisville as a Music Major. He hoped to become a worship leader after he graduated. He also had a desire to teach and mentor children. By the end of the evening, Ty seemed to have earned Greg's respect. When Phyllis left for her date, she told us breakfast would be at 7:30 am. Ty and Karen walked her out to her car before heading back to Karen's house.

Mom and Peggy came out to tell us they were heading to bed and reminded us about the tour early in the morning. I had not realized it was so late. We said our goodbyes to Greg and Austin and meandered up to bed.

The next morning, I got up early and walked down for breakfast after dressing. Greg and Austin would be helping Greg's parents set up for the BBQ and could not join us on the tour.

Phyllis was in an exceptionally good mood this morning. She had placed fresh flowers on the table. Mom was gone a lot and did not spend the money on flowers as my grandmother did. It was nice to see them. "What made you get flowers today?"

"Hal gave those to me at dinner last night. I thought it would be nice to share them with everyone," she explained. "Would you mind helping me get the plates on the table when everyone arrives?"

The sound of footsteps could be heard in the distance. "It sounds like they are coming down now," I said.

"There is coffee on the tray and hot water and tea bags, if anyone is interested," Phyllis said, as she pointed to the side table.

There was also a carafe of orange juice on the table. Mom and Peggy came down with Mechelle a few steps behind them.

"Phyllis asks for you to get your beverages. We'll be out with breakfast in a few moments," I instructed.

Mechelle asked, "Want some help?"

I asked her to make me a cup of coffee. I met Phyllis in the kitchen, and she was making us Eggs Benedict. Yum. She pulled out a tray of English Muffins that had been toasting in the oven and asked me to place two pieces of them on each plate and place a piece of Canadian bacon on each one. I did as she instructed, making sure not to disturb the fruit salad she already had on the plate. Phyllis added the poached eggs and Hollandaise sauce before sending me out to deliver the plates. The process went quickly. As soon as everyone had a plate, my mother said grace.

The meal was delicious. It was nice Phyllis could join us and get to know Peggy a little. My mother had not been on a tour and wanted to see the college, so she joined us. Everyone helped clear the table for Phyllis, and we each rinsed our plates before heading over to the campus. Surprisingly, my mother let me drive. She sat in the back with Peggy.

As we pulled in, I pointed to the buildings where I had taken classes as we found a parking spot. It was strange being here with so few cars. We met at the administrative office. Tammy greeted us. She and I had become familiar with one another because she had to help us in the library. I said hello and introduced her to our group. As usual, she made everyone feel welcome.

We walked the campus as she explained the history, registering for classes, activities, and services available to everyone. Tammy was a wealth of knowledge.

Once our tour concluded, we rushed home to get ready for the BBQ at Greg's house. Mechelle and I walked over early with the cookies and coleslaw Phyllis had made. Ty, Karen, Greg, and Austin were sitting at the patio table when we arrived. The backyard had tables with white table clothes with blue and white checkered runners on each one. The table with the food had different tiers of food. There was a variety of food to choose from. Joann motioned for us to go over to her and took the food and placed it on the display.

Mom, Peggy, and Phyllis came over after a few of the guests arrived. The day was filled with fun and friendship. We had water balloon fights and played horseshoes. It was so cute watching Austin and Mechelle together. I noticed Peggy made a point of introducing herself to him. We stayed and helped clean up after the party. Greg's parents looked exhausted. Mom and Phyllis went home after we put away the food.

We sat on the patio for a while and chatted about a variety of topics, which allowed us to get to know Ty better. He even pulled out a guitar and started singing. As shocking as that was, Greg and Karen joined him on a few songs. *That boy is amazing.* I was constantly peeling back Greg's layers and learning more about the amazing person he was.

Knowing we all had church the next morning, we left at 10:30 to shower before heading to bed. Mechelle and I chatted a bit about her possibly moving here and Austin before crashing.

The next day, after church, we took them on a tour of Louisville. Lunch followed this at Doc Crow's. Mom was pleased when she saw their Spinach Salad on the menu. Mechelle and I were both drawn to their Shrimp Po-Boy. While Peggy went for their Stuffed Baked Potato. I must admit, it sounded amazing. Mom ordered all of us Derby Pie for dessert. *Another great restaurant to return to.*

During the ride home, Mechelle and Peggy had a serious talk about her moving to the area. They discussed the pros and cons of the move. This included the cost of housing. It was so late already; she could not stay in the dorms. She would need to be put on a waiting list. In the meantime, she would need an apartment.

Once home, Mom called me into the kitchen. "I haven't talked to you yet, but I spoke with Phyllis. If you would like Mechelle to stay with us, it would be okay," Mom informed me.

So many things rattled through my head like a torpedo. *My best friend is staying here. Wow! This would help Mechelle with her depression. She could help with the Bloom Keeper's missions. Mechelle and Austin could see if they had a chance at a successful relationship. Mechelle on a farm. That I've got to see.* This thought made me chuckle. I blurted, "Of course. Yes... No doubt about it!" I kissed them both on the cheek and ran out of the kitchen. Immediately stopping in the doorway. I pivoted back to face them. I asked, "Can I tell her?" Mom nodded. I bolted out and went searching for Mechelle and Peggy. They were in the sitting room. I stopped short of the doorway and composed myself. Mom and Phyllis were approaching from behind. I waited for them and entered the room calmly.

"Mechelle, are you sure this is where you should be?" I lowered my head. "You'll be far from your family. Do you even know if the college credits you've earned even transfer?"

Mechelle looked at me, confused. She asked, "Don't you want me to come here?"

I looked down and only lifted my eyes to look at her. I took in a deep breath and blurted out in a loud voice with a giant smile, "Of course I do!" I ran over to her and put my arm around her and said, "That is why we…" I shuffled over to my mother and Phyllis, "Well, we want you to move in here."

Mechelle's eyes filled with tears. "Really?" She looked at my mother, who nodded her head yes. Mechelle's attention moved to her mother. With her hands in the praying position, she asked, "Can I?"

Peggy looked at my mother and said, "Actually, Sandra and I discussed it a few times, and your father and I think it would be a great idea."

We spent the rest of the day with us working on getting her transferred and registered for her classes for the fall. I noticed the joy on Mechelle's face as she worked on the dull paperwork. I knew this made her happy and having her here would be another asset for the Bloom Keepers and it didn't hurt that she was my best friend.

Twelve

The following morning, I dropped off Mechelle and Peggy at the airport. On my way home, my phone alerted me to a text. At the first red light. I glanced at my phone.

IMELDA L.   I haven't heard from you. Have you gotten any additional evidence?

Imelda L.? Who? Then it hit me. Imelda Lombardo, Anthony Granaldi III's cousin. I had been concentrating on finding my grandmother's killer, and I had forgotten about Imelda's son, Federico. Should I be honest and tell her I forgot about her? I could not do that. The last thing I needed was another Granaldi family member mad at me. When I got home, I texted her back to tell her what I knew.

BROOKE: The information you provided is all I know at this point. I have been dealing with another murder, but I promise to research his death this week. I will contact you in a few days.

I felt God's conviction. I had not kept my word to help her. This needed to be a priority. I was on my own for this. *Let's see, what do I know? Someone stabbed him in a park in Rome. What park? Think… Oh yes,*

Villa Fiorelli. I remember the journal entry was in April of last year. Anthony and his boys were with him. I needed to start with Joseph and Tony.

The thought of dealing with them without help worried me. I was pretty sure Juliet had returned to work today, but I had not spoken with her all weekend. It was worth a try to see if she was available.

BROOKE: Are you working?

JULIET: No. Is Mechelle still here?

BROOKE: No. Want to go to Italy?

My phone rang. It was Juliet. She asked about what to wear and bring. We thought it was important to bring our own pen and paper after the last trip. I grabbed a small backpack and threw some rubber gloves, a pen, and some paper inside it. *What to wear?* I put on some workout clothes because they would allow me to move freely if we got into an altercation. I went down to tell Phyllis who was doing laundry. She and I discussed the mission and talked about which bedroom should be Mechelle's room.

I heard a car coming down the driveway and went out to greet Juliet. She came in and said a quick hello to Phyllis. We both thought it was important to eat something before heading out. We did not need a replay of our last trip. I was about to make us peanut butter & jelly sandwiches, but Juliet pointed out someone might smell the peanut butter breath we would have. We opted for turkey sandwiches.

I took Juliet into the pantry. "I need to do one thing before going to Italy." With a hold of her arm, I teleported us to the hut.

"Where are we?"

I smiled and said, "Japan. Come on."

I knocked on the hut door, but there was no answer. Akio … Asahi! Is anyone here?"

Some rustling startled us in the bushes. "Hello?" There was more rustling.

"Brooke, should we be here?"

I looked over at Juliet. "Yes, it's probably a boar or something."

"Well, it's getting closer," Juliet advised.

Juliet grabbed a broom that was propped up against the wall on the porch.

Suddenly Akio popped through the brush with earbuds on. He seemed to have a little dance in his stride. Suddenly, he started playing the air drums. He was not paying attention to his surroundings. I teleported behind him and tripped him. He fell face forward but caught himself before landing on his face. He flung his left leg out and countered my attack, causing me to get knocked over. We both quickly bounced up on our feet.

Akio looked at me confused, "Brooke, what was that for?" He took his earbuds out.

"You were so into your music; you did not know we were here. What if it had been someone else? You need to be alert at all times," I explained.

"You're right. Are you looking for my father? He's not back yet."

"Yes. I wanted to see how the girls are doing," I explained.

"He wrote a letter to you. Come in," Akio said, heading toward the patio. "Who's your friend?"

I introduced them. Akio handed me the letter Asahi had written.

Brooke,
      Forgive my writing. Don't write English much. Girls are home. They don't want me to leave. Girls want you to come first. Look picture. I'll be there all day till you come. Gone at night.
Asahi

The picture was a postcard of the Osaka Castle Tower in Osaka, Japan. "Juliet, stay and get to know Akio. I will be back," I instructed. I teleported to the location on the postcard, making sure I was invisible. It was easy to locate Asahi. He was sitting on a bench, staring at the castle tower. I tried to talk to him using telepathy, but it did not seem to work. He seemed to be meditating or something. I tapped him on the shoulder. He swiftly reached out and grabbed my hand. Asaki looked at his hand. It appeared to be holding nothing. Only I knew the pain he was inflicting on me with his grip. "You can let go of me now," I muttered.

"Brooke?"

"Yes," I groaned.

Asahi released his grasp.

"Meet me behind that group of bushes," I said as I grabbed his head to show the bushes I was referring to. I teleported to the bushes and made myself visible. When Asahi was near me, I made myself visible. I stood up and greeted him with a hug.

He filled me in on returning them to their parents. The police saw how much they trusted him. One of the girl's parents even invited him to stay with them until he returned home. We walked for about twenty minutes to the first girl's home.

Asahi knocked on the door. A beautiful woman answered. They bowed to one another, and he introduced me, "This is Eshima. She is Aika's mother."

She invited us in. We took our shoes off before entering the home. The home was very clean and had teak furniture with pale earthy colors. We waited in the front room until she returned with both girls. It shocked me that they were together.

The girls ran in, stopped abruptly, and greeted me. I knelt and opened my arms to them. They immediately ran to me and nearly knocked me over with their hugs. They pulled back and looked at me.

The taller girl said, "I'm Aika." She turned to her mother. "Mama, this is my angel." The mother bowed to me.

I looked over at Asahi.

"I told them you are a gift from Jesus and are here to help do His work," Asahi informed me.

The small girl took her hand and ran it down the side of my face, "I'm Chie. Thank you for bringing me home." Her eyes watered. Chie just stared at me. She blinked, causing a tear to run down her face. She hugged me again, squeezing me tightly. I hugged her back. Grateful to God, she was back where she should be.

I pushed the hair that had fallen out of my ponytail behind my ear and stood up. "I'm so happy you are back with your families. Please don't talk to strangers and stay close to your families but don't be afraid to have fun. Jesus is watching over you. We need to leave. God has more work to be done," I said, turning away from them, so Eshima did not see the mirror. Asahi placed his hand on my shoulder, and we vanished from their view.

We arrived in the main room of Asahi's home. I quickly introduced Juliet to him.

Akio said, "Juliet filled me in on your current mission. Do you mind if I tag along?"

It had not occurred to me that he could help me, "Of course. That would be great."

We devised a plan. Each of us put on a pair of rubber gloves before heading to the Granaldi's mansion.

We arrived just outside Tony's room. I stuck my head through the door to see if anyone was inside. The room was empty. A journal was sitting on the nightstand. I flipped through it, looking at the dates. As I read, the content revealed the person was talking about his daughter and wife. This led me to believe it was Tony's journal. The journal began in September of last year. *Well, that's not good.* Using telepathy, I told them we needed to find his other journals for April of last year. Everyone began carefully searching the room. We discovered nothing. Juliet lifted her shoulders and hands as to ask, "what now". You're missing something. Think.

It suddenly hit me. Anthony had a secret room to hide his things. I asked the stone to reveal the secret entrance. It did. *Okay, stone. I need your help to find a secret compartment or just revealing the journal to me. Jesus, I would appreciate a little help from you as well.*

Suddenly, I saw a blue line appear on the floor. I looked over at Juliet and Akio. "Do you see that?"

Juliet looked confused and said, "See what?"

I shook my head as if to say never mind. As I pulled out my mirror, Juliet grabbed my hand and motioned for Akio to grab hold of Juliet's and my shoulders. We walked through the door and there was a pathway leading down the hall to their daughter's playroom. We heard voices. When we got to the open doorway, we witnessed Tony's wife and daughter sitting in a chair. They seemed to be reading a story. I noticed the blue line went past them and into a built-in bench by the window.

Using telepathy, I told them we need to figure out how to get them out. Juliet suggested ringing the doorbell. I explained they had a butler. Akio suggested we knock some books off the shelves and move some toys to scare them. That would have worked, but the Granaldis would immediately suspect me of being in the home.

"Brooke, use the power of persuasion. Make them want to go eat something," Juliet suggested.

"Great idea." I began working on the child. She immediately asked her mother for a cookie. The mother said no. I concentrated on the mother. Telling her to give the child some fruit. It did not appear to work at first. The child asked again for a cookie.

"No, dear, but perhaps you could persuade me to give you some fruit," Tony's wife said to her daughter.

The little girl leaned her head back and gave her mother a big grin. With her chin down and her eyes wide she said, "Yes, please."

Her mother pulled her in and kissed her on the cheek. With a big smile, she said, "Let's go see what we've got." They started walking our way.

Using telepathy. I told everyone to move out of their way. Akio and Juliet put themselves flush up against the wall. The mother's elbow got rather close to Juliet. Her eyes widened as she tried to become one with the wall as they passed.

Once they were out of earshot we entered the room, "Akio, stand guard." The blue line had disappeared, but it showed it at the bench area. "Okay, stone, show me how to get into this secret compartment."

The area left of the bench lit up with a blue glow. I whispered to Juliet, "It's over here somewhere." I pointed to the area that was glowing.

Juliet lifted the padding on the window seat. It revealed a secret storage space under the middle seat with some dolls in it, but that was not the area lit up. *We are missing something.* I began pushing on the wood next to the compartment. Nothing happened. I pushed the wood on the front of the seat just left of the compartment with the dolls. It popped open at a forty-degree angle. There was just enough room to get one journal through the door. I looked inside and found many journals. The secret compartment went to the floor. It contained five journals. I grabbed the first journal. It was for the right time frame. I flipped through it to April. I began reading,

April 7

Joseph invited Federico to join us in Rome. That little rat deserves what is coming to him.

April 10

Pops, Joseph, Federico, and I went to Rome. Out of nowhere, they attacked Federico. I almost defended him, but I saw Pops motion for us to follow him. I asked Pops if he hired a hitman. He wouldn't say. I think he doesn't trust me.

If I could get away from Pops and live a normal life with my family, I would be happy. I see no way out.

April 11

On the ride back home, Joseph told me Pops had hired Louis Dupont for the job.

Louis Dupont! Did I read that right? I read it again and confirmed it was correct.

"Brooke, Akio is motioning. Someone is coming," Juliet warned.

I put the book back and closed the cabinet. Akio was on the other side of the room. Juliet and I moved to the side of the room and were making our way toward Akio.

Tony came in carrying an envelope. He went straight for the secret cabinet. He looked around and stuffed the envelope into the cabinet.

He went down to the elevator.

Using telepathy, I said to Akio and Juliet, "Stay here and stay out of sight."

I knew there would be a greater chance of us being detected if we were together. I stood a few feet away from Tony and waited for him to enter the elevator. Tony was standing in the middle. I opened my mirror and teleported into the two-person elevator and pinned myself against the wall. Tony was only a few inches away. I held my breath until the door opened. We were on the lower level. Tony stepped out, and the door closed. I took a deep breath and stuck my head through the door. Tony was heading toward the area with the bar.

I was just about to step out of the elevator when it moved. It forced me to jump. Tony was still in the hallway. He spun around and looked in my direction. Frozen in place, I waited for him to move. He shook his head and turned left. I teleported to the family room area.

Tony's wife played with her daughter as she ate pieces of a sliced apple. His wife looked up at Tony as soon as he entered the room.

He nodded to her, "It's done."

She looked as though she was about to say something. He put his finger to his mouth and pointed to the backyard.

She picked up the plate of apples. "Daddy wants to go outside." Her daughter grabbed her hand and followed her outside.

They were well away from the house when Tony started talking to his wife, "Joseph's just as bad as Pops. I'm not going down with them. I will get the cash and passports. Once we are out of the country, we can leak everything to the police." His daughter caught his attention. He said, "Stefania, stop playing in the dirt."

Is he really wanting out? I didn't expect that.

"He's going to come after us. I think he suspects something already."

Tony turned his attention to his wife. "That is a possibility. Rosina, I love you and we need to at least try to save this family. Moldova is not that far, but they will accept us."

She hugged him.

It suddenly hit me. I was extremely far from Juliet and Akio. I teleported back to Stefania's playroom. They were gone. Using telepathy, I tried calling Juliet, "Where are you?"

"Where am I? We've been looking all over for you. Are you okay?"

"Yes, I'm fine. I'm in the playroom. We are across the hall hiding in a closet," Juliet informed me.

I popped into Anthony's closet and found them. I whispered, "Why are you guys in here?"

"The maid and butler came in, tided up the place and well…" Juliet said. She seemed at a loss for words.

"Let's just say something's going on with the maid and butler," Akio explained.

"We can go. I know what is going on," I informed them.

"I don't think you do," Akio said. He handed me an envelope.

It appeared to be in English. I lifted the stone from my neck, which revealed it was in Italian. I looked up at Akio. "You read Italian?"

"Yes, my father taught me. He made me learn it because of the Granaldi family."

I turned my attention back to the letter.

To whom it may concern,

I, Anthony Granaldi IV (Tony), testify the information in these journals that are hidden in this compartment is factual. The journals hidden in my daughter's bedroom are fake. They're used to throwing my family off my true mission to expose them. I admit I've done some horrible things in my life, but I want to correct my mistakes by disclosing the true corruption within my family. My love for my wife, daughter, and the Lord changed me. I need to fix this. I'll suffer the consequences.

Once I'm aware the authorities have my journals, I'll turn myself in. Until then, I will remain in hiding. I should also let you know; that I suspect my father has a hidden room somewhere in the house that holds many of his secrets. I've spent a lifetime trying to find it and couldn't. I suspect it is somewhere in the lower part of the house.

"We need to put this back," I instructed Akio. He nodded and grabbed my arm. Juliet followed his lead. Once he returned the letter, we traveled back to the hut.

As soon as we returned, Juliet blurted, "We need to tell the authorities about the stash of journals."

"I think we should wait a bit. If he really wants to come clean, perhaps we can help one another out. He knows Louis Dupont aka Marshall Blaise. Perhaps he can provide us more information about him," I said, trying to sway them.

"Brooke is right. If he can help provide you with information, that could be helpful. It's worth a try," Akio agreed. I could see Asahi approaching the hut with some plants in his hands. "Brooke, you need to talk with him today. People don't leave notes like that and hang around. He could leave as early as today."

Everyone greeted Asahi as he entered.

I knew Akio was correct. I needed to go back. Akio fed us a quick snack of fruit salad to tide us over until our next meal. Juliet and I would return to the Granaldi mansion as soon as we ate and rehydrated ourselves.

Thirteen

We returned to Tony and Rosina's bedroom. Two packed suitcases were sitting beside the bed. We needed to find Tony. I grabbed Juliet, and we went to Stefania's bedroom. Rosina was trying to cram a stuffed bear into a suitcase. *Where's Tony?* Using telepathy, I asked Juliet to stay with them. I knew Tony was not heading out of town without them. I popped down to the entryway and heard a commotion coming from the kitchen.

"Mr. Togno, I don't want to argue with you. I don't need to notify Joseph of my every move. My family and I are going to spend a few days on holiday in Naples. All I want from you is to bring the bags down and put them in my car," Tony snapped.

"Mr. Granaldi gave me strict instructions regarding this household, sir," Mr. Togno politely advised Tony.

"Fine, I'll do it myself, but when I get back, Joseph and I will discuss your employment," Tony snapped before heading toward the elevator.

I popped into the elevator door on the upper floor and waited for him to arrive.

Tony went immediately toward his daughter's room. Sounding stressed, Tony said, "Mr. Togno, refuses to help us. My father and brother must suspect something. We need to get out of here. I'm going to grab our bags. Can you manage that bag?"

Rosina nodded and said, "We'll meet you at the car."

Tony spun around and marched toward his room. I grabbed Juliet, and we popped into his room, but this time we were visible.

Tony rushed in and immediately stopped in his tracks when he saw us.

"Tony, we are not here to start trouble. In fact, I want to help you," I said calmly.

He stood in a defensive position and snapped, "Help me. What could you possibly want to help me with?"

"I know you are trying to go into hiding from the letter hidden found in your journal. I'm willing to help you, but I would like some information regarding Louis Dupont," I said as I relaxed my position.

He also relaxed his position. "What do you know about Louis?"

"I know that's an alias. I've been to his home, and I know his daughter."

He reached down and grabbed the suitcases. "If you've read my journals, you know what he does for a living. I'm not sure what else you could want from me."

"I need to know what he knows about my grandmother and this stone," I said as I laid my fingers on top of the stone.

"Pops and Louis worked together many times over the years. Louis is clever. It wouldn't surprise me if he wanted to find out what kind of man he was doing business with. He was good with surveillance. He probably eavesdropped on a few conversations and found out about the stone's powers," he said, putting the suitcase back on the floor.

I could hear voices in the hallway. I pulled out my mirror and grabbed Juliet and quickly made us invisible.

Mr. Togno, Rosina, and Stefania appeared in the doorway.

Mr. Togno had Stefania's suitcase clutched in his hand. "I must insist you stay here. I have contacted Mr. Joseph and he will be here shortly to sort this out."

Rosina's face looked as though she was about to cry.

Using telepathy, I told Tony, "Tell him that's fine and send him away."

Tony did as I instructed, but also asked him to leave his daughter's bag because it would need to be unpacked. With hesitation, the butler dropped the bag. Tony moved to the doorway and watched Mr. Togno for a moment before pulling his wife and child into the room and shutting the door.

Tony looked around the room and whispered, "Brooke?"

I made us reappear. "We're here."

Rosina's eyes stared at me in disbelief. She pulled her daughter to her side and grabbed Tony's arm. She asked, "What's going on? Do you see?"

"Yes, Rosina, I see them. This is Brooke. I think her friend's name is Jules or Juliet or something," Tony announced.

"I'm Juliet," she said, shaking Rosina's hand.

Tony wrapped his arm around his wife and asked, "Are you really going to help us?"

For a moment, I thought about what I was about to do. Jesus would want me to stick by my word and help them. Tony was planning on turning himself in. "Yes, we'll help you, but you must stick to your promise to turn yourself in or I'll make sure you do," I assured him.

"We have a flight to Moldova we need to catch tonight," Tony informed us.

Juliet asked, "Is it a private plane?"

"No, I need to save the funds I have for us to live on," Tony said, looking at his wife.

"Brooke, they will track them down. We need another plan. Perhaps the villa," Juliet recommended.

Juliet was right. Jacob has taught us how easily he can locate people and hack into things. The villa? They would never suspect him going there. A smile formed on my face as I thought about her suggestion, "Juliet, you're brilliant! We are going to take you to the Villa Dianella. You'll still be in Italy, but your family would never suspect you of hiding out there," I said as I placed my hand on Juliet's shoulder. "Stay here. We will be right back." I pulled out my mirror and Juliet pushed my hand down.

"We should take their suitcases. They can act like they changed their minds and unpacked. We can come back for them later," Juliet said, grabbing two of the suitcases.

"Another brilliant idea, my lady," I said as I grabbed the other one. I linked my arm through hers and peered into my mirror, visualizing my room at the villa.

We dropped their bags and set off to find Isabella or Leonardo. There were people checking in when we arrived. We patiently waited for our opportunity to speak to Isabella. I heard Leonardo's voice in the distance. He was walking with an employee. It sounded as if he was instructing him on the evening's activities. I waved at him to get his attention.

Once he noticed us, he instantly sent his staff away and walked toward us. Sounding hopeful, Leonardo said, "Well, it's a surprise to see both of you. Is this a social visit?"

I squeezed my lips together and let out a heavy exhale. "Sorry to say it's not. We need to talk."

"Follow me," Leonardo instructed as he led us to his room. "This sounds serious. Should I get Isabella?"

Juliet and I looked at one another and nodded. "Yes, this one task you will not be happy about," I informed him.

Leonardo took a deep breath and went back toward the lobby.

"Hard for him to handle. Brooke, it could be impossible. What if he's not willing to go along with this?"

I did not have time to respond to her because Leonardo returned with Isabella. "Perhaps we should sit down," Leonardo suggested.

Great idea. It'll be harder for you to lunge at me. Juliet and I sat on the sofa, while Leonardo sat in the chair across from us and Isabella rested herself on the arm of the chair.

Juliet looked over at me with a look that said she would not tell them. *Just tell them the truth.* "We've discovered some evidence to help keep Anthony Granaldi and his family in prison for a very long time," I said, as I looked over at Juliet.

"That's great news," Isabella said with a grin.

"Tony Granaldi provided this information," I said, waiting for their reaction. Neither of them said anything. They just looked at one another before returning their attention back to me. "As odd as this may sound, Tony has found the Lord and wants to fix the wrongs he and his family have done. He wants to provide the authorities with the evidence they are going to need. We have seen this evidence..."

Juliet interrupted me by saying, "Well, we have read some of it."

I continued, "That's correct. Tony has been journaling about the family for quite a while. He was going to contact the authorities to let them know where to find the evidence, but not until he was in hiding from his father."

Leonardo commented, "I see where this is going. You want us to help hide Tony?"

Isabella shot him a look and then turned to me. "You can't be serious! Do you know how much he and his family have done to us?" Isabella rose and began pacing the floor. "No! Leonardo, tell them we won't do it!"

"Isabella, I know how you feel. I can't believe Brooke is asking this of us," Leonard said as he walked over and wrapped his arms around her. He held her for a moment and appeared to be praying.

I stood up next to them and said, "Don't think for a second I don't know what I'm asking of you. I have a battle going on in me as well about this."

Isabella pulled herself away from her husband. "Then how can you ask this of us?"

"I thought about walking away from him, but I asked God what to do. He has put it on my heart to help him." Isabella turned away from me. "Look, he will pay for his crimes. He wants his family taken to safety. If they are here, I can monitor them. They have promised to be on their best behavior. If you ever have a problem, I'll stop what I'm doing and come immediately."

Juliet chimed in, "This is the last place they would look for him. He seemed sincere when he said he was trying to protect his wife and daughter. Also, it did not appear to me that his wife has any idea what really goes on in that family."

"I really need a decision now. Apparently, Anthony told the butler to report any unusual behavior from Tony to Joseph," I advised them.

"Yes, it seems Joseph has taken Anthony's place as the head of the crime family," Juliet added.

"Ladies, please give us a moment," Leonardo said before leading his wife to their bedroom.

Juliet and I made ourselves comfortable on the sofa. Without saying a word, we both just sat there and stared at the bedroom door.

About ten minutes later, both returned. Isabella's eyes were red and puffy. It broke my heart to see her so upset. "We discussed it and we're not happy with it. We'll do as you ask because it is the Christian thing to do. If what you say is true, Anthony will have Tony killed to keep his secrets. Family means nothing to that man," Leonardo stated.

Thank you, Lord! I stood up and motioned for Juliet to get up. "We will be back shortly with them. Please find them a comfortable room. If they cannot pay, please take the funds you need from my account. His wife's name is Rosina, and their daughter is Stefania. Their bags are in my room. I suggest you don't tell them about me having my room or about the secret room here. The only connection to me would be my grandmother loved to spend time here. Nothing more."

They both nodded. I pulled out my mirror. Just as I was about to place my hand on Juliet, Isabella approached me. She gently placed her hand around my arm and said, "Brooke, I want you to know we trusted Lillie with our lives as we do with you. She was right in choosing you. We both feel you are doing God's work. It's just… This is hard for us." She reached out and hugged me. Isabella turned to Juliet and told her, "You're a blessing also, young lady." She hugged her as well.

We returned to Tony's room. There was no one there. Juliet and I walked out into the hall. A maid was approaching us. Thankfully, we were invisible. I could hear yelling in the distance, but I could not make out what was being said. I placed my arm on Juliet and teleported to the foyer.

Tony and his wife were sitting at the kitchen table. Joseph, along with two other men of large stature, was standing by them.

Joseph paced. "Dad had a theory that you would betray us." He spun around. "Is that what's happening? Are you betraying us?"

Tony seemed to stay calm. He spurted out, "What? No! Rosina and I want to take my daughter on a holiday for a few days. Joseph, you do not know what it is like to be forced to have you and your family live with a parent. You have only yourself to worry about."

Using telepathy, I said to Tony, "We're back. Don't lose your temper. Lead him to believe you understand. We'll get you out of here soon."

Tony nodded, and in his mind asked, "How in the world are you doing that?"

"Don't worry about that. Deal with Joseph and his goons."

Tony went to stand up and one thug pushed him back in his chair. "Look, I don't understand what is going on, but if you don't want us to go, we won't."

Joseph stopped pacing and stared at his brother, while Rosina looked to be scared to death.

"Joseph, what makes you and Pop think I would do anything against this family? I have just as much to lose as the rest of you," Tony said as he pushed the man's hand off his shoulder.

Rosina shot him a look that told me she wanted to know what he was referring to.

Joseph looked up at the two brutes. He squinted his eyes and said, "Mr. Togno!"

The butler must have been waiting around the corner because he suddenly appeared. "Yes, Mr. Granaldi."

I noticed he changed the way he addressed him from Mr. Joseph to Mr. Granaldi. This told me Joseph was in charge.

Joseph motioned to the two men, "Show them to Tony's room and let them search it." His attention returned to Tony. "Brother, you better hope they find nothing."

I told Juliet to stay with them and I went to see what was going on in their room. I appeared just outside the door. As they walked my way, I noticed a maid taking Stefania from the hall bathroom to her playroom. I popped down there.

"Sweetie, your mother is busy. You must stay with me until your Uncle Joseph's done speaking with them. How about we play with your dolls?" the maid suggested.

Joseph had the entire household under his control. I returned to Tony's room. The men were tearing everything apart. One man pulled the dresser away from the wall. They emptied all the drawers on the bed. The larger of the two men brought a box out of the closet and put it on the bed. Tony's journals were inside.

"Well, well. Look what we have here. He opened one journal and began reading. He returned the journal to the box. "Hand me that other journal," he said to the other man. Once it was in the box, he put the lid on it and took the box with him as he exited the room.

Mr. Togno was standing outside, waiting for orders. "When he's done in there, take him to the kids' room," he spurted as he walked to the elevator. I popped back downstairs to the dining room.

I concentrated and asked, "Juliet, did anything happen?"

"Rosina asked if she could see her daughter. He told her no."

I concentrated on Tony and told him, "Tony, tell your wife your daughter is fine. She is in the playroom with the maid."

Tony rested his hand on his wife's hand. He looked tenderly into her eyes and said, "Love, I'm sure Stefania is fine. She is probably in the playroom with the maid."

The man entered the dining room with the box and placed it on the table. He snarled and commented, "We found these in his room."

Tony did not react at all.

"Tony, even though you know these are not true, you need to be upset. They are invading your privacy," I told him using telepathy.

Joseph walked over to the box and opened it. Tony must have understood because he tried to stand up, and the man shoved him back down.

"Joseph, you are not really going to read my journals. They are my private thoughts. My wife doesn't even read them," Tony pleaded.

"Give me your keys," Joseph demanded.

Tony tossed the set of keys to him.

"Rosina, I need yours," he said with less force.

"Mine are down hanging in the garage key closet," she explained.

"To ensure you don't go anywhere, Stefania will have a guard stay with her all. Until I know, we can trust you. Get out of my sight," Joseph instructed.

Rosina and Tony quickly stood up and exited the room. Juliet motioned to me she was going with them. I stayed to listen to their conversation.

"I don't want my niece left alone. One of you guys needs to be with her until we know if we can trust them. That means if you are watching her, no sleeping. Go now. They're probably on their way to see her," Joseph ordered. Once the man left the room, Joseph sat down. He put his elbows on the table and rested his head in his hands.

I popped into the playroom and found Stefania playing with her dolls. The maid was playing on her phone. I walked out to meet Tony as he approached the room.

I made sure only Tony could hear me when I said, "She's fine. Act like everything is fine. The brute is on his way here. Don't try anything. I'll come to get you tonight. Be in your room. When does Joseph go to bed?"

"Around 11:00 pm. This is so weird talking to you in my head," Tony said. He stopped for a moment, "Brooke, thank you." He continued into the room and grabbed his daughter and smothered her with kisses.

Fourteen

Greg insisted he come with me to get Tony and his family. We arrived at 6:30 pm, our time to ensure no one in the house was stirring. Tony and his wife were sitting in their room in the dark. I asked, "Are you ready to go?"

Rosina was trying to recover from our sudden entrance into the room. Confused, she asked, "How did you just appear here? Tony, who are these people?"

Tony tried to explain, "Honey, it's a long story…"

I interrupted, "But this is one story that you will not be told. Tony, if you want my help, keep my secret. I'm sorry Rosina. Just know I'm here trying to do what Jesus would do. This family has done horrific things to people I care about. Just thank God for what I do to help you because without Him, none of this would be possible."

Tony bowed his head. "You're right Brooke. I'll take what you're doing for me and my family, along with your secret to my grave."

"Come on, we need to get ya out of here," Greg instructed.

"Wait, we need Stefania," Rosina cried.

"Rosina, you're going to need to trust me. We'll bring her to you, but I can't take everyone at once. You need to disappear before your daughter. She'll be fine. We'll protect her," I assured her.

She looked at Tony, who said, "Brooke is right. We can trust her."

I asked them to hold my shoulders, and Greg grabbed my waist. I looked into the mirror above the dresser and concentrated on the wine cellar at the inn.

When we arrived, Rosina looked as though she was going to throw up. I turned to Greg and said, "I'll stay with them. Go get Leonardo."

While I waited for them to arrive, I explained to them the rules if they wish to remain in safe hiding. "While you're here, I expect you to treat everyone here with respect, especially Isabella and Leonardo. If you cannot pay for the room, you will help them in whatever way you can. That means if they ask you to wash dishes or take out the trash, you'll do it without a complaint. One word from them and this agreement is over. Do you understand?"

Tony wrapped his arm around his wife and said, "We understand. Thank you again. For what it's worth, I'm sorry for all the things I've done to your family."

Rosina turned to Tony. "What have you done to them? It sounds like something terrible."

"Rosina, he and his family have been at war with my family for generations. Tony is trying to make amends. Jesus tells us to forgive. I don't think you realized what type of family you married into, but you have made Tony strive to be a better man. If I can forgive him, you should." I turned my attention to Tony. "I forgive you, but remember, I will not forget what you are capable of. Do me a favor, read your Bible daily, and love the time you have with your family. I'll do what I can to help your family, but only you and those journals currently know your side of the story."

Greg and Leonardo entered the wine cellar. "Leonardo, this is Tony and his wife, Rosina. Stay here. We'll be back with your daughter." I pulled out my mirror, and we went directly to Stefania's room. She was in her bed, sound asleep. The man staying with her was not the one that brought the box to Joseph. He was pacing the floor.

I motioned for Greg to follow me to the side of her bed. He stood between me and the man. The man walked over to the other side of the bed. "I don't get to sleep because of you," he snarled. He was just staring at her. He looked as though he was going to poke her with his finger. Greg stuck his hand between his finger and the child.

The man closed his eyes and tried to poke her again. "What the heck?"

Thankfully, Greg kept putting his hand in his way. It was hard not to laugh at his confusion. I looked up at Greg. It blessed me to have such a wonderful man in my life.

The man looked at her again. I could tell he was trying to make sense of the force field surrounding her. His eyes glared at Stefania, and his face changed from annoyed to angry. "That's it, kid. If I'm not sleeping, you're not sleeping." He reached toward Stefania as though he was going to pick her up. I grabbed her, while Greg flung himself over her bed and plowed both his feet into the man's stomach.

Greg jumped to his feet and stood between us and the man. "Get her out of here."

As much as I wanted to stay and help Greg, I knew I needed to keep her safe. I looked in the mirror on her wall and brought us to the wine cellar. As I popped into the room, Rosina snatched Stefania from my arms.

"Thank you… Thank you. My sweet Stefania, Mamma loves you," she said, as tears streamed down her face.

"Take them to their room. I must get back to Greg," I announced as I whipped out my mirror. I arrived to find Greg was still in a battle with the man and Joseph appeared to have just arrived at the scene.

Joseph was on the phone and firmly said, "Get to my niece's room now!"

He must be talking to the larger brute.

Joseph put his phone in his pocket and looked right at me. I was his intended target. Little did he know I was no longer the scared girl he chased through my neighborhood. I ran straight for him and attempted to kick him in the head. He was successful in dodging me. We both began throwing punches. The larger brute came in and saw us. He went toward Greg. Joseph came at me again. This time, I did what Asahi taught me. I ran up the man and wrapped my legs around his neck. I held on to his head and leaned backward. My legs squeezed his throat. He wobbled. I held on until he passed out causing us to crash to the floor.

I pulled myself away from him and looked over at Greg. The smaller man had Greg's arms locked behind him and the other man was punching him. Greg's face was already swelling like someone who consumed shellfish when they were allergic. It crushed me to see him like that.

I charged at the larger man and jumped up with both legs plowed into his back. I fell to the floor and spun around. The large man was thrust into Greg and the small guy. Greg broke free. He crossed the room toward me. We both stood facing them, waiting for their retaliation. I reached over and held Greg's arm, hoping it could heal him enough to continue our fight.

The larger one was holding his head and appeared to be dizzy. The smaller guy tapped him on the back. "Come on, we got these two punks."

They started moving toward us quickly. From the angle I was standing, I could see the mirror. I looked into it and pictured us behind them. We immediately teleported and now had an advantage. I ran and jumped on the smaller man's back and wrapped my right arm around his neck. With my left arm, I held my arm in place. I squeezed with all my might.

Greg ran and tackled the larger man as if he was about to score a touchdown. They began wrestling on the ground. I noticed Joseph was stirring. I left my now sleeping attacker and went to help Greg. He was looking like he had done a few rounds with a pro boxer. I looked at them, trying to figure out what to do. They were so tightly locked together.

I concentrated on the large goon and tried to persuade him to release Greg, "You no longer need to fight, release your hold." He must have been very strong-willed, I continued until he released his hold and laid back on the ground with his arms reaching out to each side.

Greg now appeared to be the one confused. He looked over at me and must have realized what had happened. He muttered, "Couldn't ya have done that when we arrived?" Greg wobbled as he rose to his feet.

"Now what fun would that have been?" I said in a flirty way.

Greg walked over to me and wrapped his arm around me. I could feel his weight on me. Joseph must have paid a lot for these guys. They were tough to battle. We were about to leave when I saw Joseph trying to say something.

His voice seemed raspy from me, choking him, "My brother and I'll be coming for you."

I looked up at Greg as if to say should I tell him. Greg shook his head from side to side. I knew he was right. If I told Joseph we were working together, he might know where to look for Tony and his family.

"Perhaps you shouldn't have your guys watching a little girl. That one there wanted to hurt the poor child," I said, pointing to the small thug. "Don't worry about Stefania. I'll bring her back to her family, but Tony was not in his bedroom. Have Tony contact me. I'll only return her to him."

Joseph first showed a face of confusion and then anger.

I pulled out my mirror and returned to my room at the villa.

Greg plopped himself down on the bed as soon as we arrived. I called the front desk and asked Leonardo to come to my room with some water. The desk clerk informed me they would give him the message.

I climbed on the bed and sat next to Greg. My wounds had already healed. I took the stone off and laid it on Greg's chest. I curled up next to him and felt the warmth of his arm wrap around me as I laid my head on his shoulder. "You need to rest and let the stone heal you," I said as I kissed him on the chest. "You did good tonight," I told him as I lay there in the comfort of his arm. My body quickly drifted off to sleep. A knock at the door awakened me.

I instructed Leonardo to come in. He was carrying a couple of bottles of water. He looked over at Greg and watched for a second as his body continued to heal. "I have never seen this before. The healing I mean."

He turned and walked into the bathroom. I could hear some water running. He returned with a damp cloth. "For the blood," he said as he handed it to me.

I sat up and began wiping the blood from his face and hands. It was amazing there was no evidence remaining from the fight. Yet Greg was still not moving. My lungs constricted. I felt like I couldn't catch my breath. I called to him, "Honey, are you okay?"

He grabbed me by the waist and flung me under him. He looked down at me and smiled. "You are my own personal healer." He then pointed to his eye and to his heart.

Awe. I could not believe he would pick a time like this to be all sweet.

Greg suddenly seemed to remember Leonardo was in the room. He leapt off me and turned to him. "How are the Granaldi's doing?" He looked down. "I never thought I would ask about any of them. Especially about how well they are doing."

"They're happy to be together and away from their brother," Leonardo informed us. He handed Greg and me our water bottles. "I must admit it was strange having Tony be so apologetic and polite."

I grabbed my necklace that had fallen onto the bed and handed it to Greg and stood up. He put it back around my neck.

Leonardo grabbed the door handle. "It's late. I need to get some rest. Will you be here in the morning?"

"No, we need to be getting back. Greg is going to be late for work if we don't get back soon," I explained.

As soon as I shut the door, Greg turned to me with his dreamy eyes staring at me, "Why don't I call in sick today? We've hardly seen each other."

He was right. Bill demanded a lot from him, but he paid him well. The money Greg earned during the summer lasted him most of the school year. I smiled at him, and he leaned closer to me to see if I would permit him to kiss me. I did.

There was so much passion in his kiss. I leaned back and took in the moment. Greg began kissing my neck, which sent chills down the right side of my body. I wrapped my arms around him. I could feel my heart beating faster as the heat built up between us. The tenderness of his lips as he kissed my skin made me long for more. *Oh, Greg.* I longed to be with him more intimately. There wasn't a doubt he felt the same. Our arms caressed one another. The touch of his skin made me hungry for more than I was receiving. *Brooke, you need to stop.* That was what I was telling myself, but my body was screaming for more.

Greg's body froze. He buried his face beside my head. His warm breath turned me as it tickled my skin. I turned my head and began kissing his ear. His body quivered. This put a smile on my face. I grabbed him and rolled him over on to his back leaving me on top of him. He looked up at me. I leaned down and gently kissed him on the lips. Following his lead, I moved and began kissing his neck. He shivered again. He ran his arms up my back and pulled me to him. This triggered the heat to build back up between us. *Brooke, stop!* I took a deep breath and pulled away from his lips. I stared down at him. Even with his hair a mess, he was still beautiful. "I love you," I whispered.

Greg brought his hand to my cheek and took his thumb and dabbed my lower lip. I kissed his thumb. "You are my world. Life would be empty without you. I love you with every ounce of my being." He exhaled and closed his eyes for a moment. He looked up, and placed his hands on my cheeks, and asked, "Do you have any idea how hard it is to resist you? I love you. I want to spend the rest of my life with you, Brooke." He took the hair that had fallen on my face and put it behind my ears. "I know you are feeling what I am feeling."

I nodded.

He took a deep breath. "I know we both feel the same way about one another. It's the passion I'm talking about. Brooke, I want you so badly. I have had other girlfriends, but nothing serious. Nothing that tempted me to want to sin. Do you know what I mean?"

"I do. I want you, too. My mind keeps telling me to stop, but my body is craving more," I told him.

"Exactly! Oh, I love you so much," he pulled me to him and kissed me.

I leaned back and informed him, "We must stay in control." I tried to kiss him again, but he tossed me off him. *What the heck?*

Greg jumped to his feet and leaned over and tried to kiss me, but I pulled away. "Look, you said we need to stay in control and well, I'm not sure I'll be able to conquer the temptation of getting intimate. So off to work I go." He reached out his hand and helped me up.

I looked up at him and rolled my eyes at him.

"Come on, you know all of this is too much to resist," he said, motioning to himself.

I got up, and he pulled me toward him. Greg softly said, "I love you, but a man can only be tempted so long."

I knew he was right. We both longed for one another, but we both vowed to wait till marriage. He was also right. He was hard to resist.

Fifteen

When I arrived at home, my desire to feed myself was greater than my desire for a shower. I needed my stomach to stop growling at me. My mother was in the kitchen eating breakfast and Phyllis was leaning up against the counter chatting with her when I arrived.

"You got up early for your workout. Did you work out with Greg this morning? I noticed his truck was still there when I came down," Mom inquired.

I had forgotten to check to see what I looked like. I looked down and noticed my workout uniform. *Let's see... Did I work out with Greg? How do I answer that question? We fought off three attackers and saved a child and her family. That was a bit of a workout. Then, there was the moment in the bed that caused my heart rate to increase. Could that be a workout? Focus Brooke and answer the question.* "Yes, he and I have spent little time together this summer, so we had a bit of a workout. He'll be heading to work soon."

I was starving. I grabbed a banana and ate it while Phyllis made me a couple of fried eggs, hash browns, bacon, and toast. We all chatted and caught up on a few things.

Mom told us her boss was thinking about starting another company in Palm Beach County, Florida. "He's considering moving him and his family there," she announced.

Phyllis and I both looked at one another. I asked, "What does that mean for you?"

"I'm not sure. In passing, he asked if I would be interested in moving back there. He said he has not decided for sure. His family is discussing it."

I inquired more, "Would you want to move back?"

"I would love to be back at my old church and with my friends, but I don't want to leave you and Phyllis. Honestly, I hate the cold winters here and desperately want to bake in the sun with a good book," she said, getting lost in her thoughts.

"Mom, if you want to move back, I understand. I need to stay and finish my degree; besides, I love it here. I've made great friends. Even Mechelle's moving here. I've got Phyllis to help me. Unless, of course, she wants to move with you," I said, glancing over at Phyllis to see her reaction. There was not one. "We'll be fine. Besides, I hardly see you anymore. Your boss has you gallivanting around the country or working late nights. I can come to see you during my breaks and visit my old friends. Financially, we can manage both homes. If I need to, I can get a job and help. This house is paid for. I don't want to sound like I don't want you to stay, but I want you to be happy. Since you and Lance broke up, you seem lost. You've been moping around here. I think being with your Florida friends would help. What I'm saying is don't stay because of me. Make your decision based on what you want."

Phyllis chimed in, "For the record, I would prefer to stay here and be near my sister. I'll certainly be here for Brooke."

When Mom was not looking, Phyllis winked at me. I took that as a sign she knew I needed her here with me.

Mom looked up at us and said, "I've got a lot to consider." She turned to Phyllis. "Will you be able to handle two teenagers, I mean young ladies?"

Phyllis chuckled. "As long as they invite me to all their wild parties."

We all had a good laugh.

I devoured my breakfast and set off to take a shower and a nap. I lay there on my bed with my hair wrapped in a towel, thinking about everything I could accomplish because of the Bloom of Dreams. There was not a doubt in my mind my family had been doing God's work. I knew faith had healed many. *If I trust in the Lord, enough I could do the same.*

God was still working on me. He had entrusted my family with keeping such a powerful gift safe and trying to right the wrongs of the world. The more I thought about this, the more I felt the Bible calling me. I pulled it off my nightstand.

The worn leather showed its age. It reminded me of my mother and I reading our Bibles together. My father never had much to do with the Bible or church. Occasionally, he would come on holiday for a Christmas show or something, but I didn't see any point in going. I think he was convicted when he was there.

Before opening the word of God, I prayed the Lord would send me a message I needed. I opened it to 1 Corinthians 12:11. I says, 'All these are the work of one and the same Spirit, and He distributes them to each one, just as He determines.' *Wow! God, you are good.* I knew the powers of the Bloom of Dreams could only come from God. The more I thought about this verse, the more I knew I needed to make sure I was doing God's work. I continued reading until I felt I could not keep my eyes open.

A text awakened me.

MECHELLE: When do you want me to move up there?

BROOKE: Yesterday!!

Mechelle called, and we began working out the details. We thought it best she was in the room on the third floor in case we ever had guests. She agreed. We had our mothers work out the details of the move.

My hair was still damp from my shower. I pulled it back into a ponytail and dressed. My plan was to head back to the villa to have a talk with Tony.

I popped into my room and saw the bed where Greg and I had fought our desires. The memory put a smile on my face. I set off toward the foyer and found Leonardo sitting in the dining room, speaking to a young man. It sounded like he was interviewing him. I waved and continued to the front desk.

Isabella was working on her computer. She did not seem to notice me. "Excuse me, I demand to see the manager," I said in the best I could do to sound like a man.

Isabella's head flung around and seemed shocked it was me. I smiled at her and said, "Only kidding."

She came around the counter and gave me a hug. "It's so good to see you. Is everything okay?"

I assured her everything was fine, and I was only there to speak with Tony. She told me he should be outside. I strolled out to see if I could locate him. My first thought was that he and his family might sit outside. There was only a woman who appeared to be in her seventies, sitting on a bench reading a book under the canopy of a tree. It was a beautiful day. The sky was clear, with a few puffy white clouds. The breeze cooled the warmth of the sun.

I walked out away from the building and still did not see him. *Where could he be?* I walked around the path along the side of the villa toward the front entrance. Still not in sight. At the front entrance, I found the gardener with his back to me. He was wearing a hat and appeared to be cleaning the weeds out of the flower bed. "Excuse me, sir." To my surprise, Tony was the one picking the weeds.

He leaned back onto his feet and wiped the sweat from his brow with a towel from his pocket. "Brooke? Is everything okay?"

"Yes, why are you gardening?"

He stood up and brushed his pants off. "Well, you said I need to help. So, I am. My wife is with Stefania. The thought of doing this sounded miserable." He looked at his work. "Look how much nicer it looks. It's also very relaxing. A great way to relax and talk to God."

It shocked me. I did not know what to say. Who is this man? It can't be Tony. "You are doing an excellent job.

I took a deep breath and began my questioning, "I need information about Marshall Blaise. He is also known as Louis Dupont. He's after my necklace and I suspect he murdered my grandmother. Do you have any information on him?"

"I know Pops has hired him for big jobs. I don't know how he knows about the necklace," he said. He seemed to be thinking. "He's good at his job. He's a hitman. It wouldn't surprise me if he has been spying on us. I mean, we like to know who were doing business with. I'm sure he does too."

"Now, about Federico's murder. You said Louis Dupont murdered him. Is that correct?"

He looked around as if he was checking to see if anyone was within earshot. Tony said, "Yes. How could Pops just kill my cousin? That's when I knew Rosina, Stephania, and I needed to escape. If he or Joseph got wind of my intentions to come clean, we would have suffered the same fate."

"We need to prove this," I informed him.

"Everything I was aware my family had done is in the journals. I provided as much details as possible," Tony assured me.

I grabbed him and gave him a hug. "Thank you." It suddenly hit me; I was hugging Tony. *What's wrong with you?* Awkwardly, I released him and stepped back. "Well, thank you." I stepped backward, nearly stepping into the flowerbed. "Keep up the good work." I spun around and went to the main entrance.

Isabella was stapling some papers together and looked up at me. "Did you find him?"

"Yes, he's gardening," I said, knowing my face looked puzzled.

Isabella leaned to my side. She looked out the front entrance. "You think that's weird? Without asking, he started clearing the plates when people finished eating. My staff was confused. They told him the guest were not required to do that."

"Perhaps he really wants to change," I said before explaining I needed to leave.

Upon returning home, I texted Imelda to see if she could meet. She texted me her address, and we agreed to meet in an hour.

I texted Juliet to see how she was doing.

JULIET: Bored.

I asked her if she wanted to come with me to Italy.

JULIET: On my way!!

I looked on the internet to locate a picture of her home. Phyllis came into my room to drop off my towels. "Phyllis, Juliet, and I are heading to Italy for the afternoon. What's there to eat for lunch?"

"What would you like? I can make a salad, sandwiches, or soup," she hollered from the bathroom.

"You don't need to make it. Juliet and I can make something," I shouted to her.

Phyllis came out of the bathroom with her eyebrows up. They seemed to say, really.

"What? I can make something."

"Yes, you could, but we both know I can pull something together quickly. I'm headed back down. What would you like?"

"Whatever is easiest," I said with a smile. Phyllis was so good to me. As she walked out, I hollered, "I love you."

I reviewed the photograph and concentrated on all the details. Studying it for the best place to appear. The apartment building did not have bushes or anywhere to hide around it. We would need to appear invisible and try to find a discreet place to reappear.

JULIET: I'm in the kitchen.

I made my way down the stairs and noticed the bench. The journals were still waiting for me. I took a deep breath and began skipping down the rest of the stairs. Laughter was coming from the kitchen. Juliet was standing at the refrigerator. She appeared to be looking for something.

"It's on the second shelf of the left door," Phyllis told her.

Juliet returned with the mayonnaise. "It's amazing how Phyllis can make an ordinary sandwich a piece of art that tastes amazing."

Phyllis smiled. She placed the top of the croissant on the sandwiches and asked me to grab some chips. Phyllis put everything she had on a tray and asked Juliet to open the backdoor. We ate our lunch on the covered patio. As we ate, we filled Phyllis in on what had been happening. She was shocked to hear about Tony.

I took a few bites of my sandwich. It had turkey, ham, lettuce, cheese, and mayo. It was delicious. I turned to Phyllis, "How's Hal?"

She immediately blushed. "He's doing well. I'm taking him to see my sister this weekend."

"That's exciting," Juliet said as she nearly spilled her drink on herself.

Phyllis began telling us about how he always opened the car doors for her and always wanted her opinion on things. It was nice he made her feel special. When everyone finished eating, we helped clean up the dishes and popped over to Italy.

Juliet and I entered Italy from the full-length mirror in my room. The street had a few people walking around. I pointed at the building to let Juliet know our destination. The building had a rustic look. Some of the plaster had come off it. We walked through the entrance and made our way to Imelda's apartment on the third floor. We tiptoed up the stairs to the third floor. There was no one in sight, so we reappeared visibly. We made our way to her door. There was no doorbell, so we knocked and waited patiently for her to answer.

Imelda opened the door. She and I were about the same height. Imelda had dark hair and was a little heavier than me. I reached out my arm to shake her hand. "Hi, Imelda. I'm Brooke and this is my friend Juliet." She grabbed my hand and pulled me into her apartment. She grabbed Juliet's arm and yanked her in as well.

I spun around. Imelda looked down the hall and seemed nervous. She quickly shut the door and locked it. Imelda walked past us and lead us into the apartment. It was a rather plain room with dark wood floors, a table with four chairs stood just past the entrance to a dungy cramped kitchen. The kitchen was to the left. I did not see a refrigerator. There was a stovetop, a small sink, and a microwave under the stovetop. Her living room was just past It. There were two oversized chairs with a small coffee table in front of them. To the right of the living room was an open bedroom. Imelda had stunning large glass doors that opened to a small balcony.

She motioned for us to have a seat. Imelda grabbed a chair from the kitchen table and sat on it next to us. She asked, "Did anyone see you come into the building?"

I knew for a fact no one did, but she did not need to know how I was certain. "I didn't see anyone when we entered."

"And you weren't being followed?"

I looked over at Juliet and then back at Imelda. "No. Do you think someone knew I would come here?"

"It's just, Joseph came over yesterday looking for Tony. I told him I had not seen him since my son's funeral. He went through my house to make sure I was not hiding Tony and his family here."

I looked over at Juliet, who just shrugged. I turned my attention back to Imelda. "Do you know where Tony went?"

"No. I know Joseph is searching for him all over town. He has visited every one of our relatives," she said as she leaned forward. "Were you able to find out anything about Federico's murder?"

I said, "Yes, Anthony Granaldi III had him killed. All I can tell you is we are working on getting all the evidence to submit to the authorities. Right, Juliet?" I looked over at Juliet for her to confirm my statement. Juliet looked confused.

"Excuse me? Brooke, I can't understand anything you are saying. You're speaking in Italian," Juliet explained.

"I'm so sorry," I said. I explained what we had discussed. "Imelda, you need to be patient. It'll take some time to get everything lined up to prove they did it. Under no circumstances can you tell anyone I helped you with this. Mentioning Lillie is off limits too. This is the last time you will see me. I must delete my number from your phone. If the police ask you about the calls, we will both state you dialed the wrong number."

She went to her bedroom and returned with her phone. She handed it to me, unlocked. I deleted my information and handed her the phone back.

"I understand," she stood up.

We stood up as well. She hugged both of us before opening the door and looking down the hall. "There's no one out there."

Juliet and I walked out of the apartment and hurried down the stairs. "I was going to see if you wanted to walk around Florence, but Imelda has good reason to worry. Joseph might have had her watched. We need to get out of here before anyone discovers us." I pulled out my mirror, and we returned to my room.

Sixteen

Greg was finally off for the week to watch Karen. This may seem silly because she was a senior in high school, but she has a bit of a wild side. I was looking forward to getting to know her better. While I was looking forward to getting to know Karen better, I was mainly looking forward to spending time with Greg. spending time with Greg.

We took her to Hurricane Bay in the Kentucky Kingdom. Ty joined us. They had been seeing a lot of each other lately. I even got a new bathing suit for the park. It was difficult to find one that did not have my butt hanging out. I settled on a blue suit with white accents. The trim was white, and it had some white on the hips. It had three white straps connecting the front to the back. Fortunately, it covered my butt. The top was more like a sports bra, only a little more revealing. The top had the same straps on the shoulders as were on my hips, as well as a smaller section in the front that revealed nothing it should not. I had put a cover-up over it.

I went over to Greg's house to meet them. Ty was already there. After introductions we left for the water park. During the ride, Greg had the radio on, which we sang every song that came across the country music station. As I watched everyone singing, I realized I had not felt so relaxed in a long while.

We arrived at the park and got a locker for all our things. We let Karen lead us to Mt. Slide Hai. Fortunately, it did not appear there were too many people in the park. I was glad we came on a weekday.

The line went fast. We each grabbed our tubes. Karen insisted Greg and I went first. As I stepped into the launching area, the rushing water greeted my feet. The park employee held it for me while I sat down on it. Once settled, he let me loose. The tube rocked back and forth as it went down through the twists and turns. Suddenly, I could see the sun reflecting on the pool of water that awaited me.

I flew out of the tunnel and off the tube into the refreshing water. As I grabbed my tube and made my way to the exit, Greg flew out of the tunnel. I watched him as he came out of the water. His skin was glistening in the sun. He looked like a model in a sports magazine. The water accentuated his muscles. Two girls putting their tubes back stopped in their tracks and began admiring him. This made me smile. I walked past them and put my tube in the bin. I moved out of their way and waited for him.

The girls started smiling at him as he walked toward them. One girl said, "Hi.".

Greg smiled and nodded. He tossed his tube in the bin and walked up to me. On the left side of my neck, he placed his right hand. He brushed his thumb across my cheek and gently kissed me. He moved his hand down and took mine. We turned. The girls tossed their tubes in the bin. As they walked away, they looked me over.

Karen and Ty exited the pool together. Ty carried Karen's tube for her. We continued through the park's slides until our stomachs began growling. Karen and I got a table while the guys grabbed the food.

"Ty really seems to like you," I said.

This statement made her smile. She blushed when she said, "He's so nice. Mom and Dad really like him, too." She looked up at him and looked to be in a daze. "He's so cute too."

I had to admit that Ty was attractive. A thin guy with a short beard that was thick for someone his age. His personality was that of a gentleman. Ty seemed to always be concerned with Karen's needs.

They returned with hotdogs, French fries, and water for us. As we ate, we took the time to get to know Ty better. After lunch, we wandered over to the lazy river to relax while we digested our food. Greg and I went in after Karen and Ty. Greg held my tube for me as I climbed on. As he got on, I held onto the wall and waited for him.

We held onto each other's tubes as we meandered through the river. I closed my eyes and felt so relaxed as the sun reflected between the shadows of the foliage along the way. Occasionally, the tubed bumped others on the river, but it did not phase me. I was enjoying the peaceful ride.

Suddenly, cold water splashed my stomach, causing me to sit up abruptly. I looked over at Greg, who had a smirk on his face. I smiled back with a devious smile and began splashing him. Others did not seem to appreciate our antics.

I looked ahead of us and did not see Ty and Karen. I asked, "Where's Karen and Ty?"

"I'm not sure. I was not paying attention," Greg said as he pushed me toward the exit. "Let's wait here and see if we see them going around again."

We waited for fifteen minutes but did not see them. Concerned, I asked, "Do you think we should look for them?"

"Na, they are probably just wanting some private time," Greg said, pulling me in for a kiss. "We could use some private time, too. How about we head over to the wave pool?"

That sounded like fun. The waves were not moving when we entered the pool. The pool had many people, but we went in anyway. Greg and I waded out till we were chest deep. I looked around and noticed a few younger kids on floats. They seemed to wait for the waves as well. Greg and I spent this time catching up on things we had not told each other.

"I told Austin about Mechelle moving here. He already knew," Greg informed me.

"Is he excited?"

"He keeps his feelings in most of the time. Unless he's mad. Then there is no question about what he is feeling. I'd say he's excited."

"Mechelle's excited too." I pulled him closer to me and gave him a peck on the lips. I wanted more, but this was not the place for us to be affectionate.

"Look Daddy," a young child said with excitement. I turned and noticed the waves were forming. Greg and I turned and faced the waves, eager for their arrival.

Moments later, we were jumping with each wave as it arrived. I admired Greg's physique as he jumped. This caused me to jump late. I found myself underwater with several other people. We all collided. Floats surrounded me. I looked for a way to the surface. The young boy next to me was searching, as well. He looked scared. I grabbed his arm and looked up. We pushed two of the floats apart to make room for us. Our heads were being slammed between the two floats.

The boy was struggling to stay afloat. I looked around and noticed a small area behind us with an opening. Clinching his arm in mine, I pulled him to the opening. The waves made it difficult to stand. As the waves came, I pushed him up and went under as I held him up.

I asked, "Are you okay?" He did not answer. He looked scared. "Don't worry. I got you." When the waves calmed, he grabbed me by the neck and did not appear to want to let go. "Do you see your parents?"

The child looked around. Suddenly, I felt the boy pull away from me. "Troy, I was so worried about you," a man about my height said to him. The boy wrapped his arms around the man and clasped him.

I heard a woman yell, "Help! Does anyone see my daughter? She's in a pink bathing suit?"

I looked around to see who was hollering. A frantic woman was looking down into the water. I heard a whistle blow. The lifeguards began telling everyone to exit the pool. One approached the women. Greg was near the women. I began using telepathy to say, "What's going on?" Greg looked around for me. Someone had pushed me to the shallower section.

"Her daughter fell off the tube. Her mom can't find her," Greg said as he dove under the water.

I dove and scanned the area for her. I was being pushed around by the legs I saw heading in my direction. *Okay, stone, show me where the missing child is.* I looked around and saw a glowing light. I did not have my mirror on me to teleport to her. Using telepathy, I said to Greg, "She is just past you under the water."

Greg immediately dove under the water. "I see her," he alerted me.

I swam as fast as I could to him.

"Her hair's caught in this vent," he explained.

Greg returned to the surface for air. He returned to the child, to breathe into her mouth. Not needing to return to the surface, I was able to reach her at the same time he did. Greg handed her to me before resurfacing. I was sure with me touching her, she too could breathe underwater. *Why isn't it working?*

Greg pointed to the stone. It was not touching me. I grabbed it and held on to her while Greg tried to release her hair.

She was regaining consciousness. "Stay calm. We're here to help you," I said using telepathy.

The child looked at me, confused. She looked at Greg. She asked, "How can I hear them?"

I smiled and concentrated, "Let's just say God's not ready for you yet."

Suddenly, two lifeguards jumped in and swam over to us. One cut was able to free her hair.

Greg motioned for me to take her to the top, which I did. He helped me get her to a nearby ladder. One lifeguard tried to take her from me. Continuing with the telepathy, I told her, "Tell them you want to stay with me." She did as I instructed. The stone was still healing her.

"We need to get her out of the water," the lifeguard instructed.

I knew he was right. I handed her to Greg, and he brought her up the ladder. As soon as I could, I grabbed her hand. She smiled at me.

A woman ran up and pushed Greg and the lifeguard out of her way, "Joanie, Joanie, are you okay!" She pulled the girl into her arms.

"I'm fine, Momma."

The stone had cooled. "Goodbye sweetie," I said to Joannie. *Thank you, Lord, for being with us.* Overwhelmed was the best way to describe my emotions. I fought back the tears of joy I was experiencing. As the EMTs arrived, Greg and I slowly escaped into the crowd.

Greg asked, "How about an ice cream?"

I smiled at him. Karen knocked into me as she tried to steady herself to keep from falling.

Karen shouted, "You guys saved her! You're like heroes. Real heroes." She turned to a group of teenagers walking by. "Look, my brother is a hero."

Ty just smiled at her.

"Karen, please stop. We were just in the right place at the right time," Greg told her. He grabbed my hand. "We are going to get some ice cream if you want to join us.

As we ambled toward the snack area, I heard a man telling his friend, "The cops are looking for the two people that saved her. I heard someone say they took off."

I looked over at Greg. He must have heard them, too.

"I have a better idea. How about we get out of here? I'm burning," he suggested.

Following along, I said, "I think that's a great idea. I need to get out of the sun, too."

Karen looked disappointed, but I said nothing.

During our ride home, Karen kept asking questions about how we helped her. "I'm still confused. How was she underwater for so long and not have drowned?"

I explained again how Greg was getting her air when I arrived.

Greg interrupted me, "Karen, I know this is exciting to you, but perhaps Brooke and I would just prefer not to continue discussing such a traumatic event. We just need to be thankful she survived."

"Greg's right. Things don't seem to add up. God must have had a part in ensuring she survived," Ty added.

Karen changed the subject. "Greg, I'm getting hungry. What are we going to do for dinner?"

Greg looked over at me with his eyes wide. That boy had no clue.

I turned around to face the back seat. "How about we all shower and come over to my house for some Chinese? My treat. Mom is out of town and Phyllis is spending the day with Hal. We can watch a movie," I suggested.

Greg mouthed to me, "Are you sure?"

I nodded. Everyone agreed to come over in an hour. After a shower, I called Juliet to see if she and Jacob would like to join us. She said she could but would need to check with Jacob.

I did not realize how tired I was from the park until I dressed. I let my hair air dry as I decided to spend the rest of my time reading my grandmother's journals. As I grabbed my mirror and phone, Juliet texted me to tell me they would be over shortly.

I ran my right hand along the journals as I figured out which one to read. I read the first journal.

March 23, 1967

Today is my 18th birthday. My mother gifted me this journal to keep track of my new path. I'm going to be entrusted with protecting our family's secret. She asked me to journal about it to help me keep the facts straight and to help future Guardians on their path. My journals must be hidden from all wondering eyes and can only be seen by other Guardians of the stone. Mother will work with me until she feels I'm able to protect the stone. She explained not everyone in our family was trustworthy. Many are after it for the wrong reasons. She said I need to trust the stone. I don't know what that means, but I have a feeling I am about to find out. Apparently, we are wealthier than I had thought. Our family and others contribute money to help protect this secret.

Mother is going to take me to her "bunker" when I finish with my journaling. Mother explained she and I will be the only ones alive who know of its existence. I am looking forward to finding out more about the secret and her bunker. I can't imagine it is close to here. It must be somewhere on the outskirts of Louisville.

A bunker? She must refer to this room. I looked around and began thinking about the day I discovered it.

March 28, 1967

Mother brought me back to the bunker to add what has happened in the last few days to my journal. I'm still not sure where the bunker really is because we fell into it. I really do not know how to describe what happened. Somehow, we went into a mirror and came out in a type of bunker.

There were no windows and only one door in the bunker. Maps were on the walls. The furnishings comprised an apothecary cabinet, two wardrobes, an empty bookshelf, and a desk. Mother explained the bookshelf was for my journals. Mother said this room was her base of operation and it will soon be mine.

The feelings of when I found out about the stone came rushing back to me as I read the entry. She must have felt the same way I did. I remembered the weird feeling of being sucked into the mirror and being thrown out on my bedroom floor for the first time. I glanced at the clock on my phone. *They will be here soon.* I teleported to the pantry to avoid anyone seeing me return to the first floor. I called in an order of Chinese food, making sure I had a variety of items so everyone could find something to eat. I set the table with paper plates and silverware.

Greg, Karen, and Ty arrived first. I had everyone join me in the kitchen to figure out what they wanted to drink. In the kitchen light, I noticed how much sun each of us had gotten. Ty and Karen were both burnt on their faces and arms, whereas Greg and I had it more on our cheeks and noses.

We hung out in the kitchen until the bell chimed. Everyone seemed pleasantly surprised when Jacob and Juliet showed up.

Everyone found a place to sit in the sitting room until the food arrived.

During dinner, Karen told Jacob and Juliet about our rescue at the water park. "I don't know if you saw the news, but they are looking for both of you. Apparently, they want you to receive an award or something," Karen announced.

I shot Greg a look that said, oh no.

"Karen, we really don't want or need the attention. Let's just say God put us in the right place at the right time and He gave us the skills we needed to assist her," Greg said before turning to me. "Don't you agree, Brooke?"

"Yes, a miracle happened today. A child should have drowned but God saved her," I said as I grabbed another fried dumpling.

After dinner, we watched Fireproof in the library. Jacob and Juliet cuddled on a blanket I gave them for the floor while Ty, Karen, Greg, and I had the sofa. Karen fell asleep on Ty's shoulder. Once the movie was over, we woke her up and everyone left.

As I lay in my bed, I began thinking how adorable Karen and Ty were. They were still getting to know one another. This caused me to think about how far Greg and I had come since our first meeting when I nearly hit him. I smiled and rolled my eyes. He was the attractive neighbor that I tried to catch a glimpse of when he wasn't looking. Now he's my best friend that I hope to marry someday. I'm blessed.

Seventeen

Over the next few days, Greg and I returned to our normal workout schedule. Karen even joined us a few times. We took her to Parkour once. She did not seem to enjoy it much. Ty was working a lot, and he took her with him to his band practice at his church one night. That night, Greg and I took advantage of her not being around to have a date. We went on an evening horseback ride at his friend Evan's house.

As I lay in my bed, I began thinking about what still needed to be done. We needed to notify the police about Tony's journals. I wondered if Mechelle would be up here by that time. We'll work on that. I thought about how my grandmother had her mother to help her. I wish she had been here to help me. Phyllis was there for me and a big help when I first received the stone, but I was sure Lillie could have taught me more.

Mom was coming back from her trip that day and told me she had some news she wanted to discuss with Phyllis and me at a fancy restaurant. The company driver would bring her, but we would need to be there when she arrived to get her luggage.

Jacob said he was getting too many hours at work and would not be working as much. Juliet was losing her job too. The father of the children she babysits for received a promotion. They were moving to Texas in a few weeks. Greg said Austin and his family were going to Arkansas because Bill's great aunt passed away. This meant the Bloom Keepers could have a meeting.

Phyllis made us a beautiful brunch, which comprised Mini Frittatas, Blueberry Sheet Pancakes, Fruit Salad, and oven home fries with peppers and onions. As we sat around, catching up on what had been happening in everyone's lives, I realized how much I had missed this team. We were perfect. Soon Mechelle would become a part of it as well. We did not know in what capacity, but I was sure she would be an asset.

Once brunch was over, everyone assisted with cleaning up. We wanted Phyllis to take part in the meeting as well. I opened the meeting by saying, "I'm so glad we are together again. Each of you is a valuable part of the team and I have missed us working together." I took a deep breath and continued, "Now about the next mission. We need to leak to the police the location of Tony's journals. I don't remember the name of the police chief. Do any of you?"

"Bianchi," Juliet blurted out.

"Yes, we will need to compose a letter for him, but we need to get Tony to provide us with information that will be in the journals to spike his interest in investigating. Juliet, do you want to collect the information from Tony?"

"Another trip to Italy. I just don't know... Of course, I will."

"Great," I said joyfully.

"We need to make sure Tony sticks to his word and turns himself in," Greg added.

"True, lets pray for him. He is risking his and his family's life going against his father. We need to see if the authorities will go lenient on him for his information," I said as I leaned back in my chair.

"We could have two letters. One to tell them his conditions for releasing the information and the second with the location of the journals," Jacob suggested.

"Clever. I like it," Greg commented.

Juliet and I nodded in agreement.

Phyllis chimed in, "I agree. The thing is, how are you going to know if each party will agree?"

Everyone looked around the room at one another.

Jacob's fingers began clicking on his keypad.

"Perhaps send a letter to a post office box we could retrieve it from," Juliet suggested.

"No," was all Jacob said.

"Would you care to elaborate Jacob," Phyllis asked.

"Sorry, they could track us down, or at the very least track someone we know down because someone would need to set up the box." Jacob turned his computer to face us. "Do you notice anything here?" He pointed at the picture on the screen.

I looked closely at the picture. "That's the police department in Florence. What about it?"

Jacob asked, "Does anyone see what I do?"

Everyone began examining the photograph on the screen.

With pride, Greg said, "The flag! You're brilliant." They both seemed to act like they were complementing themselves.

Juliet looked as annoyed as I did. She turned to Jacob and asked, "Would you care to let us in on this brilliant idea?"

Jacob looked over at Juliet sweetly and said, "I'm sorry. The police station has a flag. We can simply ask them to remove the flag on a particular day if they agree to Tony's terms. No one would need to get information. They'll be surveillance cameras the area and probably running facial recognition software. Brooke will pop in and out undetected to see if they removed the flag."

Juliet smiled and leaned in for a kiss from Jacob. She smiled. "You're brilliant."

I turned to face Juliet. "I'll find out when Leonardo will allow Tony some time off to meet with you. We should be able to get this set up in the next few days."

"I'm available for the next two weeks. Then my family and I going to Hawaii to see my family." Juliet grinned.

Phyllis excused herself because she had errands to run before dinner tonight with my mom. The rest of us made our way to Parkour for a good workout. It was fantastic having the gang back together again. It amazed me how far along my skills had come since my first day there. Gloria noticed my advanced skills, too. It felt good to work out so hard, but I realized I needed to do more of this type of exercise because I could feel muscles burning, which I had not felt in a while.

We all returned to my house. Juliet and Jacob left because they had dinner plans with Juliet's parents and needed to get ready. Greg went home to mow his lawn. I showered and teleported back to read more of my grandmother's journal before dinner.

April 5, 1967

Mother has been disappearing a lot lately. I'm not sure what's going on. She has me training with an old man named Jeffrey. He has been showing me martial arts. It's not very ladylike, which surprises me because my mother has me learning

133

it. My mother explained to me that Jeffery taught her. I'm going to need these skills someday. I can't imagine why. She told me not to tell anyone about our training. When people drop in, Jeffrey pretends to be a repairman. He even carries tools with him every time he comes, which is nearly every day. I have bruises all over my body. Jeffrey told me I'm picking this up faster than my mother. It had not occurred to me my mother has these types of skills. She has been hiding a lot from me.

The more I read, the more I realized Grandma was not told right away about everything. It appears her mother slowly introduces her to what would become her future. I put the book back and popped back to my room to figure out what to wear to dinner.

As I moved through my closet, I saw my polka dot dress. It was a sleeveless brown dress with white dots. The dress went down to the center of my calf. It paired perfectly with a pair of my sandals. I usually wore it to church, but it was perfect for a fancy dinner.

I applied my makeup a little heavier than normal. As I looked at my hair, I was unsure what to do with it. I began scrolling the internet for ideas. I needed something uncomplicated. Finally, I settled on a ponytail that had a large loose braid going down one side. It surprised me it turned out so well.

A quick spin in front of my full-length mirror confirmed I was ready. I glanced at the clock and still had thirty minutes until we needed to head to the restaurant. I called Mechelle. There was no answer. I texted her to let her know I would check in with her another time because I had dinner plans. *What to do?* There was not enough time to talk to Leonardo. It could take me that long to find him. I grabbed my Bible. *Okay, Lord, I know you've been telling me to read your word.* I said a prayer and opened my Bible.

I plopped myself on my bed and opened the Bible to 2 Timothy and began reading. When I reached 2 Timothy 1:7 For the Spirit God gave us does not make us timid but gives us power, love, and self-discipline. This spoke to me. It made me realize the power of the stone was a blessing, but the Holy Spirit lived in me. It gives me the courage to keep going when things became tough. With the help of the Holy Spirit, I went from being a lazy teenager to a self-disciplined warrior who wanted to use these gifts to do what is right by God. Not just the gifts I have, but the gifts the stone granted me.

Phyllis knocked on the door. She asked, "Are you ready to go?"

I put my Bible down and glanced at myself in the mirror. I was ready. I nodded.

Phyllis drove us to Jeff Ruby's Steakhouse. When we arrived, we did not see the company car. Phyllis asked us to wait in the car until they arrived.

We did not wait long. Mom must have told the driver to stop in front of Phyllis' vehicle. I jumped out of the car to greet her. She and I hugged while the driver opened the trunk. Phyllis instructed us to put the suitcases in her trunk. This puzzled me. Mom only traveled with one case. I watched as the man pulled her suitcase out along with a purple one. I looked over at Mom and caught her looking at me. "What's going on?"

Mom seemed to pretend to be confused. "What do you mean?"

She seemed to hold back a smile. I looked back at the purple case. "Why do you have Mechelle's suitcase?"

"Mechelle's suitcase?"

I rolled my eyes at my mother. "Few people have that case. I've spent enough time with Mechelle to know her bag." I walked over to the company car and peeked in. It overwhelmed me with excitement.

Mechelle was sitting in the back seat smiling. "Hey there," she said smiling.

I practically pulled her out of the car. I hugged her and asked, "What? Why are you here?"

"Our parents wanted to surprise you. Well, I did too. I only packed what I could carry on the plane. The rest of my things are being shipped here," she said as she reached out for a hug. "I now officially live in Louisville, Kentucky!"

Mechelle and I started heading to the restaurant. While she explained to me how this came to be, Mom thanked the driver. She and Phyllis caught up with us at the hostess stand.

Once we were seated and had our drinks, my mother announced, "Mechelle, you have always been a part of our family, but today you are my adopted daughter. Well, in a sense." She smiled and leaned over and gave Mechelle a side hug. "I'm so glad you can be here with us. I can only speak for myself, but I have missed hearing you and Brooke giggling around the house."

We all raised our glasses and said, "Cheers."

The waiter returned. Mom ordered each of us Blue Crab Bisque as an appetizer. "This is phenomenal. You can thank me later," she joked.

I ordered the Spring Harvest salad and the Petite Filet Mignon with a Bourbon Peppercorn Sauce. My mouth was salivating just thinking about it.

"Mechelle, I thought hard about this. We are going to put you on the third floor with me because when we have guests, they might not handle the climb to the third floor," Mom informed her.

"That's fine. Will I be in the same room I was in the last time I was here?"

I knew she liked that room. I replied, "Yes. It is officially yours."

Phyllis explained to Mechelle what she expected such as picking up her dirty clothes. They should be in the hamper. In exchange she would clean and cook for her. Phyllis joked, "You'll be required to assist me periodically in the kitchen." She winked at Mechelle. She knew Mechelle enjoyed cooking.

After dinner, Mom asked if we wanted dessert, but everyone declined. "Well, now for my news." Mom paused and looked at each of us before continuing, "My boss offered me a substantial raise to move back to Palm Beach County." Another pause.

I knew where this was heading. *She's moving back.*

"I have taken it." She turned to me and said, "Brooke, you have grown into the most amazing young lady. I expect us to visit one another frequently."

Mechelle interrupted, "I wasn't supposed to know this, but I accidentally walked in on our parents talking and until your mother finds a place, she is going to be staying in my room. Crazy right?"

I agreed with Mechelle. "Congratulations!" I jumped up and hugged my mother. "I'm so proud of you. When do you need to leave?"

"In a week. I'm going to be getting the office set up and ready for him when he gets there. He is giving me a bonus for helping with that."

She filled us in on more of the details as we made our way home. Mechelle and I told her we would get the bags. Both of their bags were heavy. Mom and Phyllis began chatting in the kitchen about how things were going with Hal. Once we were out of Mom's view, I motioned for Mechelle to be quiet. I pulled out my mirror and told her to wrap her arm around me. We teleported to the hallway on the third floor. I took my mother's suitcase to her room.

Mechelle was unzipping her suitcase when I entered her room. *It's weird to call this room hers. I like it.* "Welcome home," I said as I gave her a side hug.

I closed her door and told her what had been happening with the Bloom Keepers while she unpacked. We needed to figure out what she could do to help the team.

"I don't want to be doing all this fighting everyone else is doing. Isn't there a desk job or something?"

"We have plenty of time to figure it out," I told her. We spent the rest of the evening catching up on our friends from Florida.

Eighteen

Mechelle and I dropped in on Leonardo and Isabella to find out when Juliet could speak with Tony. He told us we could come. Something seemed off with Leonardo. He looked tired. Mechelle thought so too.

We returned home. I texted Juliet to let her know anytime was fine.

JULIET: I'll be over in an hour.

We spent the next hour talking about how we could surprise Austin with her arrival. Once Juliet joined us, we sat down and composed a list of questions to ask him. Mechelle listened as we explained to her everything that was going on and what needed to be done.

With the list of questions, we arrived at my room at the villa. Mechelle seemed quiet. I asked, "Are you okay?"

"Yes. I'm just not sure what I should do," she explained.

"Just listen. Don't' tell Tony your name. He shouldn't know. Perhaps you should stay here. It's probably better he does not see your face," I suggested.

"Is it okay if I walk around the villa?"

"Of course. Juliet and I will look for you when we are done. Have fun." I opened the door and let her leave first.

Juliet and I set off toward the front desk to let Isabella know we had arrived. She was not at the desk. We ventured outside and found

Mechelle walking around and Tony trimming a bush. We walked past Mechelle, ignoring her, and continued to Tony, "I think you found your calling. You're doing a great job."

"Thanks. I find it rewarding. When I get out of prison, I want to start a company doing this. I've been reading up on this in my spare time. Isabella has been bringing me books from the library to help me," he said as he stuffed the clippings into the trash can next to him.

"We need to chat privately for a few minutes. Leonardo is aware and has no problem with you taking a break to help us," I explained.

He wiped his hands off and led us to a table away from the few people outside. When we sat down, I noticed Mechelle was talking to one of the staff.

"We need you to answer some questions about the information the police can find in your journals," Juliet informed him.

He nodded. "Sure. Are you looking for something specific?"

"If you've information about unsolved crimes connected to your family or others would be a good start," she explained.

"There are several crimes like that. Pops has orchestrated the sale of many pieces of art. These days he doesn't get his hands dirty, but he has a long list of people that owe him favors. He gets those that owe him with the right skills to do the heists or to make someone disappear," he explained. He looked over at Juliet, who was taking notes. "Give me that. I will write them down for you. It would be easier."

"Would you write it in English?"

"Sure, just don't make fun of my spelling," he said, grabbing the paper and pen from Juliet.

Immediately, he compiled a small list for us. He pushed the paper and pen back to Juliet. "This should help," he said confidently.

Juliet and I looked over the list. I noticed there was nothing about Imelda's son. "Would you add some information about who murdered Federico Lombardo?"

He took the paper back and scribbled his information on the paper.

"Thank you, Tony." I sat up and leaned in closer to him. "You have been so helpful to us. We're going to try to get a deal worked out for you." I looked over at Juliet and back at him. I told him, "We can't promise anything, but we will try."

He slid the paper and pen back to Juliet. "I can't believe you're being so helpful to me. I've treated you and Lillie so badly. My family and I don't deserve your kindness." Tony lowered his head and seemed to hold back tears.

"God has put it in my heart to help you. It's him you should thank," I said standing up. "If you think of anything else I need to know, let Leonardo know. He knows how to reach me."

He stood up, grabbed me, and pulled me in for a big hug.

I smiled and nodded. I looked over at Juliet. "Let's head back." We made our way toward the door. Mechelle was no longer in sight.

We approached Isabella's desk and found Mechelle and her talking. Once I made eye contact with Mechelle, Juliet and I walked to my room. I was sure Mechelle would not be far behind.

She did not disappoint. About two minutes later, someone knocked on the door. Mechelle quickly entered the room. She asked, "Did you get what you need?"

"We did," Juliet said, handing Mechelle the notes Tony had provided us.

Mechelle skimmed the notes. She commented, "This is great. What now?"

"Now I compose a letter and have everyone approve it before we give it to the authorities," Juliet said, taking the letter back.

Mechelle commented, "That sounds like fun."

Juliet looked confused. "Really? It's not my favorite part."

It surprised me to hear Juliet say that. She did such a good job on the previous letters, "Why didn't you say something?"

She turned to me and said, "You have enough on your plate. I just wanted to be a team player."

"Perhaps this is how I can help. This sounds like it would be right up my alley," Mechelle interrupted.

"That's a great idea. Brooke, I'll show her the ropes and when everyone agrees she is ready, we hand it over to her," Juliet suggested.

"I like it, but we need to bring it up at the next meeting," I advised.

There was a knock on the door. I motioned for Mechelle to hide. As I opened the door, I discovered Leonardo standing there. He had dark circles under his eyes. His face had lost its shine and appeared lifeless.

"I heard you were here. I hope everything went well with Tony."

"Yes, we have what we need. Are you okay? You look tired," I asked as Mechelle came out of the bathroom.

"I'm fine. Nothing for you to worry about. I have a doctor's appointment in a few days."

"I can take care of it and you can cancel your appointment," I suggested.

"Brooke, you are an angel. I know. Thank you, but I'll deal with whatever I need to. God has a plan. We may or may not like the outcome. Well, I hope to see you here again soon. Please tell Phyllis we said hello." He turned and exited my room.

I was worried about him. We returned to my room. A few moments after I shut the door, there was a knock at it. The three of us looked in shock. I composed myself and opened the door.

My mother looked rather disheveled. "Sweetheart, do you remember where we put the other suitcases?"

"Yes, there in the storage room upstairs. I'll get it for you." The girls looked at me. "I'll be back."

I retrieved two cases and brought them to my mother in her room. "There are two other cases. Do you think you'll need both?"

Mom looked at them. "Perhaps. Thank you. I have so many clothes. I think I'll leave some here, so I don't need to bring so much back and forth." She walked over to me. "I'm going to need your help packing things up when I move. I mean mainly my clothes. Because we donated everything when we moved here. I'll need to get furniture, dishes, bathroom supplies..."

I interrupted her, "You're stressing yourself out. Why don't you fly Phyllis down once you find a place? She can help you get the house set up. Besides, I think she would love it."

"Great idea." She turned to me. "Are you sure you're okay with this?"

I rolled my eyes, and assured her by saying, "Yes."

We discussed her creating a list of items she would like to have shipped to her new place. I was having such a good time. *Oh, no! Juliet and Mechelle.* "I need to get back to my friends. Perhaps you and I can have a mother-daughter day before you leave."

"Sounds like a plan," she turned and returned to her wardrobe.

The girls were sitting in the yellow chairs and appeared to be working on the letter when I returned. They must have been in deep thought because they did not even look at me. I lay on my bed and listened to them as they reviewed Tony's notes and debated how to phrase the letter.

I must have dozed off because the drool on my pillow awakened me.

"Then you will put this bloom symbol in the lower-left corner of the letter. We'll keep the letter in the plastic bag until it's delivered," Juliet said.

"Sounds easy enough," Mechelle said.

I turned my head at what sounded like papers shuffling. I asked, "Are you done already?"

Mechelle sarcastically said, "Yes, sleepy head. Did you get a good nap?"

"I must have." I sat up and went to the bathroom to clean myself up.

Juliet hollered from the bedroom, "I texted everyone to see if they could meet up."

I returned to my room. "Sounds good. What did they say?"

"Jacob said that was fine, but he was shopping with his mother and could come over when he's done. I haven't heard from Greg. We have heard from our stomachs. They are hungry," she informed me.

"Yeah, mine too."

We made our way to the kitchen to see what we could come up with.

Phyllis sat at the counter flipping through a recipe book. "Let me guess, you gals are hungry."

"You know us too well," Juliet commented.

"I made each of you a salad. They are in the refrigerator. The salad dressing is just to the left of the salad bowls."

I handed each of the girls a bowl and took one for myself. My mouth watered at the sight of the arugula, blackberry, pistachios, and goat cheese salad with a honey mustard vinaigrette. We devoured them.

After lunch, we cleaned up our dishes and went out on the patio to hang out until they arrived. Greg finally replied.

GREG: I should be there soon.

Juliet asked, "What's he been doing all day?"

"He was working on a friend of his mother's car. He works on cars all the time to earn extra money," I explained. It occurred to me that Mechelle did not have a car here. I turned to her and asked, "Where's your car?"

"Mom and Dad are bringing it when they come. Dad didn't want me driving this far," she said as she made herself more comfortable.

I could hear a car pull into the driveway.

"Oh, my honey is here," Juliet jumped up and rushed over to greet him.

Jacob and Juliet walked up the stairs holding hands. It was so sweet seeing them happy.

Jacob nodded his head toward us and asked, "So, what's up?"

I replied, "We're waiting for Greg to have a meeting."

A few minutes later Greg walked out the back door. "I'm surprised you guys are outside. It's so dang hot."

I hopped up and gave him a kiss. "Come on. Let's head in and have our meeting in the library." I held the door while everyone came in.

Greg asked, "Can I get a bottle of water?"

"Guys go on up. I'll be there in a minute," I hollered down the hall.

"Where is everyone?"

"Mom is in her room, and I don't know where Phyllis is. Why?"

Without a word, Greg nuzzled me against the refrigerator and kissed me. *Oh, I missed this.* The power of his touch had me in a hypnotic state. His hands were on my hips, and I ran my arms up his back.

Phyllis entered the room and said, "Excuse me, but do I need to put a Bible between you?"

Greg quickly pulled himself away from me, "No ma'am."

I grabbed him a bottle of water. "Sorry, Phyllis. We are having a Bloom Keepers meeting. Can you join us?"

"Not today, dear. I have a lot to do today."

Greg stopped me on the stairs. "Sorry."

I pulled him to me and said, "Don't be. I loved it." He looked around and then kissed me again.

I closed the library door to ensure my mother could not hear us. Everyone had taken over the sofa. Greg motioned for me to sit at the desk, and he leaned against the wall.

Jacob cleared his throat and said, "Okay, let's get started. We are starting the meeting of the Bloom Keepers. Brooke, the floor is yours."

"Thanks, Jacob. Today, the girls and I got the information we needed from Tony to provide to the police. Juliet and Mechelle have been diligently working on the letter and would like everyone's approval."

Juliet read the letter aloud.

Attention Chief Bianchi,

This letter comes to you because of your quick response to the Granaldi case. Below is a list of more cases that might interest you.

· The murder of Federico Lombardo

144

· The stolen paintings for both Landscape with Cottages by
  Rembrandt and Poppy Flowers by Van Gogh
· Information on Italian crime families
· The location of five Italian fugitives

You are probably asking yourself why you have received a
list of unsolved cases. Would you like to solve them? There are
some stipulations to you receiving information about these cases.
You must agree with them, or you will receive nothing.

1.   A Granaldi family member will provide the information.
A deal must be worked out to ensure they are not imprisoned.
Imprisoning this person would get them killed. They will provide
this information to you because they are working on turning
their life around. A house arrest in an undisclosed location
would be fine, but only you and your team will be made aware of
their location if an agreement is made.

2.   This person's spouse and child(ren) must be kept safe
and must not be disclosed.

3.   The evidence you receive will provide you with detailed
events about each of the crimes. This family member will testify
in court about these but would prefer to do it via video to keep
them and their family from being murdered.

4.   The house arrest will not be longer than three years.
They will be available to you and your team for as long as you
deem necessary.

If you agree to these terms, at noon three days from now,
remove the flag in front of your building. It is to remain off for
24 hours. A contract with our terms must be created for this
person. You must sign it before they do. This contract must be
with you for the 24 hours period the flag is down. We will
contact you with further instructions. Once the contract's signed
by each party, a second letter will be sent to you containing the
location of the evidence. Future meetings between your team
and this person will only occur when necessary and will not be
coordinated by you or your team.

The same team must be assigned. There is no way of
knowing who in your department is corrupt. Assemble Officer
Sartori and Detective DeSantis. There is work to be done. You
must not try to discover who is behind the Bloom. This will
cause the Bloom to end all contact with you. Bloom is working
to eradicate the evil of this world and can be trusted.
The Bloom

"Well done, ladies," Greg complimented.

"I loved how you referred to us as the Bloom," I commented.

"Mechelle came up with most of this herself," Juliet admitted.

We all complimented her. We explained the importance of writing the letter over again but using paper that has no fingerprints and things to prevent the letter from being traced back to anyone. Juliet and Jacob agreed to show her how it was done.

We began discussing how we would bring the Chief and his team to Tony. After we finished compiling the plan, we adjourned the meeting.

Everyone wanted to do some sparing. It had been so long since we had worked out together. We worked as teams to learn how to expect what our partner would do. Greg and I were together against Juliet and Jacob. Mechelle just watched us. She really did not seem interested. She would need to learn some skills. I was going to work on persuading her to at least learn a few techniques.

It seemed these teams worked well with one another. We needed to switch it up. Greg joined Jacob. Juliet and I always worked well together. Greg trained Jacob and knew him well. We seemed evenly challenged. It impressed me when Jacob tagged me a few times. It was apparent he and Juliet had been training.

In the last challenge, Jacob and I teamed up against Juliet and Greg. Neither team had worked together much. As we began sparing, Juliet and Greg came for me first. Jacob did not seem to know how to help me. I was dodging and blocking as many of the strikes sent my way.

They blocked me in the gym's corner with Juliet and Greg in front of me. I looked over at Jacob. He started running full force toward us and suddenly caused himself to slide feet first across the floor. His feet went between the two of them. As he slid through, he grabbed each of their legs closest to him. This caused them both to lose their balance. I jumped up and kicked them both in their chests. Greg and Juliet fell backward and slammed to the floor. I jumped on Greg with my foot on his neck. Jacob jumped to his feet and assumed the same position as me on Juliet. Jacob turned to me, and we gave each other a high five.

"That was amazing, Jacob," I complimented.

"Yeah, amazing. Would you get off me now," Juliet uttered.

We both looked down and realized we were still on top of them. We jumped off and helped them up.

"That really was unexpected and impressive, Jacob," Greg said as he grabbed a couple of waters from the mini refrigerator and began tossing them to us.

"I don't understand how you guys enjoy beating one another up," Mechelle said, sounding confused.

"I know you say you're not interested in this side of the Bloom Keepers, but you need to learn a few basic skills to protect yourself," Juliet told Mechelle.

"Yeah. If anyone discovers we're connected, your life will be at risk too. At very least, ya need to learn how to escape a situation," Greg added.

We began showing her some simple moves. She agreed and began allowing us to train her. We lost track of time. We had been working out for hours when Mom came in and told us Phyllis had dinner ready.

It surprised everyone Phyllis made dinner for all of us. She prepared one of my mother's favorites, Caesar salad, crab legs with a lemon garlic dipping sauce, steamed artichokes with garlic and butter, roasted brussel sprouts, twice-baked garlic mashed potatoes, and a raspberry lemon cake.

It was so delicious there were no leftovers. I told Phyllis to relax, and that I would do the dishes. Greg, Mechelle, Jacob, and Juliet got up and helped me. It reminded me of the phrase, more hands makes light work. *Thank you, Lord, for bringing these people into my life to make the burden of protecting this stone easier.*

After dinner, Jacob and Juliet went home. Mom and Phyllis sat in the sitting room, discussing the recent changes in our lives. Greg, Mechelle, and I went to the library. We just sat around talking. I rested my head on Greg's shoulder. He wrapped his arm around me and began rubbing his hand up and down my arm.

"Well, I'm going to shower and head to bed. Have a good night, guys," Mechelle said as she stood up.

"Wow, some alone time," Greg said as he kissed me on the top of my head.

I looked up at him and kissed him.

Greg pulled away and gazed into my eyes. "I thank God for you every day."

My heart melted. *Me too.* It seemed he had more to say. I waited patiently.

"Brooke, you are the love of my life. I've no desire to be with anyone else. You are it. All I want. I fight my desires all the time. I

147

know you do too," he paused and brushed my hair away from my face. "Would you pray with me?"

"Of course."

We both knelt in front of the sofa. I put my elbows on the couch and bowed my head.

Greg did the same, "Heavenly Father, we come to you in Jesus's name. Lord, thank ya for bringing us into each other's lives. Thank ya for your guidance and love. Lord, the passion between us is strong. Help us keep restraining ourselves from our desires. We hope to honor ya. We also thank ya for the Bloom of Dreams. May we do your will, and may you lead us to those that need us. Amen."

It overwhelmed my heart with joy. I had not realized it, but tears of joy were running down my face. *Thank you, Lord, for this man. I could never have imagined such a man. Only you, Lord, could have brought him into my life.* I looked up at Greg.

He looked at me and wiped the tear from my cheek. In a whisper, he asked, "Why are you crying?"

"It's just the Holy Spirit moving in me. We're blessed." Still on my knees, I grabbed Greg and hugged him. Tears of joy continued to flow.

Greg's phone buzzed. He answered. As he listened to the person, he stood up. "Yes, calm down. I'll be right there. Call Mom and let her know." He hung up. "Ty's car broke down and Karen is panicking because she told Mom she would be home by 8:30 pm. I need to go see what's wrong and give him a tow."

"Do you want me to come with you?"

"Nah. I might be out late." He leaned down and kissed me gently on the lips. "I enjoyed praying with you."

"Me too. We should do it more often. Now go rescue your sister."

I lay in bed thinking about how amazing it was to feel so strongly about another person. *Being with someone that loved the Lord made everything better. I'm truly blessed. Thank you, Jesus.* I fell asleep thinking of that special moment.

Nineteen

Mechelle's parents should arrive today just before noon. They drove Mechelle's car which was loaded with her things. Mechelle and I woke up early and helped Phyllis getting everything ready for their visit. Originally, they were flying home. They planned to rent a car because they were going to do some site-seeing on their way home. When Mom found that out, she arranged for them to take her car back. She would fly down. We helped her load a few things she had packed that would not fit in the luggage for the plane.

Mechelle's parents arrived fifteen minutes earlier than expected. Fortunately, all our chores were done. Mechelle showed them to the guest room on the second floor and let them freshen up before lunch.

I assisted Phyllis with plating the food and bringing water to the table. Peggy and Jim were sitting with Mechelle and Mom, chatting about their trip.

Phyllis served us Shrimp Patty Sandwiches with Caesar Salad and fresh fruit. During lunch, everyone caught up. Mechelle and her parents had a 3:00 pm appointment at the college to finish the registration process.

Lunch was nearly over when I received a text.

ISABELLA: Joseph is here.

I nearly choked on my food as I read the text.
Peggy asked, "Are you okay, Brooke?"

Using telepathy, I told Mechelle I needed to leave.

Mechelle's eyes widened. I knew she did not know how to help. She then told me, "Tell them you need to help a friend."

Lying to her bothered me, but Isabella needed me. I explained, "I'm fine, but I have a friend that needs some help. I'm going to eat and run, but I really need to help them.

Mom looked concerned. I asked, "What kind of help?"

Great! Think Brooke. I looked down at my phone. *Lord, I could use some help here.* "It's kinda private," I said as I stood up and excused myself. I went into the kitchen where Phyllis was cleaning up. "I need the Bloom Keepers and a way out of here. Any suggestions?"

Phyllis walked to the back door. She suggested, "Use the pantry to get to your room. Call them and I'll tell your mother, a friend picked you up. That way, we won't need to worry about what she'll think when she finds your car still here."

She motioned me to go in and opened the back door. I heard the door slam shut. I teleported to my room and called Greg, who was at work.

"Hey what's up?"

I explained, "Josephs at the villa. We need to go now!"

"Meet me at the barn," Greg instructed. I heard him saying to someone, "Hey man, I've got an emergency. I need to go." The phone went dead.

I called Juliet and explained the situation. She said Jacob was on his way over and there was no one at her house. I texted Isabella before teleporting to Juliet's house to get her.

"I have had this for a while. I suspected there would be a day when we rushed to something. There should be one to fit each of you," Juliet explained. She handed us long black sleeve shirts and black sweatpants. Juliet was already wearing hers. I helped her carry the items as we teleported back to my room.

I told Juliet to have Jacob park some where I would grab him from his car. *Greg should be at the barn by now.* I picked him up and brought him to my room. Juliet handed him some clothes. "I'm going for Jacob," I announced.

We returned. Greg was dressed. Juliet shoved Jacob in my closet with his clothes and shut the door. I ran to the bathroom and quickly changed. When I came out everyone was ready to go.

"Okay let's go," I announced.

"Wait, here are some gloves," Juliet handed everyone a pair of gloves. The guys had much larger ones given to them.

Juliet grabbed my shoulder, Greg grabbed my free hand, and Jacob placed his hand on my other shoulder. I teleported us to the entrance. We were invisible. The place was quiet. Unusually quiet.

Using telepathy, I said, "Let's spread out and see if we can find them. Are you two okay heading down toward the wine cellar?"

Jacob and Juliet nodded.

A noise came from the directions of the rooms. Greg looked at me and pointed. I grabbed his arm and teleported us closer to where we heard the sound coming from. A couple doors down from us was a young, very thin waiter. He seemed to sneak around. Greg grabbed him from behind and covered his eyes and mouth. He gripped him against his chest. "What's going on here?"

Greg lifted his hand from his mouth and held his left arm in a locked position.

In a terrified voice, he muttered, "They took everyone. They're looking for a gardener. Please don't hurt me. I was trying to get out."

"Where did they take them?"

"The cellar. The others are with Leonardo going through the rooms."

"There's no one in the entrance's direction. Get the police. Be careful going out. There may be others outside," Greg said, releasing his hold. The man looked around and seemed surprised not to see Greg. "We need to go to their room."

"I don't know which one is theirs." Greg started heading down the hall toward the other rooms.

I followed him. A commotion could be heard from outside the room I was in. Stephania came through the doorway with a man. He was holding her in his arms. Another man had Rosina by the arm. "Look lady, we just want Tony. We know he's here."

Rosina pleaded, "Please give me my daughter." She reached out for her, but the man pulled Stephania away. "I don't know where he is. Please, my daughter and I were just here on a holiday."

The man said, "That's a load of crap." He turned away from the group and yelled loudly, "Hey Tony! If you want these two to live another day, you'll come out."

The only sound heard was of them pushing the two down the hall toward the dining room.

Greg grabbed my hand. I listened to hear if he was trying to say anything.

I concentrated on Leonardo, "Leonardo, it's Brooke. Don't say a word. Just talk to me like you're talking to yourself in your head. Do you know where Tony and Isabella are?"

Leonardo said, "I think they took Isabella to the wine cellar. Tony's hiding in my closet. There is a secret compartment in it. Go help them. We are fine for now."

I grabbed my mirror and teleported Greg and me to Leonardo's bedroom.

Greg asked, "What's going on?"

I opened the closet door. "Tony's hiding in here."

Greg moved the clothes aside. "Where? Brooke, he's not here."

There's a good question. Okay, stone, reveal the secret door. The cedar-lined closet illuminated on the right side. "There," I pointed.

Greg began pushing on the panels, and the door popped open. The door slammed shut.

I stuck my head through the wall and asked, "Tony, we are trying to get you out of here."

Tony frantically looked around. "Brooke?"

I had forgotten I was still invisible. "Yes. We need to get you to a safe place."

"I'm not leaving here without my family. Leonardo told me to hide in here. He's bringing them to me."

I did not want to worry him. "Stay here. I'll get them."

I pulled my head out of Leonardo's closet wall. Greg and teleported us to the wine cellar. The guests were sitting up against the wine barrels. Isabella, Leonardo, Stefania, and Rosina were with them. Jacob and Juliet were near the entrance.

Using telepathy I asked Juliet, "What's going on?"

She looked over to acknowledge she heard me. "They believe everyone is in here but Tony. We didn't want to do anything because they're not hurting anyone."

"Smart. I'm going to get them to safety without them being discovered. This many people in one place they might not notice." Leonardo began coughing.

"Quiet, old man," one man hollered.

Leonardo's health concerned me. *Where can I take them?* At first, I thought about my home. *They will look there first if they realize I'm here.* Various places popped into my head, but none were suitable or safe. *Got it!*

I concentrated on the Bloom Keepers and Rosina being able to hear me. I told them, "We're going to get you to safety. Rosina, I'm going to take you to your husband. Make sure you and your daughter aren't touching anyone." Using the power of persuasion, I told the other guest to bot be concerned if people disappeared. *They must stay calm and not bring attention to the group.*

Before getting Rosina and Stefania, I told Greg, Jacob, and Juliet to exit the cellar and put their masks on. "When I leave, you'll be visible. I think it's best for you to only enter the room if they are going to harm anyone. I need to get Isabella, Leonardo, and Tony's family to safety." Everyone agreed and exited the room.

The man who had Rosina walked over to Joseph. I moved closer to hear their conversation.

"We can't find him."

Joseph squinted his eyes. "There's no way he would leave them. He's here. Go find him," he snarled.

Once they left, it was Joseph and two other men I did not know. Joseph walked over to them and began talking. This was my chance. I looked to make sure Rosina was not touching anyone. Rosina had her daughter on her lap. I moved next to her, making sure I was only touching them. It startled Rosina when I grabbed her shoulder. I concentrated on the cave in Japan and me arriving visible.

When we reached the cave, they were still in the sitting position and fell to the ground. It was dark. I grabbed the lighter and lit a torch.

Rosina asked, "Where's Tony?"

"He's fine. I'll be right back with him. If anyone comes here, tell them I brought you. Do not go anywhere," I insisted. I did not give her a chance to respond. I returned to Tony.

Tony asked, "Where are they?"

"They're safe, stand up. I'm going to take you to them," I instructed. I grabbed his arm. We met them in the cave.

As soon as he saw them, he leaped into his wife's arms. "Praise God you are okay."

"Stay here. I'll be back," I returned immediately to the wine cellar invisible. Isabella and Leonardo were nowhere near each other. I concentrated on talking to them. "They're all safe. I need to get you two out of here."

"Please take Isabella. I'll be fine," Leonardo pleaded.

"No. You need to go. I'm healthy. This stress is not good for you. Brooke, please take him. He's sick," Isabella pleaded.

I knew he wanted her to be safe, but Isabella was right. Leonardo did not seem like himself. I hopped over to him. Fortunately, he was sitting outside of the group. I reached down and grabbed his arm, which he immediately pulled away from me. *Like it or not, you're coming with me.* I squatted behind him. With my mirror in my left hand, I swiftly wrapped my right around his biceps and pushed myself against him to prevent him from breaking loose.

As soon as we arrived, Tony let me know how he felt about leaving Isabella. "Brooke, how could you? You better go back and get her!" He began coughing again.

I returned to find Isabella being dragged from the group.

Joseph marched up to her and yelled, "Where are they? Where's Brooke? I know she's here." It was at that moment that Joseph struck her. She fell to the floor. I was about to leave when three people dressed in black entered the room. All eyes were on them. I pulled my mask over my face and made myself visible.

The four of us had them surrounded.

I heard a voice say, "Where did that one come from?"

Joseph must have heard them because he turned to me and smiled. "Let me guess, you're Brooke."

I had my stance ready for any attack. Joseph reached into his pocket and grabbed a gun. I kicked it out of his hand. The gun slid across the floor toward the other two men.

Joseph watched it slide. "Well, well. Aren't you clever?"

The man in front of Jacob went to grab it, but Jacob kicked it out of his reach. Jacob recovered from moving the gun and kicked the man in the chest.

I focused on them and did not see Joseph take a knife from his belt. He came at me with it. I dodged his attempts at harming me. Greg kicked him in the back of the head. He nearly fell on the knife. Joseph recovered quickly.

The men searching for Tony ran in. One of them grabbed Juliet from behind. He tried to get her over toward the wall. At first, it appeared she was resisting him. She resisted less. When she was close enough, she put her feet on the wall and pushed off. This sent them both to the ground.

Jacob was in hand-to-hand combat with two of the men. Juliet battled the other man that was looking for Tony and kept knocking the man to the floor each time he would try to get up.

While I was in a fight with Joseph, Greg assisted Jacob.

I walked up the side of Joseph and wrapped my arms around his neck. This brought him down to the ground. I held on tightly.

Juliet took one of the bar chairs and broke it against the bar. She took one leg and began spinning it in her hand. *Oh, you're in trouble now.*

I was so distracted by Juliet that I did not see a man come behind me and grab me by the neck. He pulled me off Joseph. Joseph seemed to catch his breath.

Juliet ran toward the large barrel of wine and ran across the side of it and knocked the man dragging me down with her feet as they flew into his back. The man fell on top of me.

Joseph arose and staggered a bit. Greg punched him in the stomach. He fell to the ground.

Greg helped me up. No one attempted to leave the cellar because we were fighting in front of the exit. Jacob kicked a man, sending him into a rack of wine bottles headfirst. He appeared to be out of commission.

I looked back at Juliet and Greg. She had one man with the chair leg under his chin.

She sarcastically said, "Calm down, sir. We still need to show you around the wine cellar." She began spinning him around and released him in the direction of the man lying on the floor in the puddle of wine and broken glass. The man tried to stop himself, but he appeared to be dizzy. He tripped over the man and collided with the wall.

Two down, three to go. Joseph punched Greg in the stomach. I ran for him and walked up his back. In one swift move, I wrapped my leg around his neck and pulled him to the ground. As I hit the ground, it knocked the wind out of me. Jacob placed his size 13 shoe on the man's neck. The man punched him in the back of the knee, causing Jacob to lose his balance. He grabbed Jacob's foot and twisted it bringing Jacob to the floor.

I stood up and saw Juliet heading to get between Jacob and the man that knocked him over.

Greg kicked the other man in the side. He stumbled in my direction. I kicked him on the other side. He fell to the ground in pain. I turned to Greg and told him, "I believe we might have broken his ribs."

Greg shrugged his shoulders. "He should be thankful. It could have cost him an arm and a leg."

I shook my head and rolled my eyes. I could not believe he was telling jokes right now. "Duck," I hollered at Greg. He did as I instructed.

The only man on Joseph's crew was standing near Joseph. He lifted his hands and said, "I'm done."

Joseph nearly hit him over the head with a bar stool.

Greg spun around and clipped Joseph behind the legs, causing him to fall to the ground. Greg flipped Joseph over and held his arms behind his back. "We need something to tie him up with."

One hostage brought him a belt. He helped Greg tie him up. Other hostages followed suit and tied up the remaining men with their ties, belts, and shoelaces.

I could hear sirens in the distance. Jacob announced, "We need to go."

Isabella placed her hand on my arm. With concern, she said, "Jacob's right. You need to leave before the police arrive. Just put Leonardo in our room. I'll try to delay them from searching until he returns."

We ran out of the wine cellar and toward the vineyard. Once we were out of sight, I transported us to the cave.

Leonardo asked, "Where's Isabella?"

"Leonardo, she's fine. The police arrived. I need to get you back." I grabbed his arm and brought him to his bedroom as Isabella instructed. The stone heated. Leonardo broke away from me. "Leonardo, please let the stone heal you."

"No. Brooke, I appreciate your wanting to help me. I know my time here is short. I need to talk to you about that, but not now. Go before someone sees you," he said, motioning with his hand for me to leave.

Rather than returning to the cave, I went to see if Asahi or Akio were at the hut. I appeared behind a bush on the side of the hut. As I walked up to the porch, I felt someone grab me from behind. They slammed me to the ground. Without thinking, I lifted my legs up and grabbed the person's neck with my feet and pulled them forward. They came crashing down on top of me.

I kicked them in the face and sprung to my feet. Waiting for them to retaliate. The man rolled onto his back. He wiped the blood from his nose and looked at me.

"Asahi, why are you attacking me?"

He appeared to be confused. "Brooke?" He arose up. "How was I supposed to know it was you?" He pulled the ski mask from my face.

I feel stupid. "Sorry, I forgot I had it on. I'm sorry about your face."

"Don't be. You impressed an old man with your skills. Come, I need to clean myself up," he instructed.

We entered his hut, and he went to the bathroom.

He motioned for me to sit. "What brings you here?"

I explained what was going on and who was in the cave.

"You want me to let him stay here?"

"Just for a little while. I mean, he doesn't need to stay in your house, but perhaps we can get them a place here for the time being. He'll need to be as discrete as possible," I explained.

"If you trust him, I will. My grandfather has a small hut just down the pathway toward the village. I use it for storage, but it'll work for them for a short time"

A grin came across my face. I kissed him on the cheek. This was a lot to ask of him. "I don't think we should reveal how you get into the cave. I'll bring them to a spot on that path just outside the cave," I said as I pointed in the direction I was referring to.

Asahi nodded.

I returned to the cave. Everyone but Tony was sitting. He was pacing the floor.

Jacob asked, "Is there water around here?"

I was thirsty too. "We'll be out of here soon," I informed him.

Tony turned to me and asked, "Where are we?"

I responded, "This place doesn't matter. I'm taking you to a man. He has a place for you to stay. You must keep to yourselves here. The man and his son will help you with things you need. This is a very secluded area. Please be respectful of them. You need to stay away from the village. If they tell you to do something, do it without question. Do you understand?"

Tony grabbed his daughter. "Please, my shoulders."

We appeared on the pathway in the middle of the dense foliage. "This way," I instructed.

We walked along the side of the hut. Asahi was standing on his porch.

He came down and bowed. "Tony."

"Hey, I know you. You were with Lillie in Turkey," Tony commented.

"Only this time, it seems we are on the same side," Asahi responded.

We walked down another pathway. We turned down an overgrown pathway to the right. A small hut was in the distance. Asahi turned to me and asked, "Where are their things?"

I told him I would bring them to him once it was safe to return to the villa.

After retrieving the rest of our team, we teleported back to Juliet's kitchen. Once we quenched our thirst, Juliet asked us for the black outfits she had provided to be returned. She assured us she would clean them and have it ready for any future missions. Once Greg and I had changed, I returned Greg to the barn.

"Why do I need to go back to work? I'm exhausted," Greg said as he pulled me to him. As he kissed me, I could taste the salt from our sweat.

"I'm exhausted too, and we both need showers," I pulled myself away from him.

"Don't go," he urged.

I blew him a kiss. "I love you."

Greg smiled and winked.

I teleported into the garage to make sure no one saw me arrive. I entered the house and found Phyllis prepping things for dinner. "Where's everyone?"

"Sandra took them to the University. I don't expect them back for a while. How's everything?"

"Fine, I'm tired. I'm going to shower and take a nap for a little while.

Later that evening, I hung out talking to everyone about the day they had at the University of Louisville.

Twenty

I retrieved Tony's family their possessions from the villa. They seemed to settle in okay. They had made a pleasant home out of the small hut. Tony learned how to make bonsai trees, while Rosina was trying to learn how to cook.

Juliet and Mechelle had the letter ready for Chief Bianchi. We agreed it would be easier to wait until my mother moved to Florida to deal with this. There would be less chance of us being discovered. Mom and I had planned a mother-daughter day. Mechelle was invited, but she insisted we go without her.

Our day consisted of brunch, manicure, and pedicure, a tour of the Kentucky Derby Museum, and dinner at Mojito in Havana. It was good. We had not had Cuban food since we moved to Louisville. We hurried home after dinner because Mom's flight was in the morning, and she wanted to finish her last-minute packing and relax.

"Mom, I want you to know I'm proud of you."

Mom pulled me in for a hug. She said, "I'm proud of you too." She pulled herself away from me. "You have turned into a remarkable young lady. I don't think you saw me, but I saw you and Greg praying together. He is more than I could have imagined for you."

"Yeah, he's not like anyone I've ever met. I love him."

She kissed me on the forehead. "It's very apparent you both love one another. You know, secretly Joann and I have hoped the two of you would get married."

I could feel my cheeks turning red.

Mom looked into my eyes and said, "So, have you discussed it with him?"

"I didn't say that."

"Sweetheart, you didn't need to. Those pink cheeks revealed everything."

The next morning, Mom left without saying goodbye. According to Phyllis, her driver picked her up early. I sat down with Mechelle to eat breakfast and found a letter addressed to me.

My dearest Brooke,

    If I had seen you this morning, I don't think I would have gone. I enjoyed my day with you, and I'm sorry if I hurt you by leaving this way. You are the joy of my life. I'm going to miss you dearly. Take care of Phyllis and Mechelle. I may not see you real soon, but we'll get together as soon as I get settled.

Love,

Mom

I understand Mamma. Mechelle must have noticed I was on the verge of tears. She did what she always does and started a conversation about something to get my mind off the problem. "So, Brooke, do you think I have the right wardrobe for around here?"

We spent the entire breakfast discussing the style differences between Louisville and Wellington. She and I spent the day hanging out, listening to music, and annoying Phyllis. We at least tried. She seemed to enjoy us even though we were annoying.

Mechelle and I tried to think of things to do. We were trying to pass time until it was time to drop off the letter to the Italian Police Chief. An evil grin appeared on my face. I suggested, "We could have some fun with Austin. He's back in town."

"What kind of fun?"

"He and Greg are working at the farm. We could go visit them and be a little mischievous. Greg will figure it out, but Austin might get a little spooked."

Mechelle agreed. I told her to follow my lead. We arrived behind the barn invisible, but I did not tell her we were invisible. *Mechelle, it's time to have some fun.* We were about to go looking for Greg and Austin but were alerted by of something stirring in the barn. I moved to check it out and Mechelle stopped me. Her eyes got buggy and were screaming for me to stop. Using telepathy, I told her to see if she could see anyone. She quietly moved closer to where she could see better.

"Well, do you see anyone?"

"There is someone in there, but I can't tell who it is," she said, moving back toward me.

I tapped her on the shoulder and told her to follow me. We walked toward the field and avoided the door to the barn. I moved toward the field Greg was last in, but they weren't there. Mechelle tapped me on the shoulder and pointed to a tractor in the field. It appeared a few people were hanging around it.

I nodded at her, and we moved in the tractor's direction. We were about ten feet away and it appeared they were working on the tractor. Austin and his father, Bill, were just standing around chatting about the heat. They each kept looking down the dirt path for something. A moment later, a man came into view on the dirt path. He was carrying a bag.

The man appeared to be one of the farm hands, "Here ya go, boss." He handed Bill the bag. The clanking told me it was a bag of tools. He must have been the man in the barn.

Bill took the bag and said, "Thanks, my friend." He put the bag on the floor and pulled out a wrench and began banging it on the starter while Austin tried to start it. At first, there was just clicking, but after a few times of beating the living tar out of the starter, it started. "At least it's just the starter. Let's head back to the house."

Austin shut the tractor off and jumped off. He told his father, "Greg and I'll head to town and pick it up."

"Sounds good," Bill said. He turned to the farm hand and said, "Let's go see what Suzanne has fixed us for lunch."

We stayed a distance behind them as we followed them back to the house. When they all entered the house, we waited outside to see which vehicle they were going to take. They came out and strolled toward Austin's truck. I grabbed Mechelle, and we teleported to the backseat of his vehicle before they got in.

"Try not to make any noise," I advised Mechelle just before she opened the door.

"Aren't they going to see us?"

Using telepathy, I told her we were invisible.

As soon as they entered the truck, Greg said, "How was your trip?"

"It was nice seeing my cousins, but the family was bickering over who gets what. Man, it's just stuff," Austin said, shaking his head. He changed the subject, "So how's Mechelle?"

Mechelle smiled and looked over at me.

Greg smiled and said, "She's good. Are you going to ask her out?"

"I was going to call her while I was gone. I just never had a minute alone. We were all piled in my uncle's house like sardines," Austin said, turning his blinker on.

While stopped, I reached over and knocked Austin's hat off. He turned to Greg and knocked his off.

"What's the deal man," Greg commented.

"Tit for Tat, man."

Greg looked confused.

At the next light, Mechelle ran her finger gently down the side of Austin's ear. Immediately, he swatted at it. Mechelle bit her lip and looked over at me. It appeared she was laughing with her eyes. She reached up and did it again.

Austin swat again. He glanced over at Greg, "Stop."

Looking even more confused, Greg inquired, "Stop what?"

"Whatever you're doing, stop it."

Greg threw his hands up in the air, "Dude, I'm sittin' over here minding my business."

Mechelle pointed to a tow rope on the floorboard in the back seat. I smiled. She dragged it up. We started moving it across the center console. Greg noticed it first. He looked in the backseat but said nothing. He turned and started staring out the passenger window.

Mechelle pushed the rope toward Austin's elbow. When they pulled into the parking spot, she pushed it into his arm.

Austin' nearly jumped out of his seat. He looked at Greg, who had his phone in his left hand and his right arm on the window seal. "Did ya see that?"

"See what?"

Austin looked back at the rope, and he threw it back into the floorboard as if it had cooties, "Never mind." He exited the truck and asked Greg, "Aren't you coming?"

"I'll be right there."

When Austin opened the store door, Greg turned to the back seat, "Brooke?"

"Hey sweetie," I said. I grabbed his face and kissed him. He pulled back, "Okay, someone is going to look in here and think I have an imaginary friend." He unbuckled and turned back to us, "No more of that. I don't want Austin thinking his truck's haunted." He started to close the door and turned back, "Oh yea, I love ya."

This melted my heart. I grabbed Mechelle, and we returned to my room.

"This is how you feel. It's like a superpower. Part of me feels guilty if I truly scared him." She looked down and then back at me, "But wow! That was fantastic! Let's do something else."

"Like what?"

"I don't know."

There was a knock on the door. I hollered, "Come in."

Phyllis brought in some of my clothes. Mechelle filled her in on our escapade. Once Phyllis left, Mechelle asked, "Can I go with you tonight?"

This was a simple task. Drop in and put the letter on his desk and pop out. She had no experience in this and did not know how to defend herself if something went wrong. "Not this time. You need some training. Juliet, Jacob, Greg, and I have been training for these missions for a long time."

Mechelle bowed her head. She looked defeated.

"Don't worry. You're a part of this team. We'll find you a place on it. It won't be just composing a letter now and then," I explained. Trying to cheer her up. I asked if she wanted to go to the villa for a little while.

She was excited about that. When we walked past the dining room, the smell of rosemary lingered in the air. We sat down. The server asked if he could help us. We each ordered a bowl of soup. The chef always had some on hand. They served the soup with rosemary bread. Everything was amazing. We walked to the reception area. A young woman was standing behind the counter.

"Excuse me. May I see Isabella?"

The young woman looked me over, and turned and made a call, "There are two young ladies here to see you." She listened to the caller. "I will." She hung up the phone. "She'll be with you in a moment. Please have a seat.

We sat down and patiently waited for her to arrive.

About ten minutes later, Isabella came around the corner, nearly out of breath, "Oh ladies, I'm so sorry I had you waiting so long." She turned to the lady behind the counter, "Wren, these two ladies are very dear to this family. They should always be treated as if they own the place. They are never to be charged for anything."

The young woman nodded.

"Unless it's an emergency, please do not disturb us for the next thirty minutes." She turned her attention back to us, "I'm glad you both are here. We need to talk to you." We followed Isabella into her apartment. "Have a seat." She retreated to her bedroom.

A few minutes later, she and Leonardo returned. After a brief greeting, they joined us. Leonardo looked tired and his breathing seemed to be getting worse.

Leonardo looked at Isabella and back at us. "Brooke, working for Lillie and now you, has been a blessing in my life. Despite the risks associated with working with your family, Isabella and I would always choose to help your family."

Where is this going? Is he leaving me? Calm down. Hear him out.

Leonardo cleared his throat. "My health is deteriorating and before you offer, we've discussed it. We're going to let God determine my future."

It was difficult to hear, but I understood.

"I need to step down as the executor of your trust. Isabella's ready to take over, but we need to find a permanent replacement. I have buried Isabella with my work on top of her normal responsibilities. It's going to be difficult for her to run this place and take care of your finances."

I asked, "Do you think you're going to sell the villa?"

Isabella and Leonardo both chuckled.

Isabella explained, "We've something to tell you. Is it okay for us to discuss details of what Lillie had done for us in front of Mechelle?"

Mechelle was a member of the Bloom Keepers, and she was my oldest friend. I trusted her with my life. I replied, "Yes. Please continue."

"See, Leonardo and Lillie met through a mutual connection. Leonardo has a unique skill set. His connections were valuable to her. Eventually, to get them out of a dangerous situation, she revealed her secret to him. This led to a lifelong friendship and partnership. Lillie set us up with this villa. She asked us to manage it. In exchange, she provided us with a generous income and an honest career. We also helped her get whatever she needed to protect the stone and others she was working with."

"I'm confused. Are you saying my grandmother owns the villa?"

Leonardo spoke up, "Well, the trust owns it. This means you own it."

Overcome with emotions, I felt like I could barely breathe.

Isabella asked, "Do you understand?"

"Yes. I'm just shocked."

Isabella continued, "Brooke, your trust is worth more than you can imagine. You'll never need to worry about finances. You have investments that are increasing your assets daily."

Leonardo added, "We thought this was a bit much to tell you when we first met. We need to find you someone who can manage the villa and is responsible enough for the 1.2 billion in assets you hold."

I looked over at Mechelle. She looked at me.

"Did you just say billion?"

Leonardo clarified, "Yes, but that does not include the trust your mother's aware of. We would like to have this new person run both trusts. See, Mr. Thomas reports to me."

It was like a veil was being removed from my eyes. *I'm a billionaire?*

"Brooke, we have a suggestion on who can take over both positions," Isabella announced.

I sat up, waiting for her to continue.

"This person will not be available for a few more years, but they are doing exceedingly well in their finance classes. They understand the mission of the Bloom Keepers. Oh, and they are majoring in hospitality and tourism."

Again, Mechelle and I looked at one another.

"That's right ladies. We believe Mechelle would be perfect for the position once she graduates from college."

"I think that's a great idea," I said, looking for a response from Mechelle. Her mouth was hanging open, and she appeared to be in shock.

Isabella continued, "Mechelle, during the summer months, we would ask you to come here and get trained. Paid training, of course. What do you both think?"

She uttered, "Sorry, I… I don't know what to say."

Leonardo added, "My team will be there to help you with whatever Brooke, or the Bloom Keepers need. You will have a substantial income for someone your age."

Mechelle leaned forward and asked, "Are you sure I can do this?"

"Yes, you are the best candidate for the position," Leonardo encouraged.

"Please, you must take this. You are perfect for it, and you'll be living in Italy," I added.

"Then yes. This is like a dream come true," Mechelle blurted out.

Mechelle hugged everyone. She returned to her seat. "How do I explain this to my parents?"

"Before next summer, tell your parents an old family friend of Lillie's offered you an amazing opportunity. We will work around any vacations or things you must attend. You can come anytime you're bored if you want to. Lord knows we have plenty to do around here. We are currently looking for another gardener," Isabella suggested.

Everyone laughed. We socialized for a little while longer before heading home.

After dinner, I changed and grabbed the plastic bag that contained the letter from Chief Bianchi from Mechelle. I returned to the same location I did the last time I dropped off the letter about Anthony Granaldi III. His desk was cleaner than the last time. With my gloves on, I pulled the letter out of the bag. I debated on putting it on the desk but decided it was unlikely someone might put something on it if it was on his chair. There was a bloom in the letter's corner. I was proud of that little flower. *Grandma, I know you're proud of me.*

Greg came by later and we all had a good laugh about the truck ride. We also planned a double date for that weekend. That night I slept well, knowing this was nearly over.

Twenty-One

We had waited the three days to allow Chief Bianchi time to decide what he wanted to do. I suspected they would have people on cameras watching the area. It would be easy for them to do facial recognition on anyone if they were taping it. I was not worried about it because I knew they would not know I was there. What concerned me was trying to get the contract from the Chief. It was too risky to have another person with me as I retrieve it.

I arrived at the police station parking area at 7:00 am. I waited patiently for the Chief to arrive. I was invisible but still needed to be careful not to be bumped by anyone walking by. I spotted him getting out of a black vehicle. After he was clear of the area, I took a good look at the inside of his car. I left and would not return until later to check to see if the flag was down.

I worked out for an hour while Mechelle watched and cheered me on. It was great having my own personal cheerleader. I mean she really made up her own cheers for me. Classes would be the following week. Mechelle and I spent two hours trying to get our books and supplies from the campus bookstore. We grabbed a bite to eat before heading back home.

I popped in to see Tony and tell him he might be meeting with Chief Bianchi. He assured me he would be waiting for me. I went to the Police Station and noticed the flag was down. *That's good. Now stone, show me the cameras.* Nothing happened. *Stone, show me the hidden officers.* Atop a few buildings were police. They appeared to be using binoculars. *They're going to be watching the police chief.*

I moved to his office and pinned myself against the wall to stay out of his way. People were coming in and out. Detective DeSantis came in.

The chief asked, "Anything?"

DeSantis shook his head. "No sir."

"I'm famished. Want to grab a bite?"

"No, sir. I'm going to keep an eye out for this Bloom person."

"I'll be back shortly."

"Sir, do you think an officer should go with you?"

"Maybe you're right."

DeSantis walked to the doorway, "I'll have someone grab you something. Anything special you want?"

"Anything is fine. Hey shut my door," he instructed.

DeSantis shut the door. The Chief sat at his desk and began working on paperwork.

Things began rushing through my mind on how to get him to grab the papers and come with me. This was the perfect time to take him. *Surely, he will resist.* I looked around the room and noticed the reflection on the award on the wall. *Will that work? Nah... Maybe?* I focused on it, but nothing happened.

I concentrated on persuading him to pick up the contract. He did. *Okay, I've got this.* I focused again on persuading him to close his eyes and for them to remain closed until I told him to open them. His eyes closed. *Wow, I'm good.* I snatched a pen from his desk. *Here we go.* I took a breath and placed my hand on his shoulder. I took him to the cave.

I told him to remain where he was. I quickly felt for the lighter and teleported to Tony's hut. As expected, he was cleaning around the hut. "Tony, we need to go now."

"Oh, you startled me. He opened the hut door and said, "Rosina, I'll be back soon. I'm going with Brooke."

He returned to me and placed his hand on my shoulder. Rosina and Stefania had their heads in the doorway as they watched us leave. We returned to a pathway in the cave near the area where I left the Chief. It was eerily dark. I felt around on the wall for a nearby torch. Once located, I lit it to lead us to the open area of the cave where I left the chief. Just before we entered the cavern. Using telepathy, I told Tony to stop and wait for me to call for him. He nodded his head up and down. I pulled my ski mask over my face.

As I entered the cavern. I found Chief Bianchi, aiming a gun at me, "Who are you and how did I get here?"

Please Lord, don't let him shoot. I took a deep breath and slowly exhaled. *Note to self, next time you kidnap someone, check them for weapons.* "You're safe. No harm will come to you. Please put the gun away."

He shook his head and scrunched his eyes, "I'll only ask one more time. Who are you and how did I get here?"

"I'm part of the Bloom. Unfortunately, I cannot disclose how you were brought here. You need to understand we only seek to stop the evil in this world. Has the contract been signed?"

Without needing to persuade him, he returned the gun to his ankle holster. *Thank you, Jesus.*

"No, I have not signed it."

I tossed him his pen, "Please sign it." He did. "Now put them on that rock." He followed my instructions. I turned my head in the direction I entered the cavern and called out, "Tony!"

Tony entered. The two men made eye contact. The chief's eyes widened. I suspect he was surprised Tony was the one turning his family in.

Tony grabbed the contract and brought it next to me. He held the contract for both of us to read. Using telepathy, I told him everything we requested was in the contract. He nodded to confirm.

"Chief Bianchi, Tony will have his attorney look over the document. Once it is signed, we will provide it to you along with the second letter," I informed him.

"How do I contact Tony about the case?"

"When you need to see him, remove the flag in front the Police Station. I will come periodically, to check its status. I'll come to you when we're ready to see you. You need to understand, you will only have one opportunity to video tape his confession and to question him. Make sure you are prepared when it happens. Once the case is over, only Officer Sartori, Detective DeSantis, and you will be permitted to contact Tony or the Bloom. All meetings will be on our terms," I explained.

The chief shuffled his feet a bit, "Tony, we both know what you and your family have been involved in. This information better be good."

Tony took a deep breath, "Chief, you won't be disappointed in the evidence I can provide you. I'm willing to do my time but you and I both know I wouldn't be safe if I went to prison."

The chief nodded, "Yes, you'd have a price on your head. The rumor around town is Joseph's hunting for you."

"I think he suspected; I wanted out. See I turned my life over to Jesus. I just don't have the stomach for the things we were into. God convicted me," Tony explained.

"If that's true, I'm glad. Now, I need to get back to my office. I'm famished."

I walked toward the Chief and persuaded him to close his eyes and to think about a peaceful day in the countryside. I placed my hand on his shoulder and returned us to his office invisible. The door was open, and his lunch was sitting on his desk. I walked over and looked to see if anyone was nearby. His secretary was not there. I gently closed his door. I made us both visible again. I got behind him and persuaded him to not remember how he returned to his office. I turned myself invisible. I moved against the wall with my mirror ready and waited to see what he would do.

He looked around the room and picked up his phone, "Get me DeSantis!" The phone was slammed down. "I've lost my mind. Food. I'm probably just hungry." He began eating the sandwich.

The chief was halfway through his sandwich when DeSantis walked in. "What's up chief?"

The chief swallowed a big bite. "Shut the door."

DeSantis closed the door, "What's going on? We haven't seen any suspicious people out there."

"Don't ask me how, but they came here, and I don't remember leaving." He looked down confused. "I don't even know how I got back here. I...I was in a cave."

"A cave sir?" DeSantis pulled out a pad and started writing.

"They must have drugged me. I need my blood tested. Some, short lady. Well, she sounded like a teenager is with the Bloom. Tony was there. They have the contract. The flag needs to be put down. Only you and Sartori can know. We need a list of questions. How did I get to the cave?"

"Sir you're not making much since. I'm going to get the doctor for you."

That poor man. I wish I could have come up with a better way that could have been explained. Using telepathy, I said, "It's best you compose yourself. There is no way of explaining what happened today. Write down notes of things for you to remember. Stay on task and don't worry about things you can't explain."

I knew there was nothing more I needed to do here. I returned to Tony. Upon my arrival, Tony was startled. He appeared to be reading the contract.

"I've been reading over this. It is generous offer. I can't believe you were able to get them to agree to our demands."

"Tony, think about all you and your family has done. You deserve life in prison," I informed him.

Tony nodded in agreement.

"It's not me that got that sentence lightened. There is someone else that has already paid the price for your sins."

He bowed his head. "You're right. Jesus did that for me."

"You need to make an appointment with an attorney. Any suggestions, who you would like to make it with?"

"No. Everyone I know is connected to my family."

"Let me take you back. I'll find someone. I may know someone," I said, as I clutched his arm and took him back to the hut."

I grasped the contract and went to the villa to speak with Leonardo about Mr. Thomas. Wren was at the reception desk. "Good morning, Ms. Garrison, how can I help you?"

"Good morning, Wren. May I speak with Leonardo, please?"

She turned picked up the phone and began dialing.

"Hello Brooke," I heard a familiar voice say.

I turned around and saw Leonardo opening his arms for a hug. It was so wonderful seeing him doing better. "Wow! Look at you. You look fantastic."

"Thanks. Friends of Lillie's suggested I try the Hallelujah Diet. I can't remember which of the sisters, Brenda, or Judy. That doesn't matter. One of them was cured of Leukemia. I've only been on it a few days and I'm doing better. Just keep me in your prayers."

"Of course. Could we talk privately?"

He took me into his apartment.

I said, "I need to know more about Mr. Thomas, my trustee. Tony needs an attorney to look over his contract with the Florence Police. Is he someone I can talk to about it and what can I tell him?"

"Mr. Thomas is aware. He and his father have been helping your family for years. He knows all about the stone. Well, maybe not all it can do. It will surprise him you're aware of his connection. I have not told him about the plan to have Mechelle take over both trusts."

I hurried home and contacted Mr. Thomas about meeting with him. He said, "I'm available now. Actually... Give me five minutes."

"Sir, you're across town, I can't be there for at least thirty minutes."

"I need five minutes to give my staff something to do so they don't bother us. I'll lock my door and close the blinds. We both know you can arrive instantly."

I chuckled. "Yes. I'll be there in five minutes."

I grabbed my phone to tell everyone everything went well. I heard Mechelle coming up the stairs and filled her in on everything. We agreed, she should come meet Mr. Thomas with me.

He seemed surprised I had shown up with another person, "Mr. Thomas, this is Mechelle. Leonardo and I have agreed to have her take over the trusts in the future. She will be working with Leonardo.

"I didn't see that coming. Of course, it is your decision. I would still like to assist your family if I can. Lillie meant a great deal to our family."

"We are going to be needing your services. In fact, that is why we are here." I explained the situation and asked him to look over the contract.

We waited patiently as he read the document, "This seems to be a good contract, but I still need to do some research. I am not familiar with Italy's laws. I'll call you in a few days with my recommendation."

"Brooke, it might be best to have Mr. Thomas stay on even once I take over the trust. If for some reason I was unable to take care of my duties he could assist," Mechelle suggested.

"Yes, you're right. Mr. Thomas, would that work for you?" Mr. Thomas nodded in agreement. "I'm assuming you get paid a salary from the trust." He nodded again. "Mechelle don't change that. If we find we needed him excessively, we'll need to compensate him accordingly."

"That's very generous. Thank you," he commented.

"Thank you for your help," I said standing to leave.

"Brooke, Lillie would be proud of you. I'll get right on this," Mr. Thomas said holding up the contract.

Mechelle and I returned home and spent the rest of the day, shopping for new backpacks and things for the upcoming semester.

Twenty-Two

It had been three days since we had spoken with Mr. Thomas, but he finally called. He suggested Tony sign it. When I picked up the contract, he informed me I would get an increase of funds each month from my trust. This was a surprise.

Tony signed the contract. I placed the signed contract off on the seat of Chief Bianchi's car along with the second letter with the location of the journals.

Since dropping off the letter, Mechelle and I checked numerous news outlets to see if the story had broken yet, but still nothing. Classes would start soon. Mechelle and I went on a shopping spree which included her buying a cute dress for her date with Austin.

Apparently, it was date night. Phyllis was heading out for a nice dinner with Hal and his children, Eli and Addi. She seemed nervous. I was so happy for her.

Austin suggested the Porch Kitchen & Bar for dinner. Mechelle and I glanced at their menu. Austin picked Mechelle up with a beautiful flower arrangement. She was so happy. I finally found a vase for them. She placed them on the table in the foyer. They looked beautiful. It was apparent they had been talking a lot since they first met. Jacob and Juliet were already at the restaurant when we entered. The place was adorable. There were sofas in the middle of the restaurant by the bar area.

The guys must have been hungry because they ordered us Loaded Brisket Nachos. I wanted to try nearly everything on the menu. I decided on the Smoked Turkey Cobb with sunflower seeds.

Austin and Mechelle ordered the Southern Fried Chicken. Mechelle rarely ordered fried food.

The evening started off well. Everyone was excited about getting back to school. For each of us, it meant we could see one another more often. Austin was working on the farm, but not as often as before because his father hired another farmhand to replace him. Greg's parents did not permit him to work during the school year unless there was an emergency on the farm.

We were enjoying dinner when Jacob received got an alert on his phone. He interrupted everyone, "Hey, listen up. Police raid Granaldi Home."

Everyone stopped what they were doing and listened. Everyone except Austin.

"The article says the police took out several boxes of evidence. They have brought the family and staff in for questioning."

Greg asked, "Is that it?"

Jacob began going through his phone. He commented, "It just says the police are being tight-lipped about what was going on."

Austin asked, "Do you guys know the family or something?"

Everyone looked around to see who could come up with a good explanation for our interest. Finally, Mechelle answered him, "This may sound strange, but we like to research crimes going on around the world.

She wasn't lying.

"Interesting. I see people on social media posting that kind of stuff," Austin replied.

We continued talking about crimes we had seen until we left the restaurant. Greg and Austin brought us back home. Phyllis was not home yet. It was a beautiful night. The four of us sat on the back patio chatting for a short while. I tapped Greg on the knee. "Let's give them some privacy." Greg and I set off toward the library and snuggled up in our usual spot.

"It's going to be hard to keep Austin from finding out about the Bloom if he and Mechelle get serious," Greg commented.

"You're right. We'll have to be careful."

"You know you can trust him."

I suspected Greg wanted me to let him in on my secret. I just wasn't sure yet. The fewer people that knew, the better. "I know I can, but for now, I think he shouldn't know."

Greg nodded. "You're probably right."

We behaved ourselves that night. Greg left when he heard Mechelle coming upstairs. Mechelle and I chatted about the evening before we both turned in for the night.

Over the next few weeks, I returned to my routine of daily workouts, attending classes, doing homework, and checking daily to see if they had removed the flag at the Florence Police Station. I frequently went there in my pajamas. Of course, I was invisible. Not having my mother in the house, I felt more like an adult. Although Mechelle and I were roommates, we both had our own schedules. She and Austin were officially dating now. They were adorable together. The farm boy was introducing her to farming and the city girl was introducing him to enjoying the finer things in life. They accepted one another for who they were but were open to discovering new things. Apparently, Bill and Suzanne loved having her at the farm. Suzanne was teaching her how to make some of the southern foods she had enjoyed eating.

When I woke up, a text I received distracted me.

GREG: Hey beautiful. I have a special day planned for us. Let me know when you're up.

I texted him to let him know I was up. He told me to wear jeans and sneakers, and to bring a light jacket or sweater. I got dressed and hurried to get something to eat. When I walked into the kitchen, Greg was there speaking with Phyllis.

Greg asked, "You ready to go?"

"I need to eat something first."

"I've got that covered. This is for you, Phyllis," Greg informed her as he handed her a bag. She thanked him and he took me out to his car.

Once I buckled in, Greg handed me a coffee and a chocolate croissant. We began heading south. Greg did not inform me of our destination, but he assured me I would enjoy it.

After about an hour of driving, we turned into Mammoth Cave National Park. I had not been here since I was a young girl. It amazed me how he always knew how to make me feel special.

We went on a tour of the cave. The park ranger led us through, telling us about everything. Eventually, we came to an area known as Fat Man's Misery. It was a narrow winding pathway just wide enough for one's hips. We also saw Lover's Leap and the Giant Coffin. The name came from the large boulder that looked like a coffin. We finished the tour and ate lunch before going canoeing. It was peaceful listening to the paddles hit the water and seeing the vegetation. Birds were chirping and insects buzzed near us.

We glided around the bank and spotted a canoe rested on the shoreline. I figured someone needed a potty break. About twenty yards from there, I noticed a man and his son near the bank. The child was about fifteen feet from his father. He appeared to be about ten. The father said, "Don't move, you'll get sprayed." The son looked terrified.

"Greg, head over there," I instructed.

As we moved closer, I noticed a skunk about a foot away from the boy. I couldn't help but chuckle at their situation.

The father began motioning for us to move away and said, "Please stay back."

I called out to the skunk, "The boy means you know harm. Please leave the area."

The skunk stood up and looked in my direction.

"They mean you no harm. Please leave the boy."

The skunk turned and ran away from him.

"How did you…"

I interrupted the father by saying, "Have a good day."

Greg and I began paddling again.

We both had a good laugh about it.

"We should go to a zoo sometime and see what the animals will do for you," Greg joked.

While driving back, I remembered I had not been to Florence. Greg insisted I go. It was not like I had anything else to do while we drove back.

I popped over to see if the flag was down at the police station in Italy. It was down. I returned to Greg and told him the news. It was now time to figure out how to meet with the Chief. We discussed many options on the way home and agreed we would go to his house. I could easily teleport to his car later in the evening. We called a meeting of the Bloom Keepers. Everyone was going to meet me at my house for dinner. I asked Phyllis to order pizza for us.

It took us a little longer to get home than expected because of a traffic accident. Rather than leave him, I enjoyed my extra time with him. Everyone was at the house when we arrived. We came in through the back door. Laughter filled the hallway. I made a break for the dining room when Greg grabbed my hand and pulled me to him.

He drew me closer and kissed me. "Thank ya for another amazing day," Greg said with his dreamiest eyes.

"Why are you thanking me? You're the one that spoiled me today."

"Brooke, every minute I have with you is a blessing," he said before kissing me again.

Jacob was telling everyone about the new professor at the college. "Ms. Hummel insisted we call her by her first name, Chayanne. She's amazing. She has a unique way of making everyone feel like they're not in class. Everyone's encouraged to participate. She starts a discussion, and through her questions, we are learning the material. It's so much better than some instructors who just sit up there expecting you to write everything they say." Jacob looked up at us. "Hey, glad to see you guys could make it." He snickered.

The discussion about our new professors continued as we ate. Phyllis did not seem to mind not being a part of the discussion. Once our meal was over, we got to business.

Greg began, "The Police Chief wants to see Tony. We're trying to figure out the best way to get them together without them discovering our secret."

I added, "I think it would be best to bring Tony to him. When I took him to Tony, he believed we drugged him. Of course, he wasn't, but it was the only way he could account for what happened to him."

Jacob was the first to respond. "The last thing we want is for them to think we are drugging them. I agree we should bring Tony to them."

"But where? It would need to be in Italy. There are a few places we are familiar with," Juliet commented.

"Maybe Tony knows a place," Mechelle suggested.

Jacob agreed, "That's a great idea! Brooke, will the Bloom work if you're touching someone and they are thinking about a place?"

"I don't know. Let's try it," I suggested. I walked over to Jacob and pulled out the mirror. "You need to concentrate on the place and try to picture it." *Wonder where I am off too.*

Jacob concentrated and brought us to Juliet's bedroom. I asked, "Of all the places, why did you pick here? We could have gone to Fiji or the Alps."

He walked over to her nightstand and pulled out a pen and paper and wrote her a note. He took his sweet time writing it. "If we don't return soon, they're going to worry,"

"I'm nearly done." Once he finished his note, he placed it on her pillow. "That'll be a pleasant surprise for her tonight."

"Jacob, that's so sweet."

He took hold of my arm, and we joined the others.

Juliet asked, "So where did you go?"

I didn't want to lie to her, so I avoided the subject. "That worked perfectly. So, we'll let Tony pick the location. I think a few of us should go to make sure we're not being lured into a trap." Everyone agreed. "Until we know when the meeting is, we cannot determine who would be available to go."

Juliet introduced a new topic by saying, "Jacob and I've been talking about Mechelle's role. She has an incredibly important position and if anyone ever determined her link to the Bloom of Dreams, well, it could cause her to be in danger or for your funds to be in danger."

Jacob took over the topic. "Mechelle, we know you aren't interested in learning self-defense. Everyone agrees it's imperative you train. However, we don't think you should be on missions with us. That would put you and your position in the Blook Keepers at risk of being discovered. It's best you run the villa and obtain things for us from the black market."

"Both of you make valid points. Even Isabella and Leonardo are not in the limelight," Phyllis added.

"Let's vote on it," Jacob suggested.

"There's really no need. After talking with each of you and…" Mechelle chuckled, "Phyllis and I were discussing this today. Well, I agree with everything you've said. I'm not looking forward to the workouts, but it is what it is."

We ended up having a vote, and it was unanimous that her role should remain out of the limelight.

We adjourned the meeting. Mechelle and I stayed up rather late discussing her role and my new discovery of being a billionaire.

Before heading to bed, I popped in on Chief Bianchi's car at about 6:00 am, this time dressed in my black outfit and a ski mask. His home did not appear to be inside the city. As I walked up to the house, a light in the home turned on. He was in the kitchen. I looked inside and teleported myself to the dining room so I could see behind him.

The smell of fresh coffee filled the room. "Chief Bianchi, you wanted to speak with me," I whispered.

He spun around, nearly knocking his coffee off the counter. "How did you get in here?" He began moving to his right. There was a set of knives on the counter.

"Sir, I'm here about Tony Granaldi. I am with the Bloom."

He stopped moving, "Tony?... Oh yes, Tony. Sorry, I need my coffee. Do you want some?"

I knew better than to say yes. It would be easy for him to get my DNA. "No, thank you."

He poured his coffee and sat down at the small kitchen table. He motioned for me to have a seat. I declined. At first, he thanked me for leading him to the journals. He said cheerfully, "You weren't mistaken. That was a goldmine of information. We have our questions ready. When can we meet with Tony?"

"I'll let you know. We need to figure out a location, and it needs to be confidential. Joseph will stop at nothing to find him."

He blew on his coffee. "You've got that right. We've had him in for questioning. Get that boy mad enough and he has no filter. He wants his brother dead."

I replied, "I'll get back to you as soon as I can with a location and time. You need to remember, if we even suspect you have additional officers or have let others know what's going on, our deal is over."

"I understand. You've kept your end of the bargain, I will too. Can I ask, how did you know where I lived?"

"The Bloom has access to many things. The only thing you need to concern yourself with is knowing we'll keep our word if you keep yours and we're only out to help law enforcement with criminals like the Granaldi family," I assured him. "We'll be in touch." I turned and walked to the back of his house. I heard his chair move as I hid behind a door in another room to teleport back home.

Twenty-Three

After speaking with Tony, he came up with a few locations to choose from. We settled on the house of his old nanny. She had willed the house to her granddaughter, but she was rarely there. She used it as a weekend home because she no longer lived in Florence. The house was in Caldine, Italy. Tony took me there. It was a three-room flat. Jacob and I looked at the aerial photos of the area. We figured someone should be on the roof. They needed to look for people using listening devices or snipers that might be nearby. We also agreed I should be the only one talking. They already knew from my accent I was American. They knew little about the rest of the group.

We determined Juliet and Jacob would be on the roof and Greg and I would be in the flat with Tony. Mechelle, Juliet, and I surprised everyone with official uniforms. They were more comfortable than what we had been wearing. The emblem of the bloom was also on the masks and shirts. It was small and not easily detected. We had Leonardo get them from one of his secret contacts. It was great for Mechelle because she worked directly with him to get them.

At the last minute, I dropped off the address to the Chief. This gave him a minimal amount of time to have additional teams in the area. I was waiting in the hall invisible when they entered the building of the flat.

"Remember, I don't want to take any chance of not getting all the information we need. If this group can get us more cases like this, we could end many crime families. By the book," the Chief told Detective DeSantis and Officer Sartori.

181

They were each carrying equipment. The stone had not alerted me of danger. I suspected they were being truthful. Using telepathy, I asked Juliet and Jacob about the status outside.

"There's nothing going on out here," Juliet commented.

The Chief knocked on the door. That was my queue to return to the flat. I opened the door. Greg was beside Tony in the living room.

Without saying a word, I let them in.

They came in and the Chief introduced everyone to us. He acknowledged Greg, who only bowed his head. He said nothing. They began setting up the equipment, which included a backdrop to prevent anyone from knowing the location of the interview.

Detective DeSantis sat next to Tony and was within the frame of the video. "Before we start the video, thank you for incredibly detailed journals. There are a lot of search warrants being served and other investigators working on that side of the case. We understand your need for secrecy because your life and your family are being hunted down. I'm surprised you are still so close to Florence. I think that's risky," DeSantis told him.

"I can assure you; I'm doing all I can to protect them from my brother and those my family has done business with," Tony replied.

"I've just one more off-camera question. Are you behind the Bloom?"

Everyone anxiously awaited his response.

Tony looked at Greg and me. "No. I'm not worthy. The Bloom is doing God's work. I'm sure of it. They have been an unexpected blessing to me and my family." Tony looked to be on the verge of tears. "If they had not been there to help us, I'm sure we would already be dead. I don't know how they knew to find me, or what made them decide to help us, but we'll be forever in their debt."

"Interesting," DeSantis said. He turned to me. "Would you care to let us know?"

I looked over at Greg. He just nodded. My attention went from the Chief to Sartori, before returning to DeSantis, "Tony's correct. The Bloom is working to bring light to those doing evil. We know God granted us a precious gift."

The Chief spoke up, "I'm not meaning to interrupt, but your group has been an asset to my team. If we need your help in the future, how will we contact you?"

Without talking to the Bloom Keepers, I thought it best not to make a commitment. "I will see if there is a way. For now, we will continue to use the flag."

The Chief inhaled deeply before commenting, "It's just my officers and the community are aware there's something going on with our flag. Reporters are even asking questions. We really need another way."

"I'll see if we can come up with another way."

He seemed satisfied with my answer. The Chief nodded to DeSantis to begin.

"Tony, we are about to turn on the recording device. If at any point you need a break, let us know," DeSantis instructed. He turned the recorder on and returned to his seat. After a brief introduction, which included the purpose of the video, he began his questioning about the murder of Federico Lombardo.

After the first hour, Greg brought in some chairs. In the second hour, I told Greg using telepathy; I was going to check on Juliet and Jacob.

As soon as I popped in, Jacob commented, "Oh thank you, Juliet needs a restroom asap."

I quickly took her to her room. Once she finished, we talked about what they saw. Juliet assured me they saw nothing suspicious. I told her I would bring Jacob back and give them a break. "I'll return in a little while for you to relieve Greg. Oh, can you see if Phyllis could make us some sandwiches? I need five. Thanks."

Jacob was glad for the break. After a quick restroom break for myself, I returned to Greg. I filled him in. He nodded.

After another hour, they finally moved on to the location of the fugitives. Tony asked for a break. I stepped into the back bedroom to teleport back to grab the sandwiches. Everyone seemed surprised when I returned with the food. The break was needed. Greg and I ate separately in the bedroom to prevent them from seeing us without our masks.

Nearly an hour later, Greg seemed to get restless. I returned to Juliet's room. She and Jacob were watching a movie. I explained to them the need to find a new way for us to communicate because it was difficult to remember to use telepathy for such a long time. They agreed to think about it. Jacob was going to research a few things. I took Juliet back with me and brought Greg back to my house for a break from the endless questioning.

They seemed surprised when Greg disappeared and Juliet appeared, but they said nothing. After a few more hours of questioning, they shifted to questioning other crime families. It was apparent Tony was exhausted. Officer Sartori appeared to be on the verge of dozing off. DeSantis and Tony's voices were becoming raspy. An hour and a half later, DeSantis said, "We only have the paintings to discuss."

We were all having a hard time focusing. "Perhaps we should take a break and begin again in the morning." Everyone agreed. Once they had collected their equipment and exited the flat. I returned Tony to his hut. His family was excited to see him. Rosina admitted she was anxious about him because we were gone so long.

I returned to collect Juliet before popping into the attic. The guys weren't there. I left Juliet and went down to my room to change. I could hear Greg and Jacob's voices. They were in the library. They did not see me pass.

When I returned to the library, the three of them were discussing ways to have the chief contact us. Jacob hacked into some company and set up a bogus email account that only he had access to. He would let us know if they sent anything. I heard someone coming up the stairs. I peeked out the door. Austin and Mechelle were on their way.

"Quick, put the notes away," I ordered in a quiet tone.

Juliet grabbed the pad and pen from the table and slid them under the seat cushion. Jacob closed his computer.

"Hey guys," Austin said in the doorway.

"We saw your vehicles here, so Austin thought he would come in. He can't stay though," Mechelle explained.

We all chatted for about fifteen minutes before he left. The discussion changed to who would go the next day for the deposition. Jacob and I were the only ones available.

The routine was the same. They came in and set up the equipment. About two hours into the questioning, the stone heated.

"Someone's coming. Tony, we need to go," I commanded.

Jacob grabbed the video from the camera.

"What are you doing?"

Jacob said, "If he's in danger, this tape is too."

The Chief nodded. He said, "I know you'll get it to us."

There was a bang at the door. DeSantis looked out the window and commented, "I don't know how they found us, but it's Joseph's guys. Look they're surrounding the building."

"We need to get you guys out of here, too. There's no way they'll let you live knowing what you might know."

He dispatched officers to our area.

Jacob insisted we go. I took them to the cave and returned to help the officers. When I returned, I returned invisible to the bedroom. Joseph's men had them cornered in the bedroom. There was no way out. I tried to use the power of persuasion on those that were firing shots. I could not get into their heads. The noise may have been the problem. *Jesus, please let this go well.* I reappeared so the officers could see me. The Chief and Sartori were on one side of the door. DeSantis on the other.

I was near DeSantis. I told him, "Do as I say, and I'll get you out of this."

DeSantis nodded.

"Take my arm."

He did. I took us to the other side of the room next to the Chief and Sartori. DeSantis looked confused and released his hold on me. It sounded as though they were kicking the door.

"There's nowhere to hide. Just give him to us and we'll let you go," someone yelled.

"I need you to trust me. I need each of you to hold on to me," I ordered.

DeSantis locked his arm in mine. The others just stared, confused. DeSantis grabbed Sartori's arm and pulled her to me. He looked up at the Chief, "Sir, you said yourself, we can trust them."

Another bang on the door. The Chief looked at me. "Sir, please hold on." I looked into the mirror and took us to the cave.

DeSantis released his grasp as soon as we arrived. Officer Sartori continued to hold me tightly. They both looked in disbelief. The Chief turned to me and said, "Hey, I've been here before."

That seemed to give Sartori some comfort. She released her hold on me. She then muttered, "Our equipment, sir."

"I'm sure they'll destroy it," DeSantis announced.

Jacob gripped my arm and said, "Let's get in, snatch the things, and get out with it. If we each grab what is in front of us, we should be able to save it."

I nodded. I advised him, "I'll only have one hand available."

"Understood," he told me. He nodded. He was ready to go.

I looked into the mirror. One man seemed to pack up the equipment into its case.

Jacob appeared confused and asked, "What is it?"

"One guy is packing up the equipment. It will be easier to transport if we wait till, he's finished," I explained.

We waited till he was done. We returned along the wall. Joseph told the man, packing them up to hurry. As he walked out the door. He ordered another man to help him with the gear.

Jacob picked up one case and told me, "Come on, give me a hand."

I seized a case and spun around, kicking the man in the stomach. He dropped the case. The other man stopped, heading toward the cases. Jacob took two of the four cases. I grabbed the case the man had and wrapped my arm through Jacobs.

"We need the other one," Jacob announced. The handle was up. I concentrated on the mirror. The stunned man started moving toward us. Just before leaving, I stuck the toe of my shoe through the handle. We arrived in the cave with me balancing a case on my foot. Immediately, DeSantis and Sartori grabbed the cases.

After a brief explanation of what had happened when we returned, the Chief asked, "What's that thing in your hand? Is it some strange teleporting device?"

I slipped it into the small pocket of my pants. I told the Chief, "The less you know, the better."

"May I ask if this is how you got me here before?"

"Yes. I didn't drug you."

DeSantis and the Chief exchanged looks.

"Look, this is taking longer than expected. I expect each of you to stay in this cavern. Don't let your curiosity get to you. Do you understand?"

Each of them nodded. "Good. Finish your interview. I'll have someone check in on you. I'll be back in a few hours."

Sartori asked, "Where are we?"

"I'm afraid I can't tell you that." I looked at Jacob and motioned for him to join me. We teleported to Asahi's hut; he was on the porch drinking some tea. I told him what was going on. He agreed to check in on them to see if they needed anything. He assured me he would be in disguise. I returned Jacob to his room and teleported to change outfits before heading to the campus. *Wow!* I glanced at the clock and realized I was going to be late if I drove. I concentrated on arriving invisible and teleported to the ladies restroom in the building of my class. When the coast was clear, I made myself visible and hurried to my class. I arrived just in time.

Between my classes, I ran into Juliet. I filled her in quickly and rushed to my class. The instructor was excellent, but I had a hard time concentrating on what she was explaining. *Stop it. Asahi will take care of them. Trust him.* I did. I just felt it was my obligation. My team was fantastic. They were skilled people to help me with my destiny. At that moment, I gave it to God to take care of. After class, I waited in another restroom until the coast was clear. I returned home to put on what I now referred to as the Bloom uniform and returned to the cave.

When I arrived, they packed the equipment up, and everyone was chatting and drinking tea. Asahi was pouring tea into a cup for the Chief. Asahi turned and bowed to me. Strange. I was not sure what to do, so I bowed back. Asahi backed away from the group and stood near the cavern entrance.

I looked at the Chief. "Were you able to get everything you needed?"

"Yes." The Chief rose and said to me. "Your man there. He doesn't say much. None of them do. Who are you?"

I told him, "You can just call me a friend."

"Seriously, I need to call you something," he insisted.

Officer Sartori suggested, "How about Blossom?"

"Oh, I get it. I like it… Yes, Blossom, it is," the Chief announced.

Using telepathy, I asked Asahi to return Tony to his hut but not through his house. He nodded and exited the cavern in the opposite direction of his home.

I attempted to take them back to the flat, but there were police everywhere. The Chief suggested I return them to his office. I looked in and noticed his door was closed. Seeing the coast was clear, I brought them and the equipment to his office.

I was about to leave when the Chief asked, "Bloom, how are we going to get in touch with you?"

"I'll be contacting you about it soon."

"You should know, these cases could take years to resolve," he informed me.

I replied, "I understand. We'll be following them." I returned home for a well-needed nap.

Twenty-Four

Over the next few weeks. I provided the Chief with an email address to contact us. Jacob checked it regularly. I spoke with Leonardo about having a few more sets of uniforms made. Everyone loved them but, it was difficult for everyone to get them washed when their parents weren't around. This would allow them to have extra sets. Everyone would need to figure out where they would store theirs. They could keep them in their cars, room, and my house in the event they were over or needed one. Phyllis agreed to wash them as we needed and was willing to store them if anyone had concerns about them being found.

We added a symbol for each one. It was embroidered on the collar of the uniform. The Bloom emblem was on the right chest. We thought it important not to put our names on them. Jacob had a Wi-Fi symbol. Juliet's had a spear as a symbol because she is a master at using one. Greg had a throwing star and mine had a day lily in remembrance of my grandmother.

We were pretty sure we would not be needing the uniforms for a while. Things had calmed down, and I could focus on my assignments. We all worked on increasing skills that would help us protect the Bloom of Dreams. Over the past few weeks, it had become harder and harder to keep things from Austin because he was around frequently. He and Mechelle had become rather close. At the next Bloom Keepers meeting, I planned to discuss the issue.

Phyllis was out more and more with Hal. I told her I was having Italian food the night of the meeting. The menu comprised of

Lasagna, Fettuccine Alfredo, Chicken Parmesan, and a salad. I was excited to see everyone. We had seen little of one another since the new semester started. We worked our schedule at school to allow us time to train together. This was the first time in weeks we would be able to hang out and chat. The food was delivered just moments before Greg did. He and Mechelle helped me set everything up in the dining room. It wasn't until I smelled the food that I realized how hungry I was.

Jacob and Juliet came in together. Greg said grace for us before everyone made their plates. As we ate, we discussed our new professors, and new friends we were making. Jacob seemed eager for us to start the meeting. He would not disclose why. Jacob scarfed down his food and let us know he was ready to begin when we were. He even began clearing the table.

To tease Jacob, Greg started picking at his food. Jacob glared at him. Greg laughed and said, "I'm just playing with you."

We cleaned up everything, and Jacob started the meeting. After the review of minutes from the previous meeting by Juliet, Jacob said, "A few things have been in the press about the Granaldi family. There was an article posted about a family member providing authorities information about their illegal dealings. The article said there is a large police presence at Anthony Granaldi III's home where he and his two sons and their families lived." Jacob flipped the screen around on his computer. "This photo shows them bringing boxes out of their home."

Mechelle asked, "That's good, right?"

"Yes, but that doesn't mean they have enough evidence to convict them of the crimes," Juliet informed her.

Jacob continued, "The article says they cannot find Joseph and Anthony Granaldi IV, who we know as Tony. Apparently, their families are missing as well."

"It's interesting Joseph is on the run. I wonder who tipped him off," I commented.

"We know from Chief Bianchi that there are many people on the Granaldi's payroll. They could let them know once they found out about the raid," Greg advised.

Greg was right. The Chief limited the number of people on the force because he knew there were corrupt officers.

"In other news, the Chief said in a news conference that several stolen paintings have been located. The paintings are being returned to the owners once the investigation is complete. Reporters asked who stole them and he did not comment," Jacob added.

Mechelle complimented us, "That's wonderful. You guys are amazing!"

"Mechelle, remember you're a Bloom Keeper as well. Everyone plays an important role in our success. You may not be very active now, but without the management of our money and being able to access things on the black market, authorities could easily track us down," I explained.

Mechelle nodded.

Jacobs sat down and said, "That's all I got."

I stood up and said, "Austin has not found out about the stone and our group. As we all know, it is imperative we keep everything secret and only discuss things with people in the Bloom Keepers." Everyone's eyes were on me. It was as if they thought something traumatic had happened.

Jacob sat up in his chair and seemed to wait anxiously for my next sentence. Everyone was quiet and not stirring.

I continued, "Austin's around a lot lately."

Mechelle said defensively, "You're not planning on banning him from coming here, are you?"

I smiled at Mechelle. "No," I said with a giggle. "Actually, Austin could be a valuable asset to our team. He needs to train again but has skills that could be valuable to our missions. It has occurred to me that it's not always easy to have everyone we need for a mission. Although I believe we should remain small, another member to help when others can't, would be beneficial to us. With our class schedules, family commitments, and things, we are all stretched thin as it is. I'm proposing we take a vote about letting Austin become a Bloom Keeper."

Mechelle's demeanor changed. She now had a big smile on her face. "It's a yes for me."

Jacob announced, "Let's vote. All those in favor of letting him in raise your hand." Everyone raised their hands. "We're all in agreement."

Juliet asked, "Now's the hard part. How do we tell him about us?"

"Greg knows him best. He should be the one to tell him," Jacob advised.

"I think we should let him know now," Greg said as he pulled out his phone. "Now everyone be quiet. I'm going to put this on speaker." He called Austin. "Hey, Austin. What are you up to?"

"I'm trying to find the hog that's been tearin' up our crops," Austin responded.

I asked, "I've got a favor to ask. Can you get in your truck?"

"I'm already in it. I'm sittin' out here waitin' for that hog to show his face."

Greg chuckled, and said, "Put the rifle down and close your eyes."

"Man, you're startin' to worry me. Are ya out here?"

"No, just do it."

"Okay. The rifle is in my gun rack. My eyes are closed. Whatcha want now?"

Greg grabbed my hand, and we teleported to Austin's truck. We were both in the backseat.

"Hey there buddy," Greg said, announcing our arrival.

Austin jerked a bit and said, "Bro, have you been back there the entire time?"

I giggled, "No. Austin. I'm having a dinner party and you're invited."

"Sorry, I can't go. I've gotta catch this hog."

Greg responded, "Brooke, can make the hog to leave your property. Right Brooke?"

"I believe I can." I concentrated on the hog. I called for it'sit and a few minutes later, two hogs came up to the truck.

"Greg, hand me my rifle," Austin instructed.

"You're not going to need your rifle. Pay attention," Greg advised.

I opened the car door and walked out to the hogs. "Can I pet you?"

Austin's face showed fear. He said in a panicked voice, "Can she pet it? Girl, these are wild animals. Get back in the truck!"

The larger hog walked over to me and let me pat its head. The smaller one came over, and it rubbed up against my leg. I patted it on the back. "I need you to leave this farm. Your life depends on it. Leave here and don't come back here. Do you understand?" The larger hog moved his head up and down. He nuzzled the smaller one, and they ran off toward the fence line.

Austin had his mouth open. "Brooke, are you like Doctor Dolittle or something?"

This made me chuckle.

Greg chimed in, "Brooke's far more talented than Doctor Dolittle. Austin, you've always talked about going to the Grand Canyon. What if ya could be there tonight?

"That would be awesome. I wanna go to the Grand Canyon Skywalk. You know the bridge with a glass walkway," Austin said enthusiastically.

"Take Brooke's hand," Greg instructed.

"No way, she's your lady."

Greg grabbed my hand and placed Austin's hand on my shoulder. I immediately teleported us to the bridge. We arrived invisible.

Austin immediately looked around and then down at his feet. He shouted, "Oh crap!" He grabbed the railing and tried to hold on.

A few people spun around and began looking in our direction. Thankfully, they could not see us.

Using telepathy, "I told him he needed to be quiet. No one could see us."

He looked very confused. Austin began sweating and looked a bit frightened. He was holding on tightly to the rail still.

I grabbed Austin's shoulder. I felt Greg grab my arm. As I gazed into the mirror, I teleported us to the road by Austin's truck.

Austin uttered, "That was freaky! What're you?"

"She's the same person you've always known. She was just blessed with a gift," Greg started. He began explaining to Austin about the Bloom Keepers and how we needed his help. He was still leery.

I returned to the dinner party. Without saying a word, I placed my hand on Mechelle's shoulder and took her to Austin.

"There she goes again. She's here then, not here. Now Mechelle's with her," Austin spouted. He turned to Greg. "Man, I think I'm losing my mind."

Mechelle walked over to Austin and grabbed his hand. In a gentle voice she said, "I know this seems a bit much to take in, but I assure you, you are sane. I freaked out when I found out. We trust you and that is why we are revealing this to you. No one meant to scare you. We want you to join us."

"Join you doing what? I'm freaked out. My mind is racing, Mechelle," Austin said, sounding terrified.

Mechelle began telling him how she found out about the Bloom of Dreams. She explained to him she went through the same fears and things.

"You mean she can heal also?"

"Yes, she can heal," Greg stated.

Austin pulled out his pocketknife and made a minor cut in the palm of his hand. He demanded, "Heal this." He shoved his hand in front of me.

I reached down and grabbed his hand. The stone warmed. It only took a moment to heal such a slight cut. When the stone cooled, I removed my hand.

Austin looked at his hand, and his mouth dropped open. "This is crazy," he said, turning to Greg. "You're okay with this. This is like... Well, I don't know what it's like. I need to sit down." He walked over to the bed of his truck and sat down on it.

Greg began explaining how he found out about the powers of the stone. He told him about a few of the things we had done regarding the Granaldi family. As Greg talked, Austin calmed down.

"Man, that's cool," Austin told Greg.

Mechelle walked over and placed her hand on his knee. She said, "Whether or not you join us, you can't tell anyone what we've told you. Everyone feels strongly about you joining us. We know you would be an asset."

"Why don't you join us? We're having a meeting right now. Hang out with us for a while and see what you think," I suggested. Austin looked down and appeared to be thinking. "Come on. I'll bring you back in a little while. You can tell your dad the hogs left your property. We can fix the fence in the morning."

Austin agreed. I brought us to the kitchen and told him to come to the dining room when he was ready. Greg and I returned to the group. Mechelle stayed with Austin.

Jacob asked, "Where's Austin?"

"He has a lot to process. We've all been there. Give him a minute," Greg informed everyone.

We filled everyone in on what had occurred while we were gone. Once everyone was caught up, Jacob asked if I had spoken to the Chief recently.

"No, I really should check in on him and Tony. It has been two weeks..."

Austin charged into the room with Mechelle right behind him. He looks right at me and says, "You cheated!"

I cheated? "What're you talking about?"

"You cheated. I need a do over. I know I can hold my breath longer than you," Austin said, laughing.

I laughed with him. "Oh, I'm sure you could if I did it without the stone."

Once the laughter calmed down. Austin looked around the room and asked, "Everyone here is involved?"

"Yes," Mechelle said. She explained how each of us contributed to the team. Including the role, she was currently training for.

Mechelle and Austin joined us at the table. We spent the next hour providing him with more details about the Bloom Keepers. We made sure not to leave out those the behind-the-scenes players.

I explained, "For example, Greg, you know he is talented with martial-arts and is skilled at repairing or building things like you."

"Yes," he said, sounding confused.

"Well, what you may not know is Jacob is well... I'm just going to call it like I see it. He's a hack. I mean a real computer hack. He has developed self-defense skills because of our training. Juliet, she is a sweet angel, who knows Kapu Ku'ialua. You best be leery of her when she has a spear in her hands."

Juliet added, "I know you know Brooke has been training and has become quite a force to be reckoned with. She also has the stone. We are discovering more about it all the time."

Austin joked, "So what you're telling me is we should feel sorry for anyone that tries to take us down in a dark alley."

We all had a good laugh.

Greg got serious and said, "Do you think it's by chance we are all together? I believe God brought us together."

I leaned over and kissed Greg. He was right. *Only God could have made all this happen.* We began discussing our training schedules which included Parkour and how important it was to attend Bloom Keeper's meetings.

Austin told us he would seriously consider joining. He wanted to think about it some and he might have more questions before making his final decision.

Twenty- Five

I stayed up late to catch Chief Bianchi when he arrived at the station. I waited patiently for him to enter his office. When the door flung open, his eyes bulged out. He swung the door shut much like a young child would who was trying to hide a secret.

He composed himself and said, "Bloom, I'm so glad to see you. Have you been watching the news?"

I nodded and replied, "Yes. You can resolve these crimes. I saw they didn't know where Joseph went. Do you have any leads?"

"Not yet. I would like to talk to Tony to see if he can lead me to him."

"It's possible," I replied.

"Oh…" He shuffles through some papers on his desk. He pulls up a document and says, "I've signed the agreement for him. We still need a plan for his incarceration on the island. For now, I know you know where he is."

"How about we go see him? It's in the afternoon there now," I suggested.

"Where the heck do you have him in Australia or something?"

I walked over to him and wrapped my hand around his arm. I took him just outside of Tony's hut. Rosina and Stefania were picking flowers when we showed up. The Chief nodded in their direction. Rosina nodded back.

"Tony's not here right now. He's with Akio and Asahi," Rosina informed us.

I turned to the Chief and asked him to stay here. I teleported to Asahi's hut, where I found them on the porch working on bonsai plants.

"These are beautiful," I said as I looked them over.

"It's nice to see you," Asahi said with a smile.

"I've the Chief with me. The two of you need to talk," I said. I looked over at Asahi and Akio. "I'm going to borrow Tony for a bit." I grabbed him and took us back to his hut.

Tony invited us into his home. The Chief handed him the signed document and told him they would move him to a secure location when possible. I offered my help in getting him there.

They began talking about what was going on with the evidence he provided. He explained about Joseph leaving town and asked if he might know where he would go.

"I'm not surprised he left. There are several police on Pop's payroll," Tony told us.

The Chief slid his notepad to Tony. He asked, "Would you provide me with a list?"

Tony grabbed the paper and pen and began writing. He looked up for a moment. "I'm sure Joseph suspects me of turning them in. He'll find somewhere I'm not aware of to hide." Tony returned to his writing.

The Chief and I began discussing the other cases we had turned into him. He explained the murder of Federico Lombardo had made some progress toward proving Anthony Granaldi III was responsible, but they still need more evidence for their case. They had a man in custody who seems reluctant to talk. They would take the five fugitives into custody in the next few days.

Suddenly, Tony interrupted, "You need to talk to a woman named Lia... What is her last name? Fazzi. That's it. Lia Fazzi. Joseph has kept her away from family. She is his on and off girlfriend. I know very little about her other than I ran into them once. He has always kept his relationship with her a secret. She knows nothing about what he is truly capable of. Find her and you'll have a good chance of finding him." Tony slid the pad and pen back to the Chief.

"Thank you, Tony. I mean that sincerely. You've been a big help," Chief Bianchi said, reaching out to shake Tony's hand.

We said our goodbyes, and I took the Chief back to his office. I assured him I would try to find out as much as I could about Lia. We both agreed to share our information. I returned home exhausted and went straight to bed.

The next morning, I asked Jacob to meet me before class. I slipped him a piece of paper with Lia Fazzi written on it. I explained who she was and asked him to find her. He assured me he would begin looking for her after his classes.

A few days later, the following text went out to everyone.

JACOB: I have updates. We need to meet.

Mechelle was now tracking everyone's schedule. Everyone was letting her know when they had events during the week. Many of us were sharing our calendars with her.

MECHELLE: Library, Room 202 3:45 pm

That worked for me. It even gave me some time to work on some assignments at the library before our meeting. However, I was so focused on my assignments; I was nearly late for the meeting.

As a burst through the door, everyone was already sitting waiting for the meeting to start. Out of breath, I plopped myself into my chair. It was nice seeing Austin with us.

Jacob started the meeting as soon as I was settled. "Brooke asked me to see if I could locate a Lia Fazzi. She's a woman Joseph has been involved with. Well, she's been located. Her family owns a small vineyard in Sondrio, Italy. Lia lives just outside of Florence, but recently went to visit her childhood home a few weeks ago."

"That sounds promising," Greg commented.

Jacob spun his computer around. "I agree." He pointed at the screen and said, "This is her parent's vineyard. Brooke, I think you should check it out to see if Joseph is there."

I took a moment to look over the photograph. I asked, "Is that the only structure on the vineyard?"

"No," Jacob said changing the screen. "There are a few other small structures. It's a small vineyard compared to others in the area."

"I don't have a class tomorrow. I'll check it out. If I find anything, I will report it to Chief Bianchi."

Jacob continued, "It was reported just this morning, two of the five fugitives have been found and are now back in custody. Oh, I nearly forgot they found the true owner of Van Gogh's Poppy Flowers painting. The painting was returned yesterday."

Once Jacob sat down, Mechelle announced, "Austin would like to say something."

Austin's eyes got big as he looked around the room at each of us. He turned to Mechelle, "I thought you were going to tell them."

"Austin seemed a bit nervous. He has agreed to join the Bloom Keepers," Mechelle informed us.

We thanked him and he promised to protect the stone and the Bloom Keepers.

Mechelle explained she had ordered a uniform for him that have nunchakus on it.

"That's perfect for you man," Greg complemented. "He's incredible with them."

Before ending the meeting, we planned our workout schedule for the week. The schedule worked around Austin's class and work schedule to insure he could be there.

Greg and I rushed out to start our date immediately following the meeting. It was going to be a simple evening. We picked up a couple of sandwiches and made our way to the park. There weren't many people there when we arrived. We caught up on the latest news regarding our friends and family while we ate. Greg cleared the trash. He sat down next to me on the bench. His body was straddling the bench and facing me.

"Brooke, I thank God each day for you," he said playing with my fingers. "I never knew love could feel this way. Thank you for making my life better."

My heart was full of love for him. I leaned over and kissed him. We began gazing in each other's eyes as we continued to confess our love to each other. As people left the park, our gaze was broken by the commotion of people closing their car doors. I soon realized we appeared to be the only ones in the park.

Greg pushed the hair away from my neck and kissed it gently. Chill bumps ran down my body. He nestled his head into my neck and continued.

I pulled myself away and gazed into his eyes for a moment. Greg's grin was so sexy. I leaned in and kissed him. The passion built. For a moment I forgot where we were. I pulled myself away and stood up. "Oh man, you're driving me crazy," I said as I fanned myself with my hand. I took a few steps toward his truck.

Greg came behind me and kissed me again on the neck. He moved to my ear and gently nibbled on it.

I turned around and wrapped my arms around him. He grabbed me and lifted me up. He walked me over to the edge of the picnic table and placed me on it. Greg's hands pushed my hair back as he held my face. He gently kissed me on the lips. My body began to tingle. I pulled him closer to me. The intensity of our kisses increased with each moment. Before I knew it, we were both lying on top the picnic table.

Greg's hand managed to make its way under my shirt and was touching my waist. He was a gentleman and did not move it any higher than there, but he caressed my skin. I wanted more but fought the urge to move his hand higher. I was lost in the moment until I heard a car horn. Greg and I both looked up and a vehicle with bicycles on top of it drove by.

"I think that's our cue to stop," Greg chuckled. He stood up and helped me off the table.

It was so hard to stop what our bodies clearly desired. During the ride home. Greg held my hand as he drove. His thumb kept gently caressing my skin. We both were quiet during the ride. I couldn't speak for him, but I was running a movie in my head about the intense make out session we just had. Partly grateful for the vehicle stopping us and partly disappointed the moment had to end.

Greg hung out with me for about an hour before he went home to work on some assignments. I spent the rest of the evening talking to Phyllis and Mechelle. Phyllis and Hal were getting serious and had discussed getting married. I am happy for them but concerned how this will affect the Bloom Keepers. Will he move in here? Will she be moving out? There was plenty of time to figure that out.

Mechelle excused herself and returned a few minutes later. "Here, Brooke," Mechelle said, handing me a credit card. "This is for you. Leonardo and I discussed this and felt you need to have a card for unexpected purchases."

I looked at the card and said, "Um, Mechelle… This isn't mine. Who is Lillie Watchman?"

Mechelle laughed and said, "You are silly. Lillie, in honor of your grandmother and Watchman, because you are the Guardian of the Bloom of Dreams. We couldn't let you be traveling the world using your own name. This will keep your identity hidden."

"Clever," I said as I slipped the card in my pocket. We continued our conversation for a little while longer. I needed to head to bed.

The next morning, everyone was coming over early for a workout.

Twenty-Six

It had been a few weeks, but I finally got Tony and his family moved. Everything went smoothly. Rosina would be homeschooling Stefania. Despite them being confined to the home, they seemed happy. Tony and Rosina thanked me again and promised they were done with that old life. They seemed genuinely changed. I am sure he's still a work in progress. I prayed he continued moving to be the man God wanted him to be.

The Chief assured me Joseph, Anthony and their crew would spend a long time in prison. He admitted to me, that he felt Tony would not follow through. The Chief had planned on breaking his promise to us, but Tony provided him so much information he felt grateful. He said he felt he should do more time under house arrest, but he made a deal. He also told me that he would keep the existence of the Bloom a secret and he asked what he could do to repay us. I assured him we needed nothing. The Bloom Keepers would continue to work with the Chief on his cases. I would reach out to him from time to time.

With Mechelle's help, a letter was compiled and sent to Chief Bianchi with the information we had on Marshall Blaise aka Louis Dupont. The letter included his connection to the Granaldi crime family and that he was a hitman. We did not say anything about him murdering my grandmother because it would link the Granaldis to our family. The Chief left a letter for me on his desk. It informed me, that Louis Dupont was on the run, but he thanked me for informing him of the connection to Misty and her mother. He assured me it was only a matter of time before they captured him.

I had not seen Akio and Asahi since we took Tony and his family from the island. I planned on having everyone train with them periodically. For now, we planned on taking a much-needed break and would concentrate on getting through the semester. I asked for Mechelle to get them uniforms as well. Asahi would have a mining symbol and Akio would have a bonsai plant.

We spent the next few months training our team to work together and expect what the other was doing. Austin, like Greg, came in with a lot of skills. He just needed to get back in the groove of working out. Mechelle began learning the basics. I think she liked the way Austin trained with her. She could easily fend off someone trying to steal her purse, but not much more than that at this point.

We were making sure our grades came first. I had made a corporate decision to pay the Bloom Keepers from the trust. This allowed them to have more free time to work on their schoolwork and to strengthen the team.

The sudden income was hard to explain to everyone's parents. Jacob told his parents he was repairing computers on the side. He explained there was an increase in students needing his help. This was true. Word is getting around campus about his skills. He even had people try to get him to hack into the school system to change grades. He laughed it off and told them he is not that talented.

Mechelle and Juliet told their parents they were getting paid to tutor students. Greg and Austin were harder to explain. Greg was not permitted to have a job during the semester and Austin had to work at the farm all the time. Leonardo granted them each a trust to pay their college tuition. He also gave them some cash each month. The news of being granted a scholarship surprised both their parents. Leonardo instructed Mr. Thomas to create a certificate and papers stating they received funds from the Lillie Davis Scholarship. The news delighted their families.

Mom expected to have her new place finished before Mechelle, Greg, and I would come down for Thanksgiving. Greg and Mechelle's father had already decided to go hunting or at very least visit the range. Us gals were trying to come up with something creative to do while they were gone. Perhaps a day at the spa.

Austin and Mechelle were doing great. He had family coming from out of town and could not join us over Thanksgiving break. He planned on spending part of the winter break with us in Florida. We were going to head to the Florida Keys while he was down. Austin was having a hard time controlling his excitement about the trip.

Since relocating, they promoted my mother. She was very excited about her new position. Mom had been too busy to tell me the details. She planned on coming to visit soon for a long weekend, but if she was unable, we would see her at Thanksgiving.

Phyllis and Hal were doing great. Mechelle and I have made it a point to try to do more for ourselves. Phyllis had been making extra at night to allow us leftovers because she and Hal are spending more and more time together away from the house.

As for me, I continued to work to develop my skills and concentrated on what life would be like after college. I had a lot to think about. The idea of becoming a licensed private investigator had crossed my mind a few times. This would permit me to have a flexible schedule. I could use my newly gained skills. The Bloom Keepers could work for me. It would be a fantastic cover for us. I'm not sure everyone would be interested. I continued to research and pray about the idea. Leonardo and Mr. Thomas were working with me to figure out some of the financial details and the requirements for such a venture. At this point, only God knows my future.

I continued to dive deeper into reading my grandmother's journals. *Wow! She was an amazing woman.* Lillie traveled the world and helped many along the way. It was apparent in her writing, she relied on Phyllis more than anyone. She struggled with not picking my mother to receive the Bloom of Dreams until she realized I was a lot like her. She stated I was a mini version of herself. That made me proud. I wished she had a team like the Bloom Keepers, but it appeared she did not trust many people.

Greg and I were doing fantastic. Especially with the financial burden of school no longer being a problem for him. He continued to help Bill when he was in a bind. This had allowed us more time together. Our friendship and love for one another continued to grow. We suspected we would eventually marry. I have not told him, but I think about that day frequently. We continued struggling with our desires to be together intimately, but our faith kept us on the right track. Knowing God entrusted me with the Bloom of Dreams had brought me closer to Him. I was reading my Bible more frequently and spending time in prayer with Jesus. Greg and I have begun reading a chapter each night providing our schedules permit it. We started praying together each morning and each night as well. This has helped our already wonderful relationship develop more.

I have checked up on Eleni Kostopoulos a few times. She had been keeping a closer eye on her daughter, Zahara. The best I can tell she had decided not to go after the Bloom of Dreams. Only time will tell if I am correct.

Mechelle was working with Leonardo and Isabella more. I had taken her over there on several occasions. She can't seem to hold back her excitement about being able to run the villa. Leonardo had introduced her to his contacts. He refers to her as his assistant. I had let her wear the Bloom of Dreams during her meetings with them. She could read their minds. This allowed her to answer questions they had not yet asked. It seemed to give them a sense of trust. She told me it surprised everyone Leonardo would pick someone so young. Mechelle excused herself from one meeting and came back invisible to listen to the conversation between Leonardo and his contact. She told me, "They expressed concerns to Leonardo, and he set them straight. He informed them I was hand-picked by his boss. He assured them his boss was wise and knew I was capable." Mechelle stated she felt more comfortable with the position, knowing he was supporting her.

Austin and Mechelle were doing well. With Greg helping less on the farm, Austin was working more. His father, Bill, was looking for another farmhand. He wants Austin to concentrate on school more.

For now, I am grateful things are quiet. I am doing better than ever in school. We are heading to Florida for winter break. We have been talking about what we can do as a group that would please the Lord, perhaps stop human trafficking, expose corrupt politicians, find missing children, or even prevent wars. There was so much evil in the world we know we are going to be busy. We can't conquer it all, but we can do our part. The Bloom Keepers adopted a family during the break. Mom's church told us they needed help. We purchased gifts to meet some of their needs and helped the pastor repair things around their home. Maggie and some of our other friends from the area had also agreed to help.

I continued to develop my skills in martial arts and parkour. My journal writing was off to a slow start. Of course, there was little to say currently. I was thankful for that. For now, I was focused on God, school, my family, and the Bloom Keepers.

Shrimp Patty Sandwiches

Ingredients
- 4 large eggs
- 2 cups peeled and deveined cooked shrimp chopped finely
- 3/4 cups pancake mix
- 1 tablespoons cornmeal
- 1/4 teaspoon dried parsley flakes
- 1/4 teaspoon celery salt
- a pinch paprika
- ¼ cup dry breadcrumbs
- 3 to 4 tablespoons canola oil
- 4 hamburger buns
- Optional: Lettuce leaves, tomato slices, onion slices and Sriracha mayonnaise

Directions

1. In a large bowl, beat the eggs. Add the shrimp, pancake mix, cornmeal, parsley, celery salt, mustard and paprika; mix well.
2. Shape into 4 patties and coat with breadcrumbs.
3. In a large cast-iron or other heavy skillet, cook patties in oil over medium-high heat until golden brown (approximately 2 minutes on each side). Serve on hamburger buns. Top with lettuce, tomato, onion, and mayonnaise if desired.

Discover other titles by
D.A. Dwinell

Guardian of the Stone Series

Bloom of Dreams – Book 1
The Bloom's Cradle – Book 2
The Bloom Keepers – Book 3
Path of the Guardian – Book 4
Bloom of Secret – Book 5 (coming soon)

Connect with D.A. Dwinell

If you want the latest news on D.A. Dwinell or are interested in connecting on social media, please visit the following site:

Facebook: www.facebook.com/DADwinell
Instagram: d.a._dwinell

www.ingramcontent.com/pod-product-compliance
Lightning Source LLC
Chambersburg PA
CBHW020613180626
46810CB00007B/2749